THE
NURSERY

BOOKS BY SUE WATSON

Psychological Thrillers

Our Little Lies

The Woman Next Door

The Empty Nest

The Sister-in-Law

First Date

The Forever Home

The New Wife

The Resort

Romantic Comedies

LOVE AND LIES SERIES

Love, Lies and Lemon Cake

Love, Lies and Wedding Cake

THE ICE-CREAM CAFÉ SERIES

Ella's Ice Cream Summer

Curves, Kisses and Chocolate Ice-Cream

STANDALONES

Snow Angels, Secrets and Christmas Cake

Summer Flings and Dancing Dreams

Bella's Christmas Bake Off

The Christmas Cake Cafe

Snowflakes, Iced Cakes and Second Chances

We'll Always Have Paris

THE
NURSERY

SUE WATSON

bookouture

Published by Bookouture in 2022

An imprint of Storyfire Ltd.
Carmelite House
50 Victoria Embankment
London EC4Y 0DZ

www.bookouture.com

ISBN: 978-1-80314-805-2
eBook ISBN: 978-1-80314-564-8

PROLOGUE

DECEMBER 2010 – SIDMOUTH, EAST DEVON

I arrived in a blizzard of snow, climbing off the bus in the middle of the night, not knowing which way to go.

The sea roared onto the pavement, making the walk from the bus stop almost impossible, but I had to keep going, I had no choice. I had to get away, I knew she'd be dead if I'd stayed there. Now I just need to make a new life for myself, and hope nobody ever finds out who I was or what I had done.

I ran through the icy snow, head down, feeling so lost, but there in the darkness was a beacon of light, a church.

'My name is Emily,' I said when the woman opened the door. 'Please don't tell anyone I'm here.' I unfolded the blankets I was carrying, to reveal my sick child, my heart was breaking. Would she even survive the night?

ONE

TWELVE YEARS LATER – AUTUMN 2022

I took a handful of rigid spaghetti and surrendered it into a pan of boiling water, as the sauce bubbled on the hob. I was watching, thinking as I stirred slowly, breathing in the rich, garlic aroma; it relaxed me. But relaxing was a luxury I couldn't allow myself, even now.

'Ooh, my favourite.' Sofia's voice startled me. 'Are we having garlic bread too, Mum?'

I nodded. 'Home-made, it's in the oven.'

'I thought I could smell it. You're the best!'

I basked in her words, enjoying a rare guilt-free moment of motherhood. My daughter didn't throw these declarations around like confetti, 'you're the greatest,' and 'you're the best mum ever,' were usually my rewards for agreeing to buy her something or allowing her a later curfew. But still, I treasured a successful outcome from the parent/child negotiations around new mascara/jeans/trainers/music download/game download/*any* download, that I could provide.

'I *am* the best, it's true,' I said, responding to her fulsome approval of the garlic bread, 'but why are you in here buttering me up when you should be doing your homework?' I opened a tin of lentils and emptied them into the bubbling sauce.

'I *am* doing my homework,' she stressed, 'but the kitchen smells like Italy, and I'm bloody hungry!'

I smiled at this, she always made me smile.

'By the way, it's lentils, can't afford meat until I get paid,' I murmured, stirring gently.

'I do not care what she has in 'er sauce, I just want to eat ze bloody thing,' she replied.

'Love that French accent,' I joked.

She laughed. 'I was *being* Italian.' She put her hand on her hip, with mock indignation, while grabbing a spoon to test the sauce. I stood back slightly, watching her, newly surprised at her long legs now teenager thin. Her hair was long and thick, it shone with health and covered her shoulders like a shawl.

'You'll burn your mouth,' I warned, knowing she wasn't listening, her head too full of TikTok and boys.

At fifteen, she was a bundle of raw energy, hilarious and curious and confused, the world was a fabulous mystery to her, and everything had to be tried and tasted. But she had no patience – her generation didn't have to wait for knowledge or try to work things out, they googled it, and if something wasn't at the click of a button, it was too long to wait. Even now, after tentatively dipping the spoon into the bubbling sauce, she didn't wait for it to cool down but poked her tongue at the spoon. I laughed at her hand fanning her mouth to take away the heat of the sauce.

I stopped stirring for a moment and handed her a clean tea towel, which she held to her mouth. I laughed, and hugged her, trying to live in the now, knowing she wouldn't be with me for ever, like this, just the two of us in our safe little flat. In no time, she'd be off to university and a bigger life, where she'd chase her dreams and blossom. It felt like only yesterday that I was holding that chubby little baby in my arms in the hospital, we'd bonded straight away, and been through a lot, not all of it easy, but I hoped we could finally put the past to rest. I recognised in Sofia my own youth, filled with naivety, hope and an inherent belief that wearing the right lip gloss could help you achieve anything. But life isn't quite so simple, it's messy and cruel and unfair. And sometimes we do bad things that shudder through the years.

'Ruby's getting her nose pierced,' Sofia announced. I could see by the way her eyes avoided mine, though she stayed close to judge my reaction, that this was more of a request than a statement.

'Oh nice. Ruby's getting a hole put in her nose, is she? You're not,' I added, just to make it very clear. These were the kind of conversations we had most days, the veiled requests ranging from piercings, to tattoos, to hair being dyed the colours of the rainbow. 'The other day you told me Ella was having a tattoo, yet when I saw her mum in town today, she was under the impression it was *you* having a tattoo. Nice try, Sofia.'

She looked up sheepishly from the table where she'd plonked herself. 'Oh, I thought Ella was having—'

I looked at her. 'Mums don't turn into lemmings when they have kids. We don't all just think, *ooh Julie's letting Ella have a tattoo, Cath's allowing Ruby to smoke marijuana and spend the night in a hotel room with a boy band, so that means I have to let Sofia do that too.*'

She rolled her eyes. 'Cringing here, Mum, and who the hell even *listens* to boy bands anymore, let alone *sleeps* with them? And please don't call dope *marijuana*, it makes you sound like you're a hundred years old.'

'I am,' I replied, and I felt like it sometimes.

'Well, Mother, you can relax. I won't be trying any of that, and I don't even *have* a boyfriend,' she said with a sigh.

'What about Archie, I thought you and he were—'

'Oh. My. God. Archie? Really? You don't even *know* me.'

'But you're good friends, it might lead to more?'

'Stop!' She got up from her chair, huffing and puffing, apparently offended at me daring to suggest such an outrage. I reckoned she had a soft spot for Archie, the sweet boy in her class at school. She was always talking about him, and I wished she felt comfortable enough to share her feelings with me. She used to tell me everything, but I guess it was her age. I'd noticed recently she was becoming more secretive, closing her bedroom door, snapping her laptop shut when I walked into a room. I knew it was all part of growing up, but I felt slightly shut out, I only wanted to help.

I decided not to push the Archie thing, I didn't want to embarrass her. She probably talked to Ruby about him, and as Ruby was her best friend, that was how it should be. 'I love autumn,' I said, changing the subject, while looking through the window at the bright orange trees clustered around the dusky garden. Being in a ground-floor flat on the seafront might be considered prime real estate, but we only rented. We'd been here since we first arrived in Sidmouth twelve years before on that dark, stormy night desperately seeking sanctuary. We were saved by the kindness of strangers, first by the local vicar and his wife, who had allowed us to stay a few nights at the local vicarage before introducing us to his parishioners, Mr and Mrs Woods, an older couple who had offered to rent this place to me. They asked for a very small rent and also gave me a job at their shop in the town. They basically gave me my life back, and I liked to think we brought some joy into theirs. 'Look at you two, like peas in a pod,' Mrs Woods used to say of Sofia and I, and she was right, even I could see the likeness, with our red hair and green eyes. 'You're the daughter we never had, and Sofia's our granddaughter,' she would beam. And we felt the same, they'd been our lifeline since arriving here.

But as grateful as I was when they offered us this flat, I explained that we'd just escaped a dangerous situation and that

I was worried about being found. People could easily peer through the windows when walking along the front, I'd fearfully pointed out to them. I didn't offer any further information, and God bless the Woods, they never asked me any questions, they just put up some net curtains, charged me a peppercorn rent, then asked if I'd like a part-time job in their perfume shop. I had jumped at this, I had no work, I'd abandoned a career in nursing to care for my daughter, and though I'd have loved to return to a job I adored, I couldn't. The first thing my ex-husband would do would be to contact hospitals to find me, and I couldn't risk that. Besides, this was my new life, and once Sofia was at nursery school, I had started working there and loved it. So far, our lives had worked out, and no one had found us. Yet.

I loved living on the seafront, it was the same view all year round, but different every day, and each season had its beauty. Our two big windows in the flat both held spectacular views. From the front, we could see the sea, now grey, mirroring the skies, rusty Triassic sand beneath the water bleeding red into the grey. And from the kitchen window at the back of the flat, we could see the garden. I gazed at the trees in their post-summer golden glamour.

'I think autumn's my favourite season,' I said, putting two dishes in the oven to warm, as the pasta softened.

'When we go to France, shall we go in the autumn?' Sofia asked, settling herself back down at our tiny kitchen table, as I went to fill our glasses with tap water.

I stood a moment, at the sink, gazing out into the near distance. 'Yes, late summer, or early autumn,' I murmured, turning the tap on full, allowing it to run a little so the water was cold.

As a single parent, I'd never had the money to travel. But it didn't stop the two of us from making plans, looking at maps, talking about the places we'd go, the food we'd eat, it was somewhere we'd both escape to in our heads. I stood for a while, just gazing into the darkness, imagining us both in Paris, Eiffel Tower, the Louvre, the Parisian bakeries, it was a place I went to when I was scared. But I'd never been; perhaps one day?

'Mum, did we ever live near a farm?'

Sofia's question was unexpected. 'When, darling?'

'Before we came here?'

'No, we lived in a house in Manchester when you were born, and then we came here. Why do you ask?'

'We did this thing in Psychology today about memory. We had to close our eyes and recall our earliest memory, and I vaguely remembered a black-and-white cow. But it might have been a drawing... or a toy?'

I shrugged. 'You had lots of toys when you were little, but I don't recall a cow.'

'Do you think I had it at the first house, the one we left?'

I felt a chill run through me as the past crowded in, unbidden. 'I really don't remember. Perhaps you dreamt it?'

'Yeah, I suppose so. It's just so random.'

'Look, why don't you set the table, love, dinner's almost ready,' I said, her vague, grasped memories of the past making me uncomfortable.

I turned away to gaze through the window as she opened the cutlery drawer; I didn't want her to see my discomfort and sense something was wrong. But she was now happily chatting away about Ruby and how hilarious she was. I didn't hear what she said because as I looked out at the darkening trees, I saw something – or someone? My stomach jolted, pins and needles prickled my finger ends. I put down the glasses and leaned closer, trying to scrutinise the near distance. What had I seen? I placed my hand on the pane, dusk was shrouding my view. It was easy to see shapes that didn't exist, movement that never happened. Perhaps it was my imagination?

'What is it, Mum?' Sofia was immediately on alert. We only

had each other and our antennae for one another was always keen.

'Nothing, nothing,' I said slowly, calmly, tearing myself away from the shadowy glass. My instinct was to stay at the window, remain vigilant, and try to work out what I'd just seen. Was someone watching me? Had my luck finally run out?

As scared as I was, I had this urge to run out there, make a noise, and scare off whoever might be trying to scare me, even if it was just a cat. But if I did that it would make Sofia fearful, and fear was something I'd always tried to protect her from. I felt it myself all the time, the fear of being watched, being chased, being *found*. I'd wanted to protect Sofia from that debilitating dread, I never wanted her to live like I had.

'Mum? Mum?' Sofia was calling me.

I turned to her.

'Mum!' she was calling louder now and pointing at the window.

I was so terrified, I froze and couldn't bring myself to turn back and look.

'What?' I cried.

'Mum, look.' The anxiety in Sofia's voice, the urgent pointing of her finger, forced me to deal with this, and holding my breath, I turned back to the window to face whatever was waiting out there. I tried hard to focus, but all I could see in the glass was my own reflection looking back, scared, guilty. And when I leaned closer, and focused on what was outside, I saw nothing, just the trees moving in the semi-darkness, as the wind crept through the leaves. But I just knew I hadn't been mistaken, and the thought occurred to me that while I was looking out the back, whoever it was may have slipped around the front of the flat.

Suddenly, Sofia was on her feet and marching towards the window. I wanted desperately to run into the hall, to rip open the front door and face whoever it was that may have found me, but my terror rooted me to the spot. Sofia was yelling at me, but I couldn't hear her, all I heard was the roar of the ocean in my head. Then I saw what I'd tried so hard to forget, it had always been there in my head, and now the door was opening into the room. Dark, and musty, a battered old soft toy lying in a corner, a filthy blanket on the floor. I reached out, my hand touched the blanket... But before I could touch it, the door slammed in my head and I was back there, in the kitchen, the smell of garlic, the noise of water and my daughter yelling.

'MUM! Mum?' she was shouting. Then she pushed against me as she reached over and turned off the tap.

I felt the shock of cold water seeping into my slippers, it was a horrible sensation, and with leaden feet, I moved aside, never taking my eyes from the window, vaguely aware that I'd allowed the tap to run and overflow the sink. That was what Sofia had been shouting about, not someone outside the window, just the water overflowing.

'Why didn't you turn off the tap?' she asked, alarmed, as she grabbed the mop and quickly wiped it around the floor. Then she stopped. 'Are you okay?' She spun me round, looking into my face, her eyes desperately searching mine for a clue. But I couldn't let her see what I was hiding.

'Sorry, my head was somewhere else,' I replied, placing down a couple of tea towels to soak up the water. I looked up and she was standing over me, the look on her face scared me, I'd seen it before, and suddenly I felt vulnerable down on the floor. Shaking my thoughts away, I remembered this was my child, I was being paranoid.

'It's old age.' I smiled, standing up, trying to make a joke as I walked away from her to take a seat at the table and slip off my soggy slippers.

I squeezed out the slippers and left them on the radiator. I was too concerned about what I may have seen outside to worry too much about damp footwear. This wasn't the first time I thought I'd seen someone. For a few weeks, I'd had an uneasy feeling that someone was following me. I hadn't actually seen them, but a few weeks ago, walking home from work, I'd heard footsteps behind me. The road had been dark and empty, and as I'd walked, I'd heard the tap, tap behind me. When I'd stopped, *they* had stopped, and then when I had started walking again, so did they. I had turned around, and couldn't see anyone, but as I'd walked faster, so did the steps. I was so scared, I had started to run and didn't stop until I got home. My heart was pounding as I had tried to find my keys in the dark, without looking behind me. Once inside, I had run into the front room and looked from behind the net curtains to see if I could see anyone. Leaning by the street lamp outside, just feet away, was a dark figure, wearing what looked like a hoodie. I couldn't see their face, but they had seemed to be staring straight ahead. Straight into our flat. Fear had sparked in my chest, and I had heard myself whimper in the darkness.

That had been a few weeks before, and I hadn't seen them since, save a fleeting shadow passing the front window, a movement in the garden, like I'd just experienced. In daylight, when life was busy and people were bustling around, I told myself I'd imagined this, but deep down, I knew, I just *knew*.

And later that night, after eating our Bolognese and watching TV, we went to bed. My worst fear was realised when I was woken by a noise in the kitchen. At first, I thought I was dreaming and wondered if I'd imagined the noise. It may have been a car backfiring, a dog barking? But I immediately sat up, checking my phone to see the time, it was 4 a.m. Climbing slowly out of bed, I picked up the rounders bat I kept under the bed and slowly and quietly opened my bedroom door. I stood in the doorway, scared to breathe, wondering if I was going mad, my mind whirring, my heart thumping out of my chest. Movement in the kitchen, a shuffling, human sound, or was it just the wind? I had this compulsion to scream but that would only wake Sofia; I didn't want her running out of her room and straight into this... This, *whatever* it was.

I stood in my bedroom doorway, clutching the bat, swallowing down a whimper of fear. My skin prickled on hearing a drawer being opened slowly, then feet padding across the floor. Someone had broken into our home; all I could think about was Sofia, I had to keep her safe, and was prepared to do anything.

TWO

I'd never been so scared in my life as I moved inch by inch out of the bedroom and into the hallway. Vague sounds emanated from the kitchen as I stood in the darkness questioning myself again. Was I going crazy, or dreaming this? Suddenly, a flash of torchlight flooded the hall momentarily, then plunged back into darkness again. I now *knew* this was real. Someone was in the kitchen with a torch. I wasn't going mad, this was *happening*.

I tried to take a very quiet breath, and calm myself, but it wasn't working, my heart felt as if it was about to leap from my chest. The pounding in my ears was so intense, it crossed my fevered mind that whoever was in the kitchen might hear it. I had no idea what to do, but in the dark, my eyes could just make out the door of Sofia's bedroom and I instinctively moved towards it. Her room was the closest to the kitchen and the first door they'd come to if they decided to explore the rest of the flat. I moved tentatively, but with some urgency, one step at a time. It was only four steps, but each one was more agonising than the last as I tried to get there quickly while avoiding creaks in the floor.

Once there, I stood with my back against her door, so they'd have to get past me first. I prayed I couldn't be seen in the flashes of torchlight leaking every now and then into the hall. All this time, I was holding my breath. Every sinew in my body tense, my life, my whole world was in the room I stood guarding, and God help anyone who tried to get to her.

I stood there for what seemed like hours but was only minutes, allowing whoever was violating our home, our privacy, our lives, to continue. Then more careless movement, louder shuffling, a scrambling of feet and hands and a click, the window latch? Were they leaving?

I gave it a few more minutes. Then still clutching the bat, just in case, I went to move towards the kitchen. But my leg had stiffened from standing so long, and in the dark I missed my footing, falling heavily against Sofia's bedroom door.

'Mum? Mum? Is that you?' a frightened voice called out as I lifted myself off the carpet.

At first, I didn't respond. What if he was still in the kitchen? I stepped back, lifting the rounders bat in preparation. Suddenly, Sofia's door opened and she was standing there, in the shaft of light coming from her room, and I saw the look of horror on her face. She stared at me open-mouthed as I silently wielded the rounders bat in the dark.

'Mum! What's going on...?' she started, but I quickly put my finger to my lips. Realising we may not be alone, a gasp escaped from her mouth.

I waved my hand, silently urging her to go into her room and shut her door, but she shook her head vigorously, my daughter was as protective of me as I was her. I didn't hang around to argue, I had to deal with this. Aided by the light from Sofia's bedroom, I moved slowly forward, stepping carefully into the kitchen. Once inside, I quickly switched on the light with one hand while lifting the bat high with the other. I would have brought it down on whoever's head was in my home, but I felt the cold blast of air coming from the open window, their entrance and escape route. My relief that they'd gone was soon replaced with the horrible thought that someone had invaded our home.

'Mum, what's happening?' Sofia was saying, as I rushed to the window and closed it. I noticed the lock had been broken, they'd been desperate to get inside, but glancing around, there didn't seem to be anything obvious missing. I glanced in the living room, the TV was still standing. I'd have been relieved if something had been taken, if this had been a burglary – but it wasn't, it was something else. Someone was trying to scare me.

'I think someone tried to get in,' I said absently, attempting to make the situation as threat-free as possible.

'Looks like they did more than try – they actually *got* in,' she said, fear in her voice.

I turned around to see Sofia holding up a small, white, crescent-shaped piece of plastic.

'They left something. What do you think it is?' She was looking closely at it, holding it in her palm and lifting it up to the light.

I couldn't make it out and went over to see for myself. 'Where did you find it?' I asked, and she pointed to the table, where a Post-it note lay untouched. I picked it up and, puzzled by the message, I looked at Sofia.

'Here's the missing piece...' I read aloud. My heart was pounding.

'I don't understand,' she murmured.

'Are you sure this bit of plastic isn't *yours*?' I asked, unable to decipher the note and desperately hoping she'd suddenly remember what it was. 'Something you found on your way home from school?' I knew it sounded far-fetched even as I said the words.

'No, I pick up sea glass and shells, I don't pick up bits of plastic.'

'But what about the Post-it note, you're always using them,' I reminded her, again clutching for a nice, safe answer.

'Yeah, but not to write weird, cryptic notes that I leave around the house like a weirdo. Mum, aren't we going to call the police?'

If this *had* been a burglary, I would of course have been straight on the phone to the police. But this wasn't a simple break-in, someone wanted me to know they'd found me, and I had a feeling I knew who that might be. I couldn't share my theory with Sofia; like me, she believed her father was now living a new life in Australia. But not only had I gone against him, I'd walked out and taken Sofia with me. Was he seeking revenge after all these years? Was he going to reveal what I'd done and separate me from my daughter as he'd threatened to do? If so, the last thing I needed was to get the police involved.

'Yeah, yeah, of course. I'll call them in the morning.'

'No, call them *now*, I'll never sleep.'

'It's really nothing,' I said in what I hoped was a reassuring tone. 'It was probably just kids chancing their arm. They climbed in through the window and realised there's nothing here for them to take. We don't even have bottles of booze or cigarettes.'

'But why would they leave this?' She held up the crescent-shaped plastic for my inspection and I took it from her.

'I really don't get that,' I murmured.

'And the Post-it, what does that mean? It's so creepy.'

Something forced its way into the edges of my mind, this sliver of plastic *was* significant. *Very* significant, but for now, I couldn't bear to think about it – I had to push it away, I didn't want to scare Sofia.

'Hang on!' I suddenly said, hitting my forehead with the

heel of my hand. 'I remember now, I made that note the other day,' I improvised, so she didn't dwell on it.

'You did?' She looked at me, uncertain.

'Yeah, it was me...' I read it again, my mind torn between trying to work it out and coming up with a valid reason as to why I would write, 'Here's the missing piece' on a random Post-it note.

'What does it mean?' Sofia asked, rather challengingly. I think she knew I was bluffing so she wouldn't be scared, but I was finding it hard to hide my own fear and simply brush it off as something I'd written.

'It's... the title of a book. Yes, I remember now, it was a book Nancy recommended.'

She huffed. 'Nancy doesn't read books.'

'Sometimes she does,' I said, pushing the plastic and the Post-it into a drawer, a temporary holding place until I could hide them properly. 'Come on, love, let's go to bed, it's almost five o'clock, we'll never get up in the morning.'

'I'm a bit scared, can I come in with you?' she asked, wide-eyed.

How could I refuse? We were both shaken, and as much as I'd tried to smooth over it, I was more scared than Sofia.

So, after checking all the doors and windows, we went to bed. I turned off the light, but lay there wide awake, my daughter sleeping soundly next to me, my rounders bat within reach against the bedroom wall. There was no chance of sleep, the window lock had been broken, so the flat was still accessible from the outside. I would have to get it fixed later that day, but in the meantime, I would stay on high alert, trying to under-stand what had happened. Nothing had been taken, they'd just left the note, and the weird piece of plastic. But I couldn't make any sense of it, couldn't see what he was trying to tell me. The plastic was just that, wasn't it? A piece of plastic – and how on earth could *that* have any relevance?

That night, I racked my brain to think of what it might be, and how it connected me to my ex-husband, and what had happened.

But now I know, that crescent-shaped plastic was the key to everything, and the beginning of the end of our life as we knew it.

THREE

The last twelve years in Sidmouth had been the happiest time of my life. Nestled beneath bright red cliffs and surrounded by green hills, it was the antithesis of the gritty Mancunian town I'd grown up in. I wanted more for Sofia, and though the town was small and quiet, the summer season brought in the outside world just long enough to inject the area with fresh blood, so it was never boring. Sidmouth was the safe haven Sofia and I needed. But even before the break-in, something had changed. I couldn't put my finger on it, I just sensed danger. Sometimes when I was alone, it crowded in on me, making me feel anxious and panicky for no apparent reason. I guess it was primal, a survival mechanism that made me aware of threat and danger. For weeks I'd been waking at dawn, the dread gathering around me like the morning fret coming in from the sea. Consequently, when I'd woken that night to hear someone in my kitchen, it had been a horrible shock, but not totally unexpected.

And despite telling Sofia I would call the police, I couldn't. If they put my name into a computer, who knew what would emerge? I couldn't share my concerns with anyone, even my closest friend, Nancy, who worked in the art shop next to where I worked.

The day after the break-in, we had a late lunch break and met for toasted sandwiches in a local café. I had thought about cancelling; I was still shaken by what had happened the night before, the note, the message. Part of me wanted to stay in bed, keep Sofia close for the day, but I knew I needed to carry on for her sake, so I'd gone to work as usual.

Over lunch, Nancy was keen to tell me about her latest boyfriend, but I was only half-listening, finding it hard to take my mind off the break-in.

'You haven't mentioned this one before, how long have you been seeing him?' I asked, glad of the distraction, but still not engaging fully.

'A few weeks,' she murmured. 'He's great in bed.'

I wasn't in the mood for her tales of the bedroom; her boyfriends were always 'great in bed', at first, but things never seemed to work out. Unlike Nancy, I was happy to be single. I certainly wasn't going through a marriage again. I hated my ex-husband, Chris, the way he'd put me down, made me feel like a failure as a wife and mother, as a person. He was critical of my behaviour, my parenting, and we didn't share the same goals. But the moment I knew there was no hope for any future was the day he told me he didn't love Sofia, that he could never love her. I was devastated. I knew he hadn't taken to fatherhood but never realised it went so deep. When he threatened to call Social Services and have her taken away, I stood there, shaking with rage and fear and hurt. I knew then that I had to do something, so one day, when he was at work, I packed up some things and walked out, taking Sofia with me. I knew if he found us, he'd separate us any way he could, so I left no note, no forwarding address and told no one. I had to leave my old life behind for mine and my daughter's safety, and despite dreading the knock on the door, and the hand on my shoulder in the street, I really thought we'd come through. But now I could feel those dark clouds gathering.

Nancy had overheard me telling Mr Woods about the break-in as she'd waited in the shop for me to go to lunch. I had to tell him because as my landlord he would need to organise a new window lock.

'Oh no, are you both okay? What did they take?'

'Nothing, it was just kids,' I'd said, trying to make it sound insignificant, but Mr Woods was very sweet and very concerned, and said he'd have the lock fixed immediately.

Nancy had asked me if I was okay and made all the right noises, but, to my relief, once we'd left the shop, she'd dropped the subject to tell me about her boyfriend. His apparent sexual prowess was light relief compared to the torment going on in my head.

I was amused by her stories, but not envious. I had made a conscious decision not to get too close to anyone, Sofia was my priority. And it wasn't just men, I'd stayed a polite distance from the mums at the school gate too, and apart from Mr Woods and sometimes Nancy, I never discussed my business with anyone. My ex-husband had tried to have our child taken away, and if the man I'd thought I loved could do something like that, then how could I ever trust anyone again? But everyone needs someone, and Nancy was the nearest I had to a best friend. She fulfilled the only two criteria I required – she was fun and didn't ask too many questions. She'd never been married, didn't have children, and on paper, we didn't have a lot in common. But we were a similar age, shared a sense of humour, and like me, she was an outsider from up north.

Nancy's continuing search for meaning through men provided a vicarious thrill in my rather humdrum life. She left no stone unturned in her manhunt, and having been out with men from the Army, the Air Force and the Navy, she certainly liked a man in uniform. She'd sent her boyfriend from the Navy into the shop to buy perfume for her once. He was very muscular, and well over six feet tall; she said he was scared of nothing and no one. He seemed besotted, but it ended when Nancy discovered he was seeing someone else. She was devastated, and still saw him sometimes; they'd spend the night together. The other woman was long gone and he'd tell her he'd made a mistake. He asked her if they could give it another go, but she told me she was too scared to try again with him because she didn't want to get hurt. 'Navy Guy,' as she called him, was just one of many doomed relationships she enjoyed with usually handsome and *always* unsuitable boyfriends.

'If I can see the red flags from where I am, why do you miss them?' I'd said on more than one occasion. But she was desperate to meet someone, and despite her rather flighty persona, she really wanted to settle down. Recently, she'd been seeing a guy she'd met in the pub, and as the relationship had so far lasted longer than a week, she was hopeful her prince had finally arrived. I'd thought that once about my ex-husband, but how wrong I'd been; I knew better than most that there were no such things as princes.

But still, I'd see couples in cafés, or walking hand in hand along the seafront, and wonder if I was missing something. Perhaps I was naïve, but deep down I hoped that one day I'd meet someone special enough, strong enough to understand who I was, what I'd done – and *still* love me.

When I returned to the shop after lunch with Nancy, Mr Woods had already had my window lock fixed.

'I'm worried about you and Sofia,' he said. 'I wish you'd called me last night, I would have chased him off.'

'Thanks, but we're fine,' I lied, smiling at him. He was so kind, but I didn't have the heart to tell him that as a seventy-five-year-old asthmatic, he was the last person I'd call at 4 a.m. to deal with an intruder. 'I suspect it was just kids,' I said, not wanting to worry him. 'Once they realised we had nothing to steal, they went. I'm just grateful that you've sorted it so quickly, thank you.'

'Did the police take any fingerprints?' he asked.

'No, no, they just said they'd keep an eye,' I lied again.

He seemed satisfied with that and didn't ask any more questions because a customer came into the shop wanting a fragrance for his daughter, and Mr Woods, a talented perfumier who blended his own fragrances, was soon asking him all about her, hoping to sell him a bespoke perfume. But the customer said he wanted something to take away now. Mr Woods was obviously a little disappointed, his creations were gorgeous, and he took a great deal of time making something special, as he always said, 'It's a science, Emily. I'm a perfume doctor!'

'Her favourite holiday destination?' Mr Woods asked the man, who tilted his head to one side, thinking carefully about his answer. He was an older man, in his fifties, with steely grey hair that silvered at the temples, and just the shadow of a dimple in each cheek.

'I'm not sure... let me think. Madrid probably, she worked there as a student.' He smiled at me as he said this, and I saw the dimples and returned the smile. He had a quiet air of confidence, and I warmed to him as he listened politely to Mr Woods, as he waxed lyrical about 'jasmine-scented air fusing with fresh thyme'. Not once did he ask the price of any of the perfumes and when Mr Woods suggested a large bottle of *Memories of Madrid*, one of our more expensive fragrances, he happily paid the £200.

When the customer left, Mr Woods remarked on how easy the sale had been.

'Imagine spending two hundred pounds on perfume, just like that,' I said.

'He looked like a man of means to me,' he commented, as he dusted the counter.

'Yes, I suppose so. But, he had an air of sadness – I can't quite put my finger on it,' I said, 'just something about him.'

Mr Woods nodded. 'Probably his scent,' he replied. Mr Woods' sense of smell was almost superhuman, not only did he sell perfume, he created his own fragrances from raw ingredients too. His whole life was about perfume, and his observations about strangers based on their smell were always fascinating. Only that morning, a happy couple had been in to buy perfume for their wedding day, and when they'd left, I'd remarked on how happy they were.

'Ahh, it may *seem* that way, Emily, but nothing is quite what it seems there,' he had said.

Intrigued, I'd asked what he meant, and he'd slowly shaken his head, and replied, '*She* smelled of kitchens and hard work, and *he* smelled of another woman's perfume.'

'So, do you think he smelled... sad?' I asked of our recent customer.

He pulled a slightly disapproving face. 'I'm not sure. His coat smelled of damp and cooking fat, perhaps his home isn't quite as luxurious as his coat?'

I didn't get that, I definitely got sadness. My assumptions, like most people's, were based on facial expressions and body language, so I doubted Mr Woods could detect sadness in his smell. Despite his obsession with the nuance of scent, my boss sometimes saw people in rather black-and-white terms – you were good or bad, young or old, he liked you, or he didn't. He labelled people quite quickly, and wouldn't budge on his opinion. He wasn't keen on Nancy, said she was 'unreliable' – I wondered what that smelt like. I also got the feeling he wasn't enamoured with our handsome, silver-haired customer, whereas I'd warmed to him.

But Mr Woods' judgement had never been the same since

he had lost Mrs Woods. He doted on her, and she on him, and when she'd died a few years before, she took something of him with her. I sometimes felt like he lived in the past, and hadn't looked to the future since he had lost her. He still saw me as the frightened young woman who'd landed on the vicar's doorstep, and Sofia as the toddler who'd arrived with me that stormy night. He often referred to her as 'little Sofia', like he'd forgotten she'd grown, and I guessed, like me, he felt his life had stopped in the past, the day his beloved Dorothy had died. He'd stopped looking forward, only backwards.

Later that evening, as I watched Sofia texting her friends, I thought about Mr Woods' remark about people not being what they seemed; I was living proof of that.

My daughter's laughter brought me back to the moment.

'What are you laughing at?' I said, smiling at Sofia, my heart lifting at her giggles.

She handed me her phone and pointed at a cat on a treadmill. 'Archie sent it.'

'Aww, that's so nice of him to send that to you.'

She pulled a 'you're being ridiculous' face, which was a slight variation on the 'I can't believe you just said that' face. '*Nice?*' she stared at me as I handed her phone back.

'Yes, you know, boys don't usually send pictures of cute cats. He must *like* you?'

'He *likes* cats.'

'Well, good for him. You have some lovely friends.'

'Yeah, Archie sends me lots of *really nice* videos, and not just of cats,' she said absently as she gazed into the screen of her phone.

'Does he?' I asked, my interest was piqued.

'Yeah, he sends me cute videos of himself naked.' She was still gazing into her phone.

'What?' I was horrified and about to call his mother, when she looked up, her face breaking into a smile.

'Joke, Mum.'

It was my turn to roll my eyes. 'Very funny.' I was relieved though, on several levels. At fifteen, I felt she was too young for boys. I knew it would happen, but like most parents, I'd approached the concept of her growing up with fear and dread. For me it was so much worse than most parents, there was always the extra layer of concern. Would Sofia having a boyfriend mean more exposure? Would she want more freedom? And what if his family began asking questions about *me*?

She continued to scroll on her phone, as I finished my cup of tea. 'Look, darling.' I put my mug on the coffee table, as she glanced up again from her phone. 'I want you to be careful, I know this sounds stupid, but please don't talk to strangers.'

'What?' she asked, like I'd just spoken in a foreign language.

'After what happened last night. I don't want to scare you, but if they *did* take something—'

'I think they left more than they took,' she said, causing my mind to wander to the Post-it and odd-shaped plastic now hidden at the back of my wardrobe.

'I didn't mean objects,' I replied. 'I meant if they took information—'

'What *kind* of information?' she cut in.

'Well, our names, addresses, bank details... anything really.' I tried not to sound hysterical, but inside I was pretty anxious about this.

'You said they were kids, that they were harmless.'

'Yes and I still think that, but we don't *know*.'

She was looking at me doubtfully.

'Look, all I'm saying is just don't strike up new friendships with strangers at bus stops...'

'I wouldn't. What kind of weirdo do you think I am?'

'Just be aware that they could be anyone.'

I knew my words weren't landing with her, and only if something happened would she take notice, but by then it might be too late. To Sofia, this was just Mum being overprotective and making a mountain out of a molehill, but in truth it was the opposite. In the mistaken belief that after all this time we were safe, I'd let things slide, let my guard down, and it looked like he'd found us. Had Chris followed me, hung around in our garden and broken into our home? I didn't even know if it *was* Chris, but whoever it was, they weren't my friend. It was up to me to protect Sofia and myself, and after the break-in I had to be even more vigilant. So from then on, before making sure every window was locked and the front door was double-bolted at night, I'd go out into the garden with my torch and check there was no one out there.

In the mornings, I'd do the same and go outside at six thirty, when it was still dark, to check. Slipping the kitchen knife in my jacket pocket, I'd check the bins, then wander among the trees at the bottom of the garden looking for clues. One morning, just a few days after the break-in, I was walking through the dried leaves and bracken, when I saw something red on the ground. I moved it with my foot and then, holding my breath, bent down and picked it up. Clasping it between my finger and thumb, I was surprised to see it was a chocolate bar wrapper, and nearby was an empty bottle of strawberry-flavoured milk. Had he been camping out here, spying on us in the cold of night? Watching our flat? Waiting for us?

Suddenly, I heard Sofia's voice calling from the bedroom window, 'Mum, is that you?' She sounded scared, alarmed even.

'Yes, darling, it's me.'

'What are you doing?' she called down to me as I emerged from the trees.

'I thought I heard a cat,' I lied.

'It's dark and cold,' she shouted, appearing genuinely concerned.

'I'm coming in now,' I said, trying to sound casual, while discreetly throwing the wrapper and bottle in the bin, and pushing the knife down into my pocket. Did I need to be worried by this? Had someone simply thrown their rubbish in our garden? Or was there more to this? Either way, I decided that day to meet Sofia from school.

I told her I was passing the school, but she didn't believe me. I felt her embarrassment as she awkwardly said goodbye to her friends and joined me on the walk home. I knew I shouldn't have gone to the school, but I was compelled, I had this horrible feeling that if I hadn't been there, someone else might be. If it was my ex-husband playing games, then he'd know exactly how to hurt me – Sofia was the way to my heart.

'Shall we have a girls' night in tonight?' I asked in an attempt to make up for the fact that I'd turned up unannounced.

'Yeah,' she replied. In truth, most nights were 'girls' nights in' for Sofia and I, but the official title meant face masks, a girly film and popcorn. As we walked home along the seafront, the cold wind biting, something was still scratching in my head. I tried not to worry. But, later that night, as happy as I was to be in our lovely flat spending time with my daughter, I was only too aware of how fragile that happiness was for me. Just one word, one mistake, one *person* could tear everything apart. *Someone* had been in our flat, and they'd been in our garden. Whoever it was, they had started something they clearly intended to finish.

FOUR

A cool, golden autumn moved slowly into the frozen edge of winter. The mornings were frosty, the sea blustered, and the sun stayed away. It had been weeks since the break-in, I'd seen no one in the garden and, at first, I put the empty milk bottle and chocolate wrappers down to rubbish being dropped carelessly. But over the next few weeks I found the odd empty bottle of strawberry-flavoured milk and chocolate wrappers stashed in the hole of the tree, and I couldn't rest. After the first few incidents, I thought it might be Chris playing games. Had he tried to scare me, unsettle me, was this his revenge for me walking out on him? I hadn't only taken Sofia and run away that night, earlier that day I'd also taken our joint savings of £5,000 from the bank. It wasn't a huge amount, but it was all we had. After he'd threatened to put Sofia into care, I had no choice, and I'd taken it to start a new life. It had all been swallowed up in bills within the first year, but now he probably wanted it back, with interest. Was it him watching from the bottom of the garden at night, or was it someone else? My mind just kept going round in circles.

But I told myself if this had anything to do with Chris, I

would fight him if I had to, to keep what was mine. This was *my* life now, I'd built it here without him, and I wasn't going to allow him to spoil what I'd worked so hard to achieve. I would continue to be vigilant, but his shadow and the cruel threats he'd made years before weren't going to hang over me any longer. I'd finally found the peace of mind I craved here in this little town, and as long as I could keep me and my daughter safe, that's all that mattered.

Then, at the end of November, I stopped finding the strawberry milk bottles and chocolate wrappers – whoever it was had obviously found better things to do than sit in my garden in the pitch black and dead of winter.

'I reckon it's getting too cold for him to take his snacks in the dark,' I'd said to Mr Woods, who told me not to worry.

'I think it might be old Ben, you know, the homeless man. I've seen him drinking flavoured milk, he probably just throws it in the garden.'

I was comforted by this, and as the days grew colder and we started to think about Christmas, I'd put my concerns to the back of my mind. I had to push through my fear for Sofia, I didn't want to live a half-life, scared of my own shadow. Everything could be explained rationally, couldn't it?

Then, one night in early December, Sofia called to me from the front room, 'Mum, Mum, quickly!' she yelled. As a mother, you just know when they are calling you in fun or fear, and this was fear. So I ran into the room, to see her standing behind the curtains, staring out onto the dark, empty winter promenade.

'What? What is it, darling?' I asked, trying to sound calm, though, in truth, I hadn't been calm since the break-in.

'There's a guy standing by that lamp post,' she said, pointing across the road. 'He's staring at our flat.'

My stomach dropped, I felt the fizz of fear as my legs carried me to where she was standing. I looked through the window, and there under the street lamp on the promenade was a dark figure leaning, possibly staring across at the flat.

'He might be waiting for someone?' I offered feebly. 'He might not be staring at the flat, he might—'

'He was.'

'You can't really see where he's staring, it's dark,' I replied, screwing up my eyes to try to identify the dark figure shrouded in winter clothes.

'He *is*, Mum. I looked out before and he was standing even closer, right opposite our window, staring in.'

I almost fainted at this, I believed her, and though I tried to persuade her otherwise, I knew, I just *knew* after all these years I'd been found.

At that point, I considered going to the police, but what could I tell them? That someone had been in my kitchen, taken nothing, but left a piece of crescent-shaped plastic and a strange note? I could also tell them I thought I'd seen movement in my garden, that someone was leaving chocolate wrappers and empty bottles of strawberry-flavoured milk in a hole in the tree. They'd think I was mad. And then to add that I'd seen someone standing on the promenade at night looking into our flat just sounded crazy. People often wandered up and down the promenade, they may glance across into our windows now and then, nothing weird about that. But I *knew* this was weird, and only I *knew* why. But given my own history, I had to keep a low profile, and in the unlikely event that they took my concerns seriously, I couldn't get caught up in any police investigations – especially if Chris *had* carried out his threats. But I also knew that he wasn't the only one who wanted to destroy me.

The day after we saw the man across the road, I asked Mr Woods if we could perhaps have some CCTV put on the back garden of the flat. I told him what had happened and he readily agreed, and rushed into his back room to book someone to come and install it, but they never turned up. As I paid such a low rent, I felt cheeky for pushing it, especially as December was now upon us and Mr Woods would have little time or extra money to put into his properties, so I left it for the time being.

Mr Woods was in a constant state of expectation throughout the month of December about what he referred to as 'Christmas chaos'. He always started planning his Christmas perfumes months before, and I'd hear him on the phone to Italy ordering up special perfume oils. 'Musky and sweet for Christmas, with a whisper of cinnamon,' he'd say, as he mixed the ingredients in what he referred to as his 'laboratory', which was actually down in the cellar of the shop. Along with Nancy's new boyfriend, Mr Woods' Christmas plans were a pleasant distraction from my fears.

Mr Woods had been the proprietor for many years. He'd taken over the business from his mother, an Italian who'd passed down what he referred to as 'the secrets of perfume' to her son. He loved using Italian essences for his perfumes and could often be heard shouting loudly down the phone in a fusion of English and Italian. And it was during one of those loud perfume orders that the customer who'd bought perfume for his daughter a few weeks ago wandered in.

'Hello again,' I said, noting how handsome he was. His thick, steel-grey hair flopped over his face, and he pushed it back to reveal the bluest eyes. 'Did your daughter like her perfume?' I asked.

He smiled. 'She's enjoying her memories of Madrid very much, thank you.'

'Good, good,' I replied. 'Can I—'

'I'm looking for... Sorry,' he cut in and we both laughed at the fact we'd talked over each other. 'I'm looking for something for my sister,' he said. 'My daughter was so pleased with the gift, I thought I would come back.'

'Good,' I replied. 'Does she have a favourite smell?' I asked.

'I don't know. Should I know that, am I a bad brother?' he replied, pretend panic on his face.

'Not at all,' I said, giving him a reassuring smile. Mr Woods always asked about favourite smells, favourite foods, favourite places when he was helping a customer chose perfume. And in his absence I always tried to do the same and turn their favourite things into perfume.

'I know,' he offered, holding up his finger like he'd just remembered, 'she likes chocolate, does that help?'

'So she likes sweet things. What about rose? Tuberose has a heady sweetness?' I suggested.

'Sweet?' he murmured, and gave me a sidelong glance. It felt like he might be flirting, but I wasn't sure. It had been such a long time since anyone had shown that kind of interest in me, it was hard to tell. But he seemed nice and had lovely wrinkles around his eyes. Despite that air of sadness I'd noticed when he came in a few weeks before, his face seemed to slip so easily into a smile.

'There are so many fragrances to choose from, but essentially we're looking at warm, woody, floral or fresh?' I said trying to remain professional, but I got the impression my limited knowledge was rather wasted on him. I was about to attempt to charm him into buying a more expensive perfume for his sister, as Mr Woods had taught me, but before I could, he spoke.

'It must be wonderful to live in a place like this, lovely seafront, very what my mother would have called "genteel,"' he remarked.

'Yes. In travel guides, we're always described as having *a timeless charm*, which sums us up really,' I replied.

'Have you lived here long?' he asked. I thought I detected a northern accent and suddenly I felt vulnerable.

'No,' I lied, and we both stood in silence in the dimly lit shop. He moved towards me and instinctively I stepped back, my tailbone hitting the counter, sending a shot of pain through me. I looked across at him, he was still coming towards me, his arms out now.

'So, is my assistant helping you find what you're looking for?' Mr Woods' loud voice sliced into the tightness as he bowled into the shop.

'Oh, yes, she's... I'm sorry I don't know your name,' the man said, looking at me questioningly.

'I'm Emily,' I responded, unsmiling.

The chatty, friendly shop assistant had suddenly stopped smiling. For a moment, he looked confused.

'Emily's been explaining all about the fragrances,' he pushed on, 'and base notes and—'

Before he could finish, Mr Woods swooped across the shop to where we kept our most expensive perfumes in a locked cupboard. He didn't mention the £500 price tag, apparently confident that this man had the money because he picked up his keys, walked towards the cabinet, unlocked it, slowly opened the glass door and carefully reached in. This was quite a performance and when Mr Woods proffered the bottle in his open hands like it was a precious diamond, the customer caught my eye, obviously amused by my boss's theatrical performance. I gave an awkward smile, I didn't want to seem disloyal to Mr Woods, but he was unintentionally amusing at times.

'Would you like to smell?' he asked, before opening the bottle like even a sniff of this potion was costly.

The man moved across to him and Mr Woods wafted one hand above the bottle as he held it under the man's nose.

Mr Woods and I both waited in silence for the verdict. Pulling away from the bottle, he said, 'I'll take it.' And just like last time, he didn't ask the price.

Mr Woods couldn't hide his delight, this was an unexpected sale for a Tuesday morning out of season, and having taken his money, suggested I gift-wrap the perfume before disappearing into the back of the shop.

'I'm sure your sister will be thrilled with this,' I said, as I wrapped the perfume at the counter.

As he watched me wrap the perfume, I noticed he was looking at me, and each time I glanced up, our eyes met. I smiled awkwardly, surprised at how much I liked the attention, I hoped the heat in my face didn't give that away. The past few weeks had made me even more wary than usual, and when I'd heard his northern accent, I'd been triggered, remembering a past I wanted to forget. But now I told myself, here was a man just wanting to buy perfume for his sister, which in itself showed him to be a kind, caring sort of person, and the opposite to Chris. And when I looked up at him, I was reminded of feelings long ago that I'd hidden away.

He was still watching me, and I felt like he was thinking of what to say next, like he wanted to keep the conversation going.

'So you have a sister,' I said, stupidly, unable to think of anything else.

'Yeah, she's my big sister, always looked after me. Do you have any siblings?'

I nodded my head, but didn't offer any more personal information. I thought about my brother and sister, scattered to the four winds, and wondered how they were, and *where* they were.

'How many?'

I looked at him vacantly. I hated questions about my past. One of the many bonuses about living in sunny Sidmouth was that people kept themselves to themselves, and that suited me. I folded the thick gift paper around the perfume box. I was all fingers and thumbs as I tried to figure out how to answer. I was rather relieved when Mr Woods reappeared and began talking into the silence.

'So you aren't from around here?' Mr Woods asked.

'No, I—'

'I've been here all my life,' he continued, not allowing him to finish. 'Sidmouth born and bred, nothing I don't know about this place.'

I looked up from the ribbon I was now securing around the wrapped gift. Again, our eyes met and I felt there was something, definitely *something*.

'Emily's been here over a decade, haven't you?' Mr Woods was saying. 'Started work here when her daughter was at nursery school, used to bring her into the shop afterwards, my wife loved that little girl.' He smiled at the memory.

'She did.' I nodded, feeling very exposed.

'Gosh, so you have a daughter too? How old is she?' he asked.

'She'll be about twelve, thirteen...?' He looked at me questioningly. Mr Woods was never certain of her age, he still saw Sofia as the little girl who toddled around the shop.

'She's fifteen,' I said, not wanting to elaborate.

'A teenager? You don't look old enough,' he said to me, like Mr Woods wasn't even there.

I was flattered, but rolled my eyes as my boss looked on, smiling at us both, apparently unaware of the electricity in the air.

'Emily's like a daughter to me, and Sofia's my honorary granddaughter,' he added with a chuckle. 'There's nothing I wouldn't do for this one. Since Dorothy died, you and Sofia are all I've got,' he said with a sad smile. And with that, he picked up a couple of bottles from a shelf and trundled off to his cellar, without even saying goodbye.

'Was it something I said?' the man asked, after he left.

'Oh, he's a bit eccentric, but has a heart of gold. He's gone into his "laboratory."' I gestured with my head as I tied the bow.

'*Laboratory?* What the hell does he do in there, cut up the customers he doesn't like?'

I laughed. 'Yeah, I pretend not to notice the severed limbs

lying around the staffroom – I can't afford to lose my job,' I joked.

'Ah yes, single mum and all that.'

'How do you know?' I snapped.

He looked shocked at my sudden change. 'I don't, I just guessed. Your boss said that you and your daughter were all he had. Presumably, if you had a partner, he would have mentioned him? And you're not wearing a wedding ring, and I'm starting to sound like a stalker – like I've been studying you a little *too* closely.' He glanced at me from under his brows, and I couldn't help but smile.

'Sorry, I'm just a very private person.' I checked the wrapping on his perfume and handed it to him.

'Thanks, Emily. I'm Oliver by the way,' he said, taking the perfume with one hand and thrusting the other one out to shake. 'And you're right... about being a private person, not sharing everything. People share too much if you ask me – or TMI, as my granddaughter would say,' he smiled.

He was still holding out his hand, so I took it. His palm was big and warm and soft as it enclosed mine, and I was surprised at myself imagining his fingers caressing my naked skin. I was beginning to think like Nancy; what the hell had got into me?

That evening, as I made vegetable lasagne for dinner, my mind kept returning to earlier, and Oliver. I kept seeing his eyes, feeling them on me, and his soft hand that clearly didn't do manual work. In all the years I'd been single, I hadn't met anyone who I'd felt a connection with, and I felt sad that we'd probably never meet again. I felt stupid, but couldn't stop thinking about him, wondering who he was, where he lived, if he was married, and if he was interested in me, or just a good person who was warm and friendly with everyone?

Like a detective, I continued to go over and over every little thing he said, looking for clues, and trying to jigsaw together a man, a life. I only abandoned this when I detected the aroma of burning lasagne.

'Sofia, dinner's ready!' I called, opening the oven and being greeted with a blast of hot garlic air. To my great relief, the lasagne was just 'well done', not quite burnt.

With oven gloves, I carefully lifted the bubbling rectangle of cheese and pasta and vegetables and placed it on a mat in the centre of the table.

'Sofia!' I called again, but no answer.

I wandered through into the other room, where she was sitting on an easy chair, her laptop on her knee.

'Sweetie, I've been calling you,' I started, as I walked in behind her. But she didn't turn around, and I realised then she had headphones in and must be listening to music. I stepped forward to tap her gently. But as I glanced over her shoulder, her phone pinged and I was suddenly drawn to it. I wouldn't normally peer at her phone, teenagers need their space and privacy – but something pulled me in. Sofia was having a conversation with someone in private messages on Instagram. I leaned in without going too close and could just about read what it said, and as I did, I had to hold on to the back of the chair to steady myself.

Your mother isn't who you think she is.

FIVE

As I stood behind Sofia, I gasped, which immediately alerted her that I was there.

'Mum, why are you creeping up on me? You made me jump!' she snapped, in a flash of anger. She quickly clicked off her phone and grasped her headphones. She clearly didn't want me to see what was on the screen, and I hadn't had the chance to see the name of the sender on the message, I was too busy looking at the words. But they were enough to scare me.

'It's time for dinner,' I managed to say. As I walked back into the kitchen, I felt a shiver and the hairs prickled at the back of my neck. Was this simply a school friend having a joke, or was it a message from my ex? It wasn't a coincidence that someone was hanging around at the same time my daughter was being told her mother wasn't who she thought she was.

I stood in the kitchen on wobbly legs, wondering how I was going to broach this. I had to let her know I'd seen it, but I didn't want her to think I'd been snooping. If I showed too much interest, she might start hiding things from me, and until now she'd always been a very honest child. She shared most things with me, especially her concerns about school and friendships, and I didn't want to spoil this.

'Been doing homework?' I asked nonchalantly, as I cut into the lasagne, and she handed me her plate.

'Yeah.' She didn't look at me, no twirling around the kitchen, no gasps of delight when she saw the garlic bread like she usually did.

I put her plate of food in front of her and still she seemed unable to look at me. Fear creeped into my stomach and snaked around. I'd worked hard, sacrificed friendships, relationships and my nursing career to make our life here, and keep us safe. But just as I'd dared to believe we were home and dry, now my life seemed to be unravelling. I felt quite tearful just thinking about it – surely after everything I'd been through, I deserved some peace?

I sat down at the table with Sofia, who was already tucking in. I had to ask her about the message. I appreciated that a fifteen-year-old wouldn't appreciate her mother prying into her private conversations. But this wasn't about privacy, it was about safety and her security.

'Hey, I have to ask,' I said, picking up my fork, pretending to be distracted by my lasagne, 'I couldn't help but see your message just now.'

Her head shot up from her dinner and a scowl slowly formed on her face. 'What message?'

'It said something about... about your *mum not being who you think she is*?' I tried to sound vague while shaking my head slowly. 'What's that about? I wasn't actually looking, but I caught it in the corner of my eye.'

She flushed slightly, and from the guilty expression on her face, I realised I was right to be concerned, this wasn't a school friend having joke.

'Has this person sent other messages too?' I hear myself

croak, my fork and my heart now poised, waiting for her response.

She shrugged, and continued eating. 'No. Just some weirdo, I guess.'

'Do weirdos often send you private messages on Instagram?' I asked, showing my alarm at this by putting down my fork. Her flippant response angered me, she had no idea of the danger she might be putting us both in. 'Because if so, I don't think you should be going on there, or any other social media platforms for that matter. After the break-in, I specifically asked you not to speak to people you don't know.'

She knew this was a genuine threat, that I would make her delete all her accounts and might even confiscate her phone. Her friend Ella's mother had recently done this and the other girls had lived in fear of the same thing happening ever since. I sent a silent thank you to Ella's mum for showing the way.

Sofia was now shifting in her chair and instead of wolfing down the lasagne and garlic bread, she was playing with it. I waited in the silence for more information, but when it was clear there wasn't any forthcoming, I had to speak.

'I need you to talk to me, Sofia, because this is important. I'm your mum and you can't hide things from me. You know the score, I will just have to go through all your private messages on *all* your accounts, because you're fifteen and vulnerable.'

She was looking down, still messing with her food, not responding.

'I'm only asking because I'm concerned for your safety, I *worry* about you.' I reached out and touched her hand.

She looked at me, then immediately looked away.

'So, what's going on? Are you chatting with someone I don't know?'

She rolled her eyes, but the mention of confiscating her social media had made her think about the potential outcome of this conversation, so she turned to me. 'She's my friend.'

My mouth went dry, had my daughter developed a 'friend-ship' with someone who wasn't who she thought they were? Who could be anyone.

'*Who* is she? Is she even *female*?' I asked.

She didn't answer me, just tapped on the edge of the table with her fingers. My heart was beating fast to the same rhythm, as panic rose inside me.

'Sofia, answer me. Are they saying they're the same age as you? What's their name?'

She dragged her eyes up to meet mine, and unsmiling, she replied, 'She's a couple of years younger than me; she's called Pink Girl.'

I couldn't believe what I was hearing; it all felt so ominous to me.

'Pink Girl isn't a *name*, it's something people call them-selves when they don't want to reveal their real names. "She" could be anyone? A forty-year-old man, someone we know who's just weird... anyone!'

I couldn't help but wonder if this was Chris, my ex. Sofia didn't really remember him, but she'd often asked about him, and I feared she had created something quite different in her head about what and who he was. *Could* this be him?

'It's not a *man*. She's my age. At first, I thought it was someone from school... one of the boys...' She looked embarrassed.

'Who?'

'Jake, Archie?'

'Okay, so do you *know* it isn't them?'

She shook her head. 'No it isn't.'

'So it's not someone from school? It's someone you've *only* met online?' I'd never wanted her to be on social media, and had only allowed her an Instagram account a few months before. I'd figured that she'd go online anyway, and by allowing her to be on social media, she wouldn't do it behind my back as kids sometimes do. I also thought I could keep an eye on what was going on – so much for that.

She hesitated for a moment, then nodded.

'So, what sort of things does she say to you?' I asked.

'Nothing creepy. She just messaged me saying how cute my top was in my profile pic and asking about my favourite music.'

It may have seemed innocent to Sofia, but to me it sounded like the way a predator would befriend a child. What the hell was going on?

'What else?'

She was staring at me, and I had the feeling she was deciding what to tell me and what not to tell me. For the first time, I felt the sting of my daughter's duplicity. 'Just stuff...'

'Like what?' I pressed.

She sighed like she really couldn't be bothered with this. 'I dunno, just *stuff*,' she repeated, but when she looked up and saw my face, she realised I meant business. 'Like, she asked what's my favourite café, where do I hang out, do I like living here and—'

'You told them where you *live*?' I was now in full-on panic.

'I didn't *tell* her, she knew... that's why I thought it was someone from school.'

I couldn't speak. I was horrified. And scared. Her reaction suggested that she most likely *did* give the details of the town where she lived, the places she went. Sofia thought this was a new friend. *But I knew it wasn't.*

I took a breath, trying to calm myself. 'How long have you been messaging?'

'A couple of weeks, that's all?'

I wasn't sure I believed her. 'So you never spoke to anyone before the break-in?'

'That was weeks ago – no, I swear it's only been a couple of weeks. A month tops,' she added quickly. 'Sorry... I'm sorry.'

I heard her voice break, and it hurt my heart, but I couldn't comfort her, I couldn't just say it's okay, no harm done, because harm *had* been done. And I needed her to know that. This was serious, dangerous.

'Swear to God, Mum, I didn't tell them *anything*,' she said, her dinner abandoned now.

All this time we'd lived here in secret, no one from outside had a hope in hell of finding us. I'd never had accounts on social media and had trusted Sofia to have privacy settings on, and be aware of dangers, but this had been happening under my nose. I could have kicked myself for being so stupid and not more vigilant.

'You *have* to come off social media,' I said firmly.

'Mum, no,' she whined. 'Why? I haven't done anything wrong. Other kids at school chat to people they haven't met.'

'Well, they shouldn't, and *you* especially shouldn't—' I started.

'Why me?'

I couldn't go down that road. 'Because we're vulnerable, a woman and daughter living alone are targets for online criminals.'

'It wasn't *my* fault we were burgled,' she yelled. 'I didn't know Pink Girl then.' She was angry, frustrated, but so was I.

'You obviously can't be trusted, I should never have let you talk me into having social media accounts.'

'But, Mum, my privacy settings are on. *Strangers* can't see my page, you're being so unfair!'

She was flustered now, embarrassed and, despite the bravado, probably worried too. Only *she* knew what she'd revealed to a complete stranger, and she wasn't going to share it with me.

'But you don't know Pink Girl, they could be anyone! So you're telling a *stranger* where your favourite café is. They could be watching you in that café with your friends, they could follow you home. What if it's some old man who likes school-girls?' I said, aware this was probably unsettling and creepy, but if scaring her meant she'd stay safe, then so be it.

'God, it's just a *chat*,' she huffed, but by her tone I could tell my words had got through and she was finally questioning what she'd done. 'I chat to people all the time,' she said, with an air of defiance and teenage arrogance that angered me.

'You think you're so grown up and yet you're potentially putting us *both* in danger. You clearly aren't responsible enough to be on social media.'

Tears sprang to her eyes and I immediately hated myself. I'd hurt her feelings and that was the last thing I ever wanted to do. She started to cry, and I reached my hand across the table to touch hers, but she flinched and pulled it away, leaving my hand, palm down on the table.

'You're being so mean, Mum,' she said through the same tears she'd cried when she'd fallen off her bike when she was little.

'I'm sorry, I don't want to make you cry, but I thought you understood the dangers. I'm concerned about what you've been doing.'

She was full-on sobbing now, but I told myself that perhaps this was what had to happen to make her understand how serious it was.

'Look, whoever it was said something about your mum's *secret*, what was that about?' I asked, gently, trying to get to the root of this. 'Because that doesn't sound like the kind of thing a friend would say to another friend.'

She shook her head. 'I don't know, I saw the message, but I haven't responded.'

'It's just a weird thing to say to someone you don't know, doesn't it creep you out? If it were me, I would have immedi-ately blocked them.'

'She's my friend,' she whimpered. 'I like her.' She wiped her eyes with her cardigan sleeve.

'It sounds creepy to me,' I said, standing up and grabbing the box of tissues from the dresser. 'Can I see the messages?' I touched her shoulder as I put the tissues in front of her in what I hoped was a reassuring way.

She pushed her phone towards me.

'No, let's look together,' I said. I needed her to help me navigate this brave new world.

She reluctantly turned on her phone, opened up the screen, and pulling my chair up next to her, I focused, bracing myself, as she ran her fingers along the keyboard. One click and all the Instagram messages were suddenly displayed, and as she began to scroll through, I leaned closer, screwing up my eyes to focus on and devour each and every word.

Slowly, thoroughly, I read through the conversations, and they were pretty much as she'd said, nothing creepy or controversial, just chatting about *stuff*. In itself it would be nothing to worry about, except for that final, stinging comment.

Your mother isn't who you think she is. My stomach jolted again at the sight of it, and I knew then, it *must* be him.

'You've been speaking to this person for longer than a few weeks,' I remarked, noting the dates on the messages.

'Yeah,' she replied, a little on the defensive again now she'd wiped away her tears.

So this could have been Chris, and if it was, that's how he discovered where we lived before the break-in. He had found Sofia on social media and made it his mission to get his revenge on me.

'Let me see Pink Girl's page,' I said, businesslike.

She pulled a face, but turned back to the screen, and I watched as she brought up Pink Girl's profile. I leaned in closely to look at what was on the page. I was after some clues that this was a forty-six-year-old man posing as a teenage girl, but again, it seemed very plausible. The photos were of a teenage girl with her dog, her friends, there were even videos of her applying make-up. Was I barking up the wrong tree after all? Was this nothing to do with Chris or me or anything else, just two girls meeting online? But why the message about me?

'Where does she live?' I asked, something else suddenly sliding into my brain.

'Somewhere up north, I think,' Sofia replied.

And with that the worry returned. I didn't know who this Pink Girl was, I couldn't trust them.

'I'd like you to block them now please?'

Sofia looked at me like I'd just told her there was a bomb under the table. 'Are you serious?'

'I'm deadly serious. I want to see you do it, and if you don't, I'll confiscate your phone and you'll only be allowed to use the laptop for homework. I mean it.'

I watched as she slowly clicked the button.

'Shall we finish our dinner now?' I said, standing up, moving my chair back.

'Not hungry,' she muttered. 'I'm going to bed.'

'Okay. But before you go, can I please have your password.'

'*What?* No, that's not fair!' she protested.

'I'm sorry but until you can be trusted, you have to give it to me. Your choice, if you don't, your phone will be—'

Before I could finish, she spat the words and numbers at me.

'Will you write it down please,' I insisted. I didn't plan to use it but hoped the fact I had it might mean she wasn't tempted to unblock her online *friend*. I dug out a pen and a Post-it from the drawer, put them on the table and she snatched them, scribbling the password before storming off to bed.

I sat for a long time in the silence, left in the wake of the storm, wondering how it had all escalated so quickly and kicking myself for not managing it better.

I'd left my life behind to keep her safe, and though I'd lived in fear until now, I'd naively thought after all this time there was no danger of being found. I'd taken so much care not to risk our safety, and to keep our little family of two under the radar. But as I sat in the silence without her, I knew the worst had happened, and I was very, very scared.

SIX

The morning after I saw Sofia's message, she was very quiet when she wandered into the kitchen for breakfast. We were both hurt and a little tender after our argument as it was unusual for us to fall out and I was keen to offer an olive branch.

'I don't want to be the mother that shuts everything down, I don't want to stop you from doing anything you want to do. But if I feel it's unsafe, then I have no choice,' I said, trying to justify my reaction to the whole Pink Girl situation.

'I get it, Mum,' she murmured. 'But you're wrong. Pink Girl isn't dangerous, she *is* just a friend. We talk about stuff I talk to my school friends about. How would a paedo know about make-up and clothes?'

'They would make it their mission to know, it's called grooming,' I replied. I couldn't tell her my real fears, I had to create a bogeyman to keep her alert. 'If she's just a friend, why would she make that comment about me not being who you think I am?' I asked.

'I don't know, it was probably a joke, but I'll never know now because you made me block her,' she groaned.

'Look, you've watched *Catfish* on the TV, you know what

happens. These poor teenagers fall in love, or they make friends with someone—'

'Yeah and it's not a prince in a castle, it's some weirdo living in a truck. I know what catfishing is, Mum.' She rolled her eyes and picked up her school bag. 'I gotta go,' and she headed for the hallway.

'Let's not fight, Sofia,' I said, following her.

She stopped in the doorway, shrugged, and with a slam of the door she was gone.

I knew to her this was huge; I'd basically asked her to cancel who she thought was her new best friend, but I couldn't risk her being online until I'd found out what was going on. I had a right to worry as this wasn't the first time my daughter had become so enamoured of someone that she didn't pick up on potential danger.

The previous year, Sofia had spent a lot of time with a girl from school called Zoe, who was new to the area. I didn't know her, so suggested she invite her new friend over for tea. Sofia asked if she could sleep over too, which I agreed to. I bought them popcorn, strawberry face masks and assumed they'd have a girlie evening watching a romcom. However, the next morning the face masks were unused, the popcorn all over the bedroom, and there was a distinct smell of something thick and sweet in the air. And when I asked what film they'd watched, they had looked at me like I'd just spoken in Mandarin. Despite hearing lots of giggles coming from Sofia's room, apparently the only screens they'd been watching were the ones on their phones. I suspected the girls had been vaping, the cloying sweet odour that clung to the bedlinen and curtains transported me straight back to *that* room – curtains shrouded in cigarette smoke, the teddy bear reeking of nicotine. I felt the despair; was I fighting a losing battle now as a mother myself? Was this the beginning of something else, smoking, drugs, a different life? I felt hopeless, and wondered, not for the first time, if it's possible to fight our destiny, or if our lives are dictated by genes and history?

I didn't want to cause a scene and embarrass Sofia in front of Zoe, so asked her about the smell after her friend had gone.

'Oh my God, Mum, we wouldn't vape. It was probably perfume you could smell. You are such a drama queen,' she'd said, and laughed about it with such gusto, I'd believed her. But now I wondered if I could trust my daughter as much as I thought I could. Perhaps she was capable of deception after all? Perhaps it was in her blood?

Unlike Sofia's other friends, Zoe was quite surly and didn't really acknowledge me, despite stopping by the flat with Sofia after school, often staying for food and the occasional sleepover. Being in a small town, I'd heard her mother spent most evenings in the pub and I guessed Zoe spent a lot of time alone or looking after siblings. If I'd thought I could help this child in any way, I would have taken her under my wing, brought her into our family, but she wasn't receptive to me at all and would whisper behind her hand to Sofia, which I felt was quite rude. I reluctantly accepted this friendship until I noticed Sofia copying Zoe's mannerisms, avoiding eye contact, shrugging and sulking. It wasn't like Sofia at all and she was also becoming slightly withdrawn from me.

'What is it about Zoe that you like so much?' I'd asked, treading gently, trying not to be too negative. 'She always seems rather unhappy, and you're not like that. And you know what they say, don't let anyone dull your sparkle,' I said, repeating some cliché I'd seen on a birthday card.

She had rolled her eyes. 'Oh my God, Mum, you've been in the card shop again, haven't you?'

I'd had to smile at this. 'I *might* have been, but it's true, you've gone quiet and morose since you started hanging out with Zoe.'

Another shrug, just like her new friend. 'I dunno, I just like her,' she'd said.

'But you don't seem to have much in common. She doesn't go to art club or gymnastics class like your other friends,' I'd pointed out. Worryingly, I'd also heard from one of the other mums that while Sofia and her other friends were working with charcoal at the after-school club or doing cartwheels in the church hall, Zoe was hanging out in the park vaping (which would explain the oversweet, fruity smell in the bedroom after she'd stayed over).

'No, she hates shit like that. Zoe wouldn't be seen dead at gymnastics or an after-school club.'

I flinched at the way she now peppered her sentences with words like 'shit'. I knew it was the way Zoe spoke, and I didn't like it, they were fourteen-year-old girls. But I saved that fight for another day; I'd learned the hard way that one had to be strategic when dealing with teenagers, and not just go in at the deep end.

'Oh, well, that's Zoe's choice not to do extracurricular stuff, but you enjoy the art class, don't you?'

She'd nodded.

'I just don't understand why you're friends, when you seem so different from each other. I mean, what do you talk about?'

She didn't immediately respond, was probably trying to think of the best way to broach this, but eventually she'd looked up and said, 'We talk about our dads.'

I felt like I'd been hit in the face. I'd always tried to be sensitive to the fact that after I split with Chris, Sofia didn't have a father figure in her life, and consoled myself with the fact that Mr Woods was like a slightly distant grandfather figure, and preferable to Chris. I'd thought Sofia understood that, and it wasn't an issue, but apparently it was. I'd tried so hard to be a good all-round parent, to provide her with everything she needed, and it hurt to think I hadn't been enough, that I'd failed her in some way.

'Where's Zoe's dad?' I'd asked.

'Prison,' she'd replied matter-of-factly. I didn't want to judge, but I wasn't surprised, it explained the way Zoe was. It made me even more concerned about Sofia hanging around with this girl, but if I tried to stop the friendship, it might make things worse. I decided to just keep an eye on things and hope it fizzled out naturally.

One evening, a couple of weeks later, Sofia had asked if she could go to Zoe's house for a sleepover. Instinctively, I didn't want her to go. I trust my instincts, always have, so I had explained that I didn't know her mother and I'd really rather she didn't.

Predictably, Sofia had objected strongly to this, so I'd conceded and said she could stay until late on a Friday or Saturday evening. 'But the deal is that I come and collect you.'

Sofia was easily swayed, easily impressed by other girls, and as a mum I wanted to be there for her in a way my own mother couldn't be there for me. Mum had been ill for a long time with breast cancer, and as my father had walked out before I was born, she was all I had. I used to make a wish every night before I went to sleep that Mum would get better, and along with that wish, I'd make a second wish, that my father would come back. Mum never spoke about him, and so I imagined this prince-like figure on a white stallion coming to rescue us. I used to envy the other girls at school who had dads and had this daydream of him turning up at the school gate one day, his arms open wide. But it never happened, and I had to count my blessings that I had a lovely mother; but tragically, my sister and brother never really got to know her. They were only two and five when she died; I was twelve, and as Mum had been poorly on and off for most of their short lives, my little siblings saw me as their mum.

My mother had been a single parent like me, and having

seen her struggle, I was only too aware that children were a huge responsibility for one person. I had no one else to share any decisions with; sometimes I'd run things by my friend, Nancy, or Mr Woods, but neither of them had been parents, so invariably I just went with my gut, as I always had when it came to Zoe.

My real fear about Sofia spending time at Zoe's house was that her mother might not be around, and might leave the girls to their own devices. I imagined Zoe would probably have a house party, or worse still, maybe her father was out of prison now and living with them at the house. What if he was hanging around there with his friends? My daughter was only fourteen then, and I didn't want her exposed, or vulnerable, to any bad influences. I remember being upset about the situation when I was at work one day and told Mr Woods all about it. He was as horrified at the vaping as he was at the fact my daughter might be forced to socialise with middle-aged ex-prisoners. I probably exaggerated the whole thing, I've always catastrophised slightly, particularly when it comes to Sofia, but it was good to have someone to share my fears with, even if I did worry him with my concerns.

'I don't like the sound of this Zoe one little bit,' he'd said. As a single parent, I always felt alone in my concerns for Sofia, so it was nice to know someone else cared and saw the same dangers I did. He'd asked if I wanted him to talk to her. It was very sweet of him, but I doubted he could get through to her, and I wanted to tread carefully. She was at a tricky age. Treading the line between childhood and adulthood was always going to be a worry. Having seen what had happened to my sister, who went off the rails around sixteen, I didn't want the same to happen to Sofia.

But then, miraculously, after just a few months, Zoe seemed to disappear from the conversation. Sofia never mentioned her, and began to reconnect with her old friends.

'How's Zoe?' I had asked one day, curious. 'You don't mention her much.'

'Haven't seen her,' she'd replied. 'She missed loads of school, then got into a fight with a teacher. She's been suspended.'

'I had a feeling she was heading for trouble that one,' I'd said.

'You never liked her,' she'd snapped. 'You're probably glad she got suspended.'

I admired my daughter's loyalty to her friend but couldn't help but feel it was misplaced. 'I'm not glad she's been suspended, but I admit, I always worried when you were with her.'

'You *hated* her. She always said, "your ma hates me."'

'I didn't *hate* her, she was just a young girl, I hardly *knew* her,' I'd said, in an attempt to defend myself, at the same time feeling guilty, because it was true I wasn't sad to see the back of her.

'You *did* hate her, always asking why I was friends with her,' she'd snapped, her face flushed with pent-up anger. She'd never said this before, and I remember being shocked at how much she'd held on to.

'Sofia, please don't be so aggressive, she *was* a bad influence. I always felt uneasy when you were with her.' What I really wanted to say was, 'That girl is trouble and the very idea of you spending time with her gives me sleepless nights.'

It turned out my instincts around Zoe weren't wrong, and one evening, I saw for myself the dark little pockets of life that lie in wait for a teenage girl, even in an old-fashioned seaside town like ours. I'd been working late, stocktaking then walking through the park when I saw Zoe with a group of older teenagers. They were laughing and shouting, the language was vile. As I got closer, I realised that some of the older boys in the group looked like they were in their twenties. It was dusk, the trees were black against the sky and blocking out much of the weakening light, but I heard someone say, 'She's going, she's going.' I slowed down, almost rooted to the spot, and that's when I saw her. She looked completely out of it, dark shadows under her eyes, her hair matted, and she was just staring ahead.

'Zoe?' I murmured and stepped towards the group, aware of the panic, the fear in the suppressed voices.

Instinctively, they immediately formed a protective circle around her.

'Is she okay?' I asked, but the reaction was visceral as one of the men broke away from the group to walk slowly, menacingly, towards me.

'Fuck off, just fuck off...' he muttered under his breath.

I glared at him, and he glared back, both of us standing in the semi darkness, the others watching in scared silence. In that instant, I knew if I challenged him, he would hurt me. So I slowly backed away, almost stumbling as I went, and then I ran, only turning back when I reached the park gate.

I called the police as soon as I got home, and they immediately dispatched someone to the park, but apparently there was no one there by then.

A few days later, Sofia had told me that Zoe was back at school.

'Oh, did you sit with her at lunchtime?' I'd asked, hoping she'd say no.

Sofia had shaken her head. 'No, she's been in trouble with the police.'

'Oh?' I'd tried not to look too interested.

'Yeah, she was with some of her friends in the park and someone grassed on them to the police.'

'What?'

'She says it was you, and she hates me now,' she spat accusingly. 'She says she's going to beat me up if she sees me, says it's all your fault, she says she'll hurt you too.'

'That's just nasty,' I replied.

'She's upset, you've ruined her life, Mum!' she hissed.

'I'm sorry she feels that way,' I'd replied, 'but they were clearly using drugs. Instead of threatening violence, I'd have thought she might thank me for saving her life. If I hadn't done anything, she might be dead by now.'

Sofia had rolled her eyes.

'You really don't get it, do you?' I had yelled, angry now. 'It's about life and death, and the way you live your life now dictates your future. Don't you dare roll your eyes at me,' I'd added, as Sofia stomped off to her room.

Knowing Zoe was back at school bothered me, and unbeknown to Sofia I went to the school the very next day and had a meeting with the Year 11 teacher, making it very clear that they needed to keep an eye on Zoe.

'She needs support,' I'd said. 'She's threatened Sofia because I reported her and her friends for taking drugs in the park, and I'd prefer if they were kept apart.' The year head had said they would be putting 'safeguarding methods' in place, for both Sofia and Zoe.

My daughter never found out I'd asked for them to be kept apart, she didn't need to know. I was just keeping her safe, I'd seen what the heady cocktail of youth, drugs and peer pressure could do.

It wasn't long afterwards that Zoe's mother moved her and her siblings to Scotland, apparently in an attempt to leave all the trouble behind. But it seemed that Zoe got in with a bad crowd, and her problems became worse after the move. Just a few weeks after leaving Sidmouth, Zoe took what was considered to be an accidental overdose and died.

Sofia was devastated by the news, it was the first time she'd ever known death and as it was a friend her own age, it hit her hard.

'With support it could have been prevented,' I'd explained, 'but given her background, her life, she had no chance.'

Even now, I sometimes see Zoe's face in the shadows, the hollowed-out cheeks, sunken eyes emanating fear and hate. Then she morphs slowly into my sister, the same haunted look, the same tortured face. I think of my sister often, she's never far from my thoughts. She never stood much of a chance in life, some people can't escape their childhoods, and they go on to recreate them. I'd run as far away as possible from my past and from what I'd done, hoping to erase it, but now I know I was fighting a losing battle. The past can't be erased, because it lives inside you, and however hard you try, you will never escape. Even when you think you have...

SEVEN

Despite Sofia blocking her online, I still worried about Pink Girl, who she really was, and what she wanted. It played on my mind, but I didn't want to keep going over and over it with Sofia, I wanted her to move on, so on a quiet day in the shop, I found myself talking about it to Mr Woods. He was a good listener, didn't judge and was always on our side, and with no family around, that meant a lot.

'You know, I think perhaps Sofia is attracted to difficult people. She was the same with that Zoe girl,' he said, shaking his head.

He made the same connection I had and I nodded. 'Perhaps I've been too protective,' I said, 'and she's attracted to dangerous characters?'

'Ahh yes, forbidden fruit always tastes sweetest,' he said with a smile. 'But I do think the internet is evil. I think you should simply ban it!'

'If only it were that easy,' I murmured.

'It is, you just switch it off at the mains!'

He was seventy-five and didn't really understand the inter-net's potency and power, and turning off the mains didn't solve the mobile phone issue. Besides, it was now in children's DNA. For parents today, the Pandora's box had already been opened, and it was up to us to manage it. But I did take his point about Sofia being attracted to people who might be difficult, or potentially dangerous. It was something I'd also seen, but when someone else confirms it for you, it's hard to shake off – and it bothered me because it made her more susceptible to people who might want to do harm.

Later, I met up with Nancy, and shared my concerns. As a serial online dater, my friend understood both the allure and the complexities of social media.

'I'd love to "ban it", as Mr Woods suggests, but his solution is too extreme,' I said with a sigh.

She laughed. 'He's a mad old bugger, but he has a point.'

'Yes, but it's more complex than internet or no internet – she's a young girl, she's vulnerable, and yet she doesn't seem to realise this,' I explained, biting into a flapjack. 'I asked Sofia to surrender her password, which meant opening up her online life to her mother – and at fifteen that's a big ask. Sofia and I only have each other – and I feel like she hates me right now.'

'You have no choice, if she's talking to paedos or—'

'I don't think this is a paedophile,' I replied. Though grooming was a very real danger, and something I'd considered, it was quite different to what I feared was actually going on. 'Sofia has blocked her, but I still feel uneasy that this person is out there, I want to know who it is... and more importantly where they are.'

'Don't put yourself in danger, you don't know who this person is, it could be anyone.'

It could be anyone, but my first suspect was definitely still my ex, but I couldn't tell Nancy that.

'I just want to scare this bloody troll, that's all. I'm not exactly sure how I can find them though.'

'Even if you *did* find Pink Girl, she might tell Sofia. Sofia freaked out the last time you interfered, with that Zoe, the girl who died.'

'But it's not the same,' I said, taking a sip of my coffee. It wasn't the same, it was very different: Zoe was every mother's nightmare, Pink Girl was just *my* nightmare. I put down my coffee cup. 'Thing is, I wanted access to Sofia's social media because I needed her to understand I didn't trust *her*, but now I feel like it's been flipped and she doesn't trust *me*.'

'Why do you feel that?'

'Well, last night for example, she was on her phone and suddenly got a text and was looking at it, and responding, but wouldn't even tell me who it was from when I asked.'

'That's fair enough, isn't it?' she answered. 'She's a teenager, it's what they do.' She was looking at me like I was mad.

'I know, but that's not Sofia, she'd usually say, "It's Ruby or Archie and they're asking if I can go to the cinema." Or it might just be that someone sent her a funny cat picture and she'd show me. She used to share everything with me and now she doesn't share anything.'

Nancy lifted her hand in the air, a halt sign to stop talking. 'It may have *seemed* like she was sharing with you, but I bet it was always totally censored. She didn't show you any dick pics, did she?'

'No!'

'I rest my case. *Everyone* gets dick pics, so she *wasn't* sharing everything.'

'She's a *child*, Nancy!' I was shocked at the suggestion.

'Yeah, that's what my mum thought about me. And your mum about you probably.'

I took a breath, it made me uncomfortable talking about Mum. I worried I might reveal something. 'My mum died before I was old enough to deceive her,' I said with a wistful smile.

'Yeah, sorry, I meant—'

'No, don't apologise, my kid sister had a lot of issues later with her stepmother. We had different fathers, and when our mum died, her dad took her. She was only two years old, cute as a button.' I smiled, fondly remembering my baby sister with the red curly hair. 'I found out later that she had this wicked stepmother who locked her in her room and was vile to her. She ended up in a children's home, and from the age of twelve, she started drinking, sleeping with men and was soon taking drugs,' I said, tears pricking my eyes.

'I'm sorry, love,' Nancy said, looking down at her coffee.

'Oh it's life, isn't it? But I got sidetracked there, what I was trying to say was that's why I want to stay close to Sofia, keep an eye on what she's doing. My sister once told me that her stepmum told her to run away to make life easier for them, and eventually she did, she was seven years old. She had such a horrible childhood.'

'Yeah, I can relate to that,' she said, typical Nancy, gently bringing the conversation back to her. But I was glad; the past was a dark place I didn't even want to talk about, but too often it nudged me, reminding me that it was there, and always would be, in the pit of my stomach.

'I had a horrible childhood too, and ended up running around town with unsuitable boys, smoking weed, drinking underage... and I turned out okay, didn't I?'

'Erm. You're not making me feel any better,' I joked with raised eyebrows.

'Okay, I'm not exactly a role model for teenage girls,' she conceded with a smile. 'But all I'm saying is you don't have to know *everything*. She's sixteen soon and it's probably best if... well, if you don't interfere *too* much?'

She posed this like a question, but the implied criticism that I was an interfering mother was clear. I could see why she'd think that, but even as my closest friend in this town, she didn't really know my struggle, and had no idea just how much I had at stake.

'You're probably right,' I said, not finding this conversation particularly helpful. 'I guess what I'm worried about is that I've ruined the trust we both had, the lovely, easy friendship.'

We'd talked about this before, and Nancy didn't believe that Sofia and I had a *true* friendship, she was one of the 'I'm your mother, not your friend' brigade. Her own mother had told her that, and though at the time she said she'd felt hurt by the remark, she now knew her mother had been right.

Unsurprisingly, Nancy jumped on this now. 'If you were a true friend, you wouldn't try to control every single aspect of her life, though, would you?'

'I don't,' I snapped, offended.

'I'm sorry if you think that's harsh, but—'

'Let's not,' I cut in. I didn't want to go over this again, we had to agree to differ. She clearly had a perception of mother/daughter relationships that were different from mine, and she'd never understand because she didn't know the half of it.

'Okay,' she replied, stirring her coffee.

The atmosphere had suddenly turned prickly, and I was about to say I had to go, when Nancy suddenly looked up from her drink. She was sitting opposite and gazing at someone behind me, across the coffee bar, her eyes widening. After searching her face for clues and not getting any, I turned around to see a familiar face, smiling at me and lifting his hand in a gesture of hello.

'Do you know him? Cos he seems to know you.' Nancy seemed surprised.

It was Oliver, the customer who'd bought perfume for his daughter a few weeks ago. I lifted my hand awkwardly from the elbow, a faint smile on my lips.

'A customer,' I said to my friend. 'Memories of Madrid, it

cost a fortune, then he came back and bought more perfume for his sister.'

'Oh *really*?' She continued to gaze at him.

I smiled. 'He made Mr Woods a very happy man, spent hundreds of pounds.'

'Memories of Madrid, eh?' Nancy raised her perfect eyebrows in both wonderment and interest. 'Invite him over to join us,' she said under her breath, without moving her lips.

'No, that would be weird.'

'It would be *delicious*,' she murmured, not taking her eyes off him. I was surprised at the prickle of jealousy on my skin.

'*You* shouldn't be looking. Anyway, how are things going with the new man in your life?' I asked, in an attempt to distract her. I didn't want her calling Oliver over, I would feel very uncomfortable fraternising with a customer, especially as Nancy was now fluffing her hair and apparently ready to flirt for Britain. 'Go on then, how are things with Mr Great in Bed?' I asked.

'We're on a break.' Her face dropped, and she looked down, shuffling sugar sachets between long, red nails.

'Oh, Nancy, I'm so sorry.' I was annoyed at my clumsiness. 'Why didn't you say?'

'Oh, it's not over – just a break while he sorts his life out. I'm okay, it's all good,' she replied, which wasn't like Nancy at all, her relationship endings were usually Shakespearean and had played out in various coffee houses throughout our friendship. Nancy loved *big*, and consequently when it ended – which it always did – she hurt *big* too, and she always, *always* had to share.

'When I saw you last week, everything was going well. What happened?'

'I'd really rather not talk about it, not now. He has some shit to sort out,' she added with a nervous smile.

I guessed that he was most likely married, she'd found out,

and he'd told her he was going to leave his wife. But straight from the classic cheater's playbook, he couldn't leave his wife just yet, so while he did that he and Nancy had to take a break. He presumably thought he was off the hook, but poor old Nancy never read the subtext in these relationship endings and had probably chosen her wedding dress and was now waiting for him to appear back on the horizon. It wasn't the first time and wouldn't be the last.

She finished her coffee, gazed into the distance and said, 'That guy keeps looking over.'

'Perhaps he wanted more than memories from Madrid,' I joked.

She dragged her eyes up to me. 'He is just a customer, isn't he, nothing else?'

I laughed. 'No, nothing like that.' I produced an outraged expression, then paused. 'But he's good-looking, isn't he?' I discreetly turned my head to glance at Oliver as he stood in the queue to be served. 'He made Mr Woods tremble with excitement,' I said with a chuckle.

'He's doing the same for me right now,' Nancy replied, a glint in her eye.

'His name's Oliver... I think.'

'Oh, you're hilarious.'

'Why, what do you mean?'

'*I think...* I *think* he's called Oliver,' she said in a girlish voice. 'You know damn well what his name is. You fancy him, don't you?'

'No, I *don't*. Stop!' I wafted her with my napkin.

I noticed that Oliver was now leaving the queue with his tray and before I could stop her, Nancy beckoned him over. He looked slightly uncomfortable and just smiled back, but she wasn't one to let things go and began calling him.

'Hey, why don't you come and join us?' she was saying loudly.

'No, Nancy, don't,' I urged, while dying of embarrassment. Being polite, Oliver had no choice but to walk to our table. I was mortified; Oliver seemed like a nice, quiet man and I didn't want Nancy to start some flirtatious conversation, making us both look like desperate housewives.

'My friend says you bought some lovely perfume for your daughter,' Nancy said in a sing-song voice, the minute he stopped by our table. She was staring right at him, being overfamiliar, like a cocky schoolgirl. I was mortified. Oliver shifted on one leg, smiling awkwardly.

'Yes, yes...' He soon regained his composure and smiled. 'She loved it.'

'I *bet* she did,' Nancy said slowly, while looking him up and down.

'I'm glad she liked it,' I responded, desperately trying to make this a grown-up conversation.

Nancy was now flashing her eyes at him, and he was looking from me to her, clearly not knowing what the hell was going on, so I politely introduced them.

'This is my friend, Nancy, and this is Oliver,' I said.

'Oliver Foster.' He put his tray down on the table and, leaning forward, shook Nancy's hand. I felt a little thump in the chest. She was beaming, her big brown eyes full of promise, her lips pouty and full. Hell, even her long dark curly hair seemed bouncier and shinier.

'I was just saying to my friend, who *is* that man over there,' she purred. She certainly knew how to lay on the charm.

But it didn't seem to be working on Oliver, he never met her eyes. I knew he was a quiet person, and women like Nancy probably scared him. I wasn't at all surprised when he wrapped things up with her quickly, unable to cope with her rather overblown performance. 'Well, it's good to meet you, Nancy, and lovely to see you again, Emily.' He nodded at us both. 'I'll pop into the shop later this week,' he said, before leaving. 'I need some Christmas gifts.'

I was both surprised and flattered that he'd remembered my name and felt myself blushing. 'Oh yes. Please do. Mr Woods will be delighted to see you.'

'Great, great,' he replied, lifting his tray and walking away from us, through the café. He took a table at the far end. From where I was sitting, I could see him drinking his coffee and gazing out of the window.

'He seems lonely to me,' I said to Nancy.

'I'd keep him company any day – or night?' she simpered, but it was half-hearted, she'd obviously realised he wasn't interested.

I looked back over at him, and just then he looked up from his coffee and our eyes accidentally met. We both smiled awkwardly, but there was something about him. I definitely felt like we had a connection.

After the recent issues, I'd felt more vulnerable and exposed than I had in years, and seeing him alone reminded me how alone I was. Perhaps I needed a man in my life after all? I certainly wouldn't want any man, but Oliver Foster seemed kind and gentle and intelligent. He was tall and solid, and perhaps it was the way I was feeling, but he seemed just what I needed at that time, a big rock to hold on to. I sipped on my coffee and wondered what his story was, and if I could ever trust him enough to tell him my story?

EIGHT

I thought about Oliver a lot over the next few days. I was surprised how much of an impact this stranger was having on me, and after seeing him in the coffee bar, I'd wondered if there was a chance he might have felt that same connection I did. I was looking forward to seeing him again and headed into work with an added spring in my step each day.

One morning, there was a sprinkle of snow.

'Mum, look outside,' Sofia called from the living room.

I was still putting my make-up on in my bedroom, and for a horrible moment, I thought she'd seen something, or *someone*, in the garden. I was always uneasy, always on high alert, but after recent events, I'd become even more suspicious and ready for bad news.

'It's snowing, Mum,' she called, and my first reaction was relief. I loved the excitement in her voice and realised that even at fifteen that little girl with pigtails who longed to make a snowman was still there.

So instead of looking at the garden from my bedroom window, I rushed down the stairs and joined her in the living room. This was our chance to get back to how we'd always been, and I took my place next to her, pressing my face against the glass with her.

'Look at us, like two little kids,' I said, and we both giggled. 'If this gets deeper, I think we may have to have a snowball fight this evening,' I suggested, waiting for her to pull a face or roll her eyes.

'You're on!' she said. I saw this as a sign that things between us were getting back on track and Pink Girl wasn't such a spectre any more. I still needed to deal with that at some point, but for now, I just wanted to enjoy having my daughter back.

After breakfast, Sofia ran around looking for her books, I put my boots on and we trudged outside. The shop and Sofia's school were just minutes from home, and half a mile from each other, so we usually walked some of the way together. That day, as Sofia and I took our usual route, chatting and laughing like old times, enjoying the wintry scene, it was perfect and I felt like everything had been restored.

Arriving at work, Mr Woods greeted me. 'I think we'll need to be playing our carols soon, Emily,' he said. 'We need that tape.'

I smiled. A couple of Christmases earlier, I'd asked Sofia to make a Christmas playlist for the shop, just to add some atmosphere. Mr Woods always referred to it as 'that tape'; it was a permanent mystery to him how the music played without a cassette deck.

There was something magical about the shop at Christmas. The dark panelled woods and bottle-green walls were the perfect backdrop to the traditional tree that the late Mrs Woods used to decorate. Mr and Mrs Woods had always done 'the switch-on' in mid-December and invited their regular customers for mince pies and mulled wine.

As the couple had no children of their own, Sofia and I were always invited to their home for Christmas dinner, and at the Christmas opening of the shop, I would dress Sofia up as a fairy.

She'd serve mince pies smiling shyly at everyone, and when customers congratulated the couple on their beautiful grand-daughter, no one corrected them.

'It wouldn't be Christmas without our girls,' Mrs Woods used to say, and Sofia and I felt the same. It was like fate had landed us there in each other's lives.

When Mrs Woods was diagnosed with cancer five years earlier, I had helped nurse her, as I had my own mother. I was happy to do whatever was needed, but she only lived for a year. Both Sofia and I felt her loss keenly. We broke down in tears when we found out Mrs Woods had left Sofia a small legacy in her will to help her in her first year of university. She'd also made her husband promise to look after us. He told me my job was for life, as was living in their lovely flat for a very small rent.

We loved them like family, and despite Sofia growing up, nothing was too much trouble for her when it came to Mr Woods, who now lived alone surrounded by photos of his darling Dorothy. Even the previous year, at the age of fourteen when *nothing* was cool, Sofia had agreed to walk round with a plate of mince pies at the shop's Christmas launch – though not surprisingly she had baulked at dressing as a fairy.

'This snow has put you in the mood for Christmas,' I said to Mr Woods now.

He smiled, but I knew the festive season was bittersweet for him, because Mrs Woods had died four years before, on Christmas Eve.

'It's never quite the same, is it?' I said, touching his arm.

He patted my hand. 'No, but we carry on. We fight the fight.' He made a fist with his hand and then went into the back of the shop. Christmas was not just about being with loved ones, it was about remembering the ones you'd lost. I felt it too every year.

. . .

A little later that morning, I was gathering together my seasonal window display on the counter, when the door jingled. And in walked Oliver Foster, looking very tall and handsome. He banged his feet on the mat to shake off the snow, which sadly had now turned to heavy sleet. So much for a snowball fight with Sofia later, I thought, but we could still have a cosy night in.

'It's filthy out there,' he muttered, leaning out of the open door, shaking his umbrella onto the street.

'Yes, it was so pretty and Christmassy this morning, and look at it now,' I said with a sigh.

He leaned his umbrella against the wall and walked in, closing the door behind him, and just as he did, Mr Woods bustled into the shop. They said good morning, but Mr Woods had his coat on and was heading out. Just as he was standing at the door, he turned and asked, 'Did your sister like the perfume?'

'She loved it,' Oliver replied. 'In fact, she wants some more for Christmas.'

Mr Woods nearly passed out with pleasure at the prospect of another big sale, but before he could answer, Oliver quickly added, 'But I've told her, only landmark birthdays at that price.'

Mr Woods' head went to the side, he observed a moment of grief, then turned to me. 'I'm going to Exeter for flower petals, so I probably won't be back in the shop today, will you lock up?'

'Of course,' I said. 'Have a nice time.'

Mr Woods nodded as he left and closed the door, leaving just me and Oliver Foster in the shop. I suddenly felt really nervous, my heart was beating and I was desperate to say something intelligent. This man made me feel like I wanted to impress him, it mattered to me that he liked me.

'So, you're looking for some Christmas gifts?' I said, realising that in the morning's excitement with the snow, I may not have put mascara on both eyes and hadn't powdered. My face was probably now very shiny, and one eye looked bigger than the other, but I tried not to think about that. I hoped Oliver found things like intelligence more attractive than powdered faces and mascaraed lashes.

'I'd like some perfume for my daughter, oh and my granddaughter too. But then again, she's only thirteen, so perhaps she's too young?' he asked uncertainly.

'We do have some very fresh, light fragrances for young girls?' I suggested.

He seemed open to the idea and I reached under the counter and brought out Mr Woods' signature perfumes.

'This one is quite lovely. It's one of Mr Woods' own perfumes, it's called Dorothy, after his late wife.' I took a blotter, sprayed perfume on it and handed it to Oliver. As he took it from me, our fingers touched. For a few seconds, it was as though time had stopped, the perfume hung in the flower-filled air, and our eyes locked.

'What's this perfume called again?' His voice broke the spell, and I realised to my deep embarrassment, I hadn't let go of the blotter. Oliver was gently trying to take it from me and I immediately relinquished it, with an uncomfortable giggle, feeling such an idiot.

'Dorothy,' I repeated, and he smiled that big, warm crinkly smile that lit up his face, and I melted.

Yes, he was an older man, perhaps even as much as ten years older than me, but watching him put the blotter to his nose and close his eyes, it was easy to imagine his face in ecstasy. And when he opened them again, they were looking right at me, and it seemed so intense, so penetrating, I had to look away.

I sprayed another blotter and handed it to him to ease the tension.

'What's this one called?' he asked.

I had to gather myself together and do my job.

'It's called Sofia,' I replied. 'Actually, it's named after my daughter,' I added. It always filled me with pride when I told customers this. There was something so special, so touching about Mr Woods having created these bespoke perfumes and bestowing them with our names. And somehow Mr Woods had seemed to capture each of us in these scents. Sofia was a light, youthful, clean perfume.

'Oh how lovely, as you say it's light and fresh and... Yes, I like it. I'll take one of those for my granddaughter.'

'Lovely,' I murmured. 'I'll wrap it for you. And for your daughter?'

'Yes, my daughter – perhaps something from the same collection?'

'This is a lovely rose with a spicy undertone. I wonder if you can smell it?' I asked. 'I think you'll get a better idea if it's actually on the skin.' I sprayed the perfume on the inside of my wrist and offered it to him. Mr Woods always told me to test perfume on skin – 'It smells very different on everyone,' he'd say, and I was doing as I was told, even if it wasn't my skin that would be wearing it. I just had this urge to get close to Oliver, and this was a great excuse. As he was tall, he had to stoop slightly for his face to reach my wrist, and having not been near a man in twelve years, I found the intimacy of this quite shocking and gasped inwardly.

'Yes, I can almost taste that hint of spice,' he murmured, his eyes on me. I couldn't speak, and had to move away, the intensity of his closeness, and his stare was too much.

He said he'd take both perfumes and I unrolled the sheet of gold paper and began to gift-wrap them.

'My daughter would have been delighted to have a perfume named after her,' he said.

Despite the charged atmosphere, or perhaps because of it, my mind had gone blank. 'Yes, Sofia was thrilled, Mr and Mrs Woods have been so kind to her – well, both of us really,' I said, slowly wrapping the first bottle, taking my time, enjoying his presence.

'Did you say one of those perfumes was named after Mrs Woods?'

'Yes. Sadly she died a few years ago. Mr Woods hasn't really been the same since.'

'Oh dear, that's sad. Always hard to get through those times, and whatever anyone says, you *never* get over it. Time doesn't heal, you just adapt to being without them,' he added, like he was speaking from experience.

I gave him a sympathetic smile, wondering who *he'd* lost.

I was intrigued to know what had happened for him to seem so haunted. Despite the fact he'd seemingly opened up to me, I didn't feel it would be appropriate to question him about his loss.

'So, you've moved here recently?' I asked.

'Yeah, I'm living a few miles down the coast, it's just a rental.'

'Oh, so you aren't planning to live here permanently?' I was disappointed at this. Despite only having met him a handful of times, I felt like we'd clicked.

'I guess. I don't know. I have some things I need to fix. Then I'll probably kick back and enjoy my free time.' He smiled. 'I'm fifty-six next birthday. I've taken early retirement and so I could, in theory, go and live anywhere.'

'Ooh how lovely. The Bahamas perhaps?' I smiled.

'Perhaps? But not sure I could live anywhere too hot. I'm from Yorkshire and we're used to more inclement weather up there.'

'I'm from Manchester,' I heard myself say. I wasn't accustomed to sharing personal details with people I didn't know, but Oliver was different. 'I prefer wintry weather, too.'

'I go back up there sometimes, but it's a long drive.'

'I'm not sure my car would survive a journey that far.' I widened my eyes to signify horror at the very thought.

He chuckled. 'What do you drive?'

'A hundred-year-old Fiat,' I joked.

'My wife used to drive a Fiat, said it was the best car she ever had.'

My wife! At this, my heart plummeted and bounced around the floor for a few moments. I was surprised at my disappointment – no, devastation at the fact he was married.

'So I guess your wife will have a say in where you retire to?' I managed to say.

He shrugged. 'No, sadly not. I'm afraid, like Mr Woods, I'm a widower. She died last year.'

'I'm sorry, I just thought—'

'No, please don't apologise. I just get through each day, I have to.'

That explained his earlier comment about time not healing. I was surprised at his honesty, I was a stranger and yet he opened up so fully about his feelings. I'd sensed his sadness the first time he came in the shop, and again when I saw him in the café with Nancy, he'd seemed lost, without an anchor. Now I could see why, and was touched by his continuing love for his wife. I wasn't sure what to say, how could I respond adequately to something like that?

I finished wrapping the first box and, taking the second, started wrapping the gold paper slowly around it.

'You're quite a perfectionist, aren't you?' he observed.

'I do everything the best I can,' I replied, 'something my mother instilled in me.' I carried on in silence. It was so quiet, I could hear the clock ticking. 'I hate ticking clocks,' I remarked.

'Me too, makes you realise life is being eaten up, children are growing, we're all dying.' It was an uncomfortable thought and I felt as if speaking about his late wife had left a tense atmosphere.

I finished wrapping, then handed him the perfumes. He thanked me, paid and said goodbye, but seemed to take ages walking to the door.

I busied myself tidying up the ribbon ends and bits of paper cut-offs, and just as he opened the door to leave, he turned around, cleared his throat and said, 'Emily, I hope you don't mind me asking—'

At that moment, Nancy appeared in the shop doorway.

'Oh, hi, Oliver,' she said, almost snuggling up to him in the doorway, making out she couldn't get past him. I hate to admit it, but in that moment, I hated my friend.

'Hi there,' he said uncertainly; it was obvious he'd forgotten her name. 'I'll get off then, thanks for these.' He looked back at me and half lifted the bag of perfumes. 'Happy Christmas,' he said, leaving us both staring after him.

'Happy Christmas indeed,' Nancy murmured, after he'd gone.

Her timing was rubbish. What had he been going to say to me? It could have been anything, but what if it was something wonderful? What if I never saw him again, and I never found out?

NINE

Nancy wandered into the shop and flopped against the counter like a stroppy teen. I wasn't really in the mood for this; she knew Mr Woods didn't like people hanging around who weren't customers, and it made me uncomfortable. But she'd probably seen Mr Woods leaving earlier, so knew the coast was clear, and as things were quiet next door she wanted something to amuse her. I wondered if it was a complete coincidence that she'd gate-crashed my moment with Oliver.

'So?' she said, eyes wide.

'So what?'

'Did he flirt with you?'

'Oh, Nancy, it's nothing like that,' I lied. 'He bought some Christmas presents, that's all.'

'He was in here for ages.'

'Were you spying?' I smiled at this so it didn't sound too accusatory.

'No, he walked past our shop about twenty minutes ago; he must have been in here all that time.'

'Stalker,' I teased her. 'He told me he retired, I wonder what he used to be?' I said, to myself really. 'I reckon he was a doctor, or a bank manager?' I mused.

Nancy shrugged. 'I saw old Woody leaving,' she said, instinctively checking behind her to see he hadn't suddenly returned.

'You're safe, he's taken the rest of the day off. He's gone to Exeter for flower petals.'

'Is that a euphemism?' she asked, opening bottles, sniffing the contents.

I chuckled. 'No, he really has gone for petals. You know what he's like, he's obsessed with his perfume ingredients,' I said, hoping Mr Woods didn't return unexpectedly and find Nancy with her nose in his precious bottles.

She sprayed one of our more expensive fragrances lavishly all over herself, which irritated me, because if Mr Woods did happen to come back, he would smell it and assume it was me who'd been spraying it. He wasn't keen on Nancy; he never said anything, but I could tell by the way his lip curled if ever I referred to her – and he never called her by name, just 'the girl that works next door'.

'Are you quiet in the shop this morning?' I asked, wishing I hadn't told her Mr Woods was gone for the day, because she was now making herself at home.

She nodded and, to my relief, put down the crystal glass perfume bottle she'd been holding aloft. 'John's at an art exhibition; he's taken most of the stock with him, so no point in me working today.' John was the owner of the art shop next door where she worked, and someone she'd fantasised about for the first three years she had worked there, until she discovered he had a boyfriend. 'So did Oliver say anything outrageous?' she asked, giving me a wink.

'No, of course not, he isn't some sleazeball,' I said. She loved the teenage chats about whoever she was going out with that month, and I was happy to listen, but I was never going to tell.

My life had been a secret for so long, I wasn't suddenly going to start spilling now. So I started dusting the shelves, ready for the Christmas stock that had just been delivered, hoping she'd take the hint and head off. But she perched herself on the glass counter that Mr Woods polished himself, making herself at home.

'Tell me honestly, if he asked you out, would you go?'

'Oliver? Actually, he said he wanted to ravish me in Mr Woods' cellar, but I told him I was too busy.'

She rolled her eyes. 'Do you know where he lives?'

'No, funnily enough, I didn't ask him,' I replied sarcastically.

'I just wondered if you took his address for delivery?'

'No, he can carry a bottle of perfume.' It was my turn to roll my eyes. It crossed my mind that she might be interested in Oliver herself and it made me slightly uneasy. Nancy was so attractive, she was used to the company of men, knew just what to say and do, and she could have anyone. For me, Oliver was different, he wasn't like the men she went out with who drank in the pubs and leered at women, he was special. I didn't want to lose him to Nancy, although I was aware he wasn't yet mine to lose, but just talking to him made me feel something that I hadn't felt in a long time. 'Why the interest in Oliver? He's fifty-five, you know, I thought you preferred them younger?' I lifted a large box of perfumes onto the counter and started opening it, taking out the small bottles.

She leaned on the counter in front of me and rested her chin on her hands. 'In the summer, I like them younger. But nice to have someone older in the winter to snuggle up with, you know? The younger blokes are good for a roll in the hay and an ego boost, but ten years from now, where will I be?'

'Where will any of us be?' I replied.

She stood upright. 'I don't want to be alone, Em,' she said, like the thought had just occurred to her. I waited for the punchline, but she wasn't joking, she looked bereft. 'You'd think someone like Oliver would be flattered to go out with a forty-year-old woman.'

I shrugged, feeling a little prickly at this. Was I invisible? Didn't it occur to her that I might like Oliver, or he might like me even? I felt like I was back at school and rather childishly thought, *I saw him first!*

'Are you still on a break with that guy you're seeing?' I asked, wondering if she was at a loose end and that was why she was lusting after Oliver.

She pursed her lips. 'I don't know, he isn't answering my calls, or texting me back. What do I do wrong, Em? Is it really that hard to be with me?' She started to pick up the bottles I was taking from the box and sniffing them, 'Ooh Midnight in Sidmouth!' she joked. She wasn't comfortable with the truth, she always had to coat it with sugar.

'That's too exciting to bottle,' I said with a chuckle. I was equally uncomfortable with the truth.

Suddenly her phone buzzed, and she plucked it out of her jeans pocket. I saw her face drop.

'Is everything okay?' I asked.

'Probably not.' She didn't look at me, just glared into the phone for a few seconds.

'Can I help?'

'No. No it's fine,' she said, pushing it back into her jeans pocket.

'You upset?'

'No, I'm *fine*, okay?' she snapped, then seemed to compose herself. 'Sorry.' She turned and gazed out of the window at the street.

'He finally texted you back?'

'No, just some handsome stranger asking me if I'd like to go on a romantic trip to Paris,' she said sarcastically.

Whatever had been in the message had clearly shaken her up.

'I understand,' I said, 'life just overwhelms you sometimes, doesn't it? It's like there's nothing to look forward to.'

She nodded. 'Yeah, I sometimes wonder if I should just run away, but then I've always done that.'

I could tell there was more going on but didn't want to press it. 'We may not be whisked off to Paris any time soon, but we can pretend,' I said, opening up one of our most expensive French perfumes. 'This smells like Paris. Mr Woods ordered the rose petals all the way from Grasse,' I explained, spraying the fragrance of roses around her. 'There you go, Paris in the springtime!'

'Thanks, that's gorgeous, I feel better already,' she said, unconvincingly. She pulled away from the counter. 'I'd better get off. John will probably be phoning the shop just to check I'm behind the counter.'

'Okay.' I smiled. 'Let's try to have a lunch break at the same time tomorrow, eh?' I suggested in a vain attempt to cheer her up.

She nodded and went to the door. As she opened it, she said, 'Thanks, Em.'

'What for?'

'For the perfume, and the laughs, and for being... oh I don't know, for being there.'

Before I could answer, she'd gone, and I was left with the feeling she had more she wanted to share with me. I couldn't help but wonder about the text she'd received, but it was a long time before I found out what that was about.

I spent the afternoon taking a delivery, twenty boxes of exotic ingredients for Mr Woods' perfume making. I'd planned to start the slow but regimented task of positioning all the Christmas stock and decorating the window, but the delivery had taken up most of the afternoon. I was just getting ready to leave when Sofia called me.

'Will you be long, Mum?'

'No, sweetie, I'll be ten minutes tops, I'm just about to leave,' I replied. 'I made a chilli, so if you want to start warming it through that would be great.'

'Okay.'

'I thought I'd make some cakes tonight, for the church bake sale on Saturday.'

'Can I help?' she asked, which was a joy to my ears.

'Of course, and you can talk me through your Christmas list?' I added, with a smile. Sofia's Christmas list was always several pages, and there was always a heated debate about the items she *really* wanted, and how we whittled it down. 'I'm on my way,' I said, grabbing my coat and heading for the door. I locked it after me and set off walking the few minutes home.

It was cold now, and even though it was just 5 p.m., there were very few people around. I liked that about living in a small town, everything closed and everyone went home. I passed a few houses, warm lights at the windows, families already inside, their kids safe. I was so happy heading for home and Sofia. For now we'd overcome the slight bump in the road, and although I knew I couldn't afford to let my guard down, that night, as I walked home, I was happy. Everything was back to normal, Christmas was coming, and I was about to enjoy an evening with my daughter. Then my phone rang. It was Nancy. By the time I'd picked up, she'd gone, but she'd left a message:

'Hey, babe, I'm sorry about today. I... took some pills. I've drunk a bottle of gin, I'm going to a better place, just wanted... to say goodbye...'

TEN

I immediately called Nancy back, trying to gather my thoughts as the phone rang. Had she been trying to tell me something earlier and I'd missed it? How could I not pick up on something like this?

The phone kept ringing, she wasn't picking up and now I was really frightened. My head was swirling with images of her lying on the floor of her cottage, seconds from death. If she'd meant to do this, she wouldn't have called me. Our mutual loneliness echoed in my head as I realised I was the only person she had and she was asking me to save her. But I didn't know what to do first, or which way to run. I was five minutes from home but about ten minutes away from Nancy's and had to make a decision now! My instinct was to run home and call an ambulance, and jump in my car to get to Nancy's. But as I ran along the seafront towards home, I realised that this was life and death, and in the minutes it took to go home, I could be on my way to her. So I turned back and began running to Nancy's house in desperate hope that I'd get there in time. I called for an ambulance as I ran.

In those few minutes, running back into town, through the

little streets, my head was in a whirl. What had made her do this? Yes, Nancy was desperate for a relationship, and there was obviously trouble in her current one, but she'd been there before and got through it. I thought about the text and wondered if that might be the catalyst, but not knowing what it was, I had no idea if it was relevant. We think we know our friends and their lives, but we don't really. When we go home and close our doors, we all take off our masks. In my case, I didn't even take it off when I was home, so why was I surprised that Nancy's happy-go-lucky persona wasn't quite as it seemed? After all, I knew that she was lonely, that she didn't have anyone, so should I have tried to do more?

By the time I reached Nancy's rented cottage, I was breathless, my mind filled with so many horrible thoughts as I banged on the door, calling her name. I peered through the window, but the house was in darkness, so I went back to the front door and thumped again, and again, yelling her name into the quiet street. I could hear the waves crashing in the distance, spits of rain on my face, the wind was starting to blow in from the sea, and I was shivering now with cold and fear.

'What's all that noise?' I heard a woman's angry voice, as she emerged from the darkness of the cottage next door. 'If you want Nancy she's probably out. Always in the pub that one, why don't you try there?'

'No, no, she called me, I assumed she called me from *here*. I think she might be in some difficulty, she might have hurt herself,' I said, not wanting to actually tell this woman everything.

'Oh? Drunk more like,' she replied.

'Are you Mrs Robinson?' I asked. Nancy hated her neighbours, particularly this one, apparently she was very nosey. I'd add judgemental to that too.

'I am,' she said rather defiantly.

'Look, it's kind of an emergency,' I said, not wanting to add any more to her no-doubt large portfolio of nasty gossip. 'I've called an ambulance.'

'Oh!' Her demeanour changed somewhat at this. Presumably at the promise of some drama, she walked unsteadily through her little front garden to join me.

While she did, I called Nancy's number again. It rang and rang and now I could hear it coming from inside, until the answer phone picked up.

'She's definitely in there,' I said, as Mrs Robinson trundled up the path. She then gave a rather frail bang on the door and shouted Nancy's name through the letter box, which wasn't very helpful.

I was frantic, desperate to do something. How much longer would the ambulance be?

'I might have to smash a window,' I murmured, almost to myself, as I weighed up the latch I knew was on the inside that I could potentially open if I could get my hand in.

'You don't want to go smashing windows,' Mrs Robinson muttered, then she bent down and started moving some plant pots by the front door. 'She's always losing her keys, I think she used to hide a set under a plant pot, but I don't know which one.'

Why hadn't I thought of this? I immediately turned on the torch of my phone and got down on the floor with her, shining it where she was looking.

'That's better, I can see now,' she said, as I helped her lift the pots and check underneath, our hands scrabbling in soil, until we saw something glinting.

'Yes!' I said, and grabbing the keys, I asked Mrs Robinson to hold the phone and shine the light on the lock so I could see where to unlock the door, which she did, with a running commentary.

'You need to twist it, not like that. Doesn't look like there's anyone in to me...'

Eventually, I managed to open the door. As I stepped in, Mrs Robinson was right behind me.

'Would you keep an eye out for the ambulance?' I asked. The last thing Nancy would need right then was Mrs Robinson peering over her, making unhelpful remarks. I didn't give Mrs Robinson a chance to protest and headed into the hallway.

It was pitch black and deathly quiet inside, a faint smell of unwashed clothes and damp hung in the air. I almost stopped breathing, I was immediately back there in that dark, shabby little room, the battered teddy bear, the smell of neglect. It was never far away that room, it was always just beneath the surface, waiting in my head for a smell, a taste, a feeling. And there it was, like yesterday, all the guilt and fear and tears wrapped up in baby blankets and something like love.

I suddenly remembered where I was and why I was here and pushed it from my head, stepping further inside. I'd been in Nancy's home a few times in the years I'd known her, but it was usually just for a cup of coffee, a quick chat as I was passing. I didn't *know* this place and had no idea where the light switch was, so I ran my hands along the walls as I walked down the tiny hallway.

I called Nancy's name, it echoed through the little cottage, bouncing back at me, but no response. I lifted up my phone to shine the light again, aware it was draining my already low battery, but I had no choice. I called out again, desperately looking for the light switches. Eventually, I located one on the hallway wall. The light was weak and came from a single bulb in a shade hanging above me. But still no sign of Nancy, just a dimly lit hallway, cold and dank. I was reminded as always of the past, the musty smell, the darkness, the neglect. I immediately pushed these thoughts from my mind, there wasn't time for this – so I moved to the bottom of the stairs where I suddenly heard a creaking from above. I immediately ran up the rickety little cottage stairs two at a time, still calling her name. I pushed at what looked like a half-opened door, bracing myself for what I might find. But as the door opened, something seemed to jump out at me. I yelped and fell backwards, landing hard on the wooden floor. I dropped my phone, but the light was shining on a pile of material, which I realised was towels and bedding. I'd opened a linen cupboard and its contents had landed on me.

Shaken but relieved, I got up and I found the light switch for the landing, which was also weak and dimly lit up the landing. I went towards the next door, again half-opened, and entered a bedroom, holding my breath, terrified of seeing Nancy lying there and being too late. Before I could locate the light switch in this room, I became aware of a sour, rancid smell and shuddered. It smelt like vomit and urine and I almost gagged as I moved further into the room.

Suddenly I heard a groan, I turned my phone in the direction and saw movement on the bed and rushed over to where Nancy was huddled under the covers.

'Nancy, it's me, it's Emily.' I was close to tears, relieved she was still alive, but scared to death she might just go any minute.

'What have you taken?'

There was no response.

'Nancy, Nancy,' I could hear myself saying her name, over and over like a mantra.

I turned the lamp on by her bed, and now I could see she was covered in vomit. She was lying on wet sheets and had obviously lost control of her bladder. Her eyes were closed, and her breathing shallow, but she seemed to be shivering, which gave me hope. I gently turned her over into the recovery position. I checked her airways, and they were clear. As a trained nurse, I knew that without medication or a stomach pump, there was little I could do. I just hoped the paramedics arrived quickly. Her breathing was now irregular and I was concerned that even if she received treatment and survived, there could still be brain damage. I remembered cases like this coming into the hospital, and you could never say for sure what would happen, especially without knowing what she'd taken and in what quantity.

I didn't hear the sirens, just the thundering footsteps coming up the stairs and two paramedics running in. I was holding her hand but, as I expected, the paramedics asked me to move, and I left the room, knowing they probably wouldn't want me to be around while they treated her. I knew from my nursing days that it can be distressing to see loved ones being brought round from something like this – if indeed they could bring her round? My stomach lurched at the possibility she might not come through this.

And as I sat at the top of the stairs waiting, I wondered if it was already too late.

ELEVEN

Eventually, Nancy was taken to hospital in Exeter, and I left and walked home. My phone was dead, so I couldn't call Sofia and just hoped she was okay.

Sofia was in the hall waiting for me when I got home.

'Where have you been? I've been so worried,' she said, hugging me.

'I was on my way home, but had to go to Nancy's—' I started, but didn't get around to telling her about Nancy because she just burst into tears.

I put my arms around her and just kept telling her how sorry I was. I wanted to cry myself, how could I have let her down so badly? I explained that my phone had died, but she kept shaking her head.

'Can you imagine what you'd be like if I'd just told you on the phone I was on my way – and then I never turned up?' she said coldly. I felt the sting of her pain, she'd been worried about me, our roles were temporarily reversed. 'And then I'm trying to call you and I get the answerphone. I walked out onto the front in the dark to see if you were there. I thought you'd been run over or hurt or—'

'You're right, you're absolutely right,' I said. 'My phone wasn't dead at first, I could have phoned you, I should have phoned you. But I didn't just go to Nancy's for a casual visit, she called me and I—'

'I'm sorry, but I have to do my homework now,' she cut me off and, picking up her laptop, walked out of the room.

'Sofia...'

She stopped in the doorway of her room. 'I warmed up the chilli, it's probably cold now.' She closed her door, leaving me in the hall, still with my coat on. She hadn't given me a chance to explain properly why I was late and would now feel hurt thinking she was second place to my friend. Sofia was second to nothing and no one, she was first and always had been.

As I plugged my charger into my phone, I saw ten missed calls from her and, looking at the time, realised I must have been at Nancy's for almost two hours. No wonder Sofia was so upset. I thought about her walking along the front alone in the wind and the rain, desperately looking for me. There was no one for her to call. It had always been like this, just the two of us – but I'd never had this kind of emergency before. Being alone at night when your mum is inexplicably late is scary for a child, even a mature fifteen-year-old. I'd let her down and needed to explain.

I walked to her room and knocked on the door. When she didn't respond, I opened it tentatively.

'Sofia, I'm so sorry, love. I realise you must have been out of your mind with worry. It was thoughtless of me.' She was lying on her bed and quickly clicked her phone off. I would usually have asked who she was talking to, but not tonight. 'You are justifiably angry with me. And I have no excuses, except that Nancy was in trouble.'

She shrugged. 'So what?'

'She'd taken an overdose.'

'An overdose of wine?' She rolled her eyes.

'No, actually she'd taken pills and gin, and when I got there, she was out of it,' I explained. 'I called the ambulance and she's now in hospital.'

Sofia turned to look at me and, clearly feeling bad, asked, 'Will she be okay?'

I saw this as a thawing, so moved to sit at the bottom of her bed.

'I don't know,' I answered truthfully. I told her all about what had happened and she moved from indifference and hurt to asking questions. Then I said, 'Am I forgiven?'

She grudgingly nodded, and I suggested we have dinner.

'I've no idea what it will taste like, I reheated it twice,' she said, following me down the hall to the kitchen. 'But that's what happens when you don't call and let me know where you are!' she added, grumpily.

'Now you sound like me,' I replied with a chuckle and put my arm around her shoulder.

I microwaved two bowls of rewarmed cold chilli, Sofia set the table, and I called the hospital. As the phone rang, I tried not to think about Nancy's cold, clammy hand and the way she seemed unresponsive as the paramedics carried her past me on a stretcher. As I suspected, as I wasn't next of kin, they couldn't give me any information apart from that she was 'comfortable'. I remember saying the same thing to concerned callers over and over again at the hospital. Comfortable could mean anything, from sitting up in bed and laughing, to being in intensive care with minutes to live. I clicked off my phone with a long sigh, and Sofia looked up as she placed our knives and forks on the table.

'Well, at least she's alive,' I muttered, putting down the phone.

'Good. You're not going out again, are you?' she asked.

'Not if I can help it, but as I seem to be the only friend she has, the hospital took my number. So in the event of... If she worsens, they might call.'

'You can't go to Exeter tonight,' she said.

'But, Sofia, she's got no one else.'

'I just think it's not your job to pick up after her, she's just an old drunk.'

I was shocked at Sofia's seeming lack of care, her callousness. 'She tried to kill herself, Sofia? People don't do that as a leisure pursuit. She could have died, she still might!'

'Okay, okay, calm down,' she snapped.

'Please don't tell me to calm down,' I shot back at her, as I put our bowls of food on the table. 'This isn't like you, Sofia, why are you being so unkind?'

'I'm not, but if I had a friend like Nancy, you'd give me the speech you gave me about Zoe, about how some people aren't good for us, that they aren't really our friends.'

I looked at her, shocked and not sure how to respond. I did say those things about Zoe, but it never occurred to me that she was *still* holding a grudge. She now seemed to be using it against me because I'd helped Nancy. I didn't want an argument now about this, I felt too raw, my nerves jagged.

'Well, I'm sorry you feel that way, but Nancy will need some support, and if the hospital calls me to say she's... dying, I will drive to Exeter tonight.'

'And leave me here, I suppose?'

'No, of course not. I could ask Mr Woods to come over and sit with you, or I could take you with me?'

'I don't want to go.'

'Okay, fine,' I snapped, and stared at my plate of uneaten chilli. I just wasn't hungry anymore.

Sofia did the same, and we sat opposite each other, our bowls in front of us like two chess players reaching stalemate. I'd never felt this detachment, this coldness before from my daughter. Our relationship had always been so easy until now, and I didn't know how to handle it.

'This isn't like you. What's the matter, love?' I asked, going for the simplest approach.

She just glared in front of her, not willing to engage. Unsmiling, she picked up her bowl, emptied it into the bin and walked over to the sink, then ran the hot water and squirted in the washing-up liquid. I couldn't work out what was wrong with her, but at the same time, I knew it was probably her age. The other mums I knew with sons and daughters Sofia's age had been struggling with their kids' hormones for a couple of years. And I don't think anyone believed me when I said she was happy and easy-going. I guess I'd been lucky so far and this was bound to happen at some point.

As she placed her bowl and cutlery to dry on the rack, I said, 'Look, Sofia, I'm sorry I didn't call you, but I've explained now and I thought you'd be mature enough to accept my apology.'

'I have,' she replied sulkily.

'So why are you being like this?'

'I'm not being like anything, I just need to go and do my homework.' She walked to the door.

'But I thought we were going to bake together tonight?' I reminded her.

She paused in the doorway. 'You're always nagging me to do my homework, and now you're freaking out when I'm doing it.'

'I'm not freaking out, I just thought—'

'I can't bake now, I have to go through my notes for a test tomorrow.'

'Okay, fair enough,' I said. I knew I was doing this all wrong, my emotions were getting the better of me and I was behaving even more like a child than she was. But I couldn't see a way forward.

After she left the room, silence landed like a heavy cloud

over me and alone now at the kitchen table, I felt the walls slowly closing in, the light dimming. At first, I just sat there thinking about my argument with Sofia, how I could have handled it differently, and if I needed to be more understanding, or more firm with her. That night had been so tough and it wasn't over yet. As a nurse, I'd been used to illness and dying, but finding Nancy like that had shaken me. She was my friend, my only *real* friend. She wasn't perfect, could be a bit wild and reckless, she could also be unreliable sometimes, but she wasn't a *bad* person. She'd always been kind towards Sofia, which is why I was surprised at my daughter's sudden animosity towards her.

Sitting there in the dim lamplight, going over what we had said, I suddenly had this feeling that someone was watching me, it came from nowhere, and feeling vulnerable with my back to the open kitchen door, I immediately stood up and turned around. Nothing, just the dark hallway, and silence. I turned on the hall light and checked I'd locked the front door, then walked back and into the living room without turning on the light. I walked over to the window, to look out onto the promenade. I gently opened the net curtains, and as I did I came face to face with someone!

The face was pressed against the glass, and in the darkness all I saw was the outline, the shape, and two eyes staring back at me. I opened my mouth to scream, but nothing came out, I was so frightened. I quickly pulled the curtains together and shot back from the window, cowering in the corner of the room. Sofia had pointed out the man standing under the street lamp, she'd said he was looking in, staring from the front garden. This could be the same man, it was hard to tell in the dark, it was just a head, two eyes, and then nothing.

Eventually, after some time had passed, I gathered my courage and walked very carefully back to the window. I lifted the curtain slowly, my whole body braced for what might be on the other side of the glass. This time I was going to yell and scream and bang on the windows, scare them instead of me. I opened the curtain, and keeping my face at a distance from the glass, I screwed up my eyes to see if they were still there, but nothing. I was so relieved, tears started running down my cheeks. I really thought they'd still be waiting by the window, or worse still trying to break in. Then, as I looked up, my eyes searching the promenade, my chest thumped. There he was, a dark figure huddled against the wall, standing in the distance, just staring in the direction of our flat. I stood behind the net curtain watching, but when I heard a noise in the garden, I turned away for a few brief seconds.

When I looked back, the figure was gone, the promenade empty and rainswept, a cold bleak place on a winter's night. What was going on? Was it Ben the poor homeless man again? Or was it something, someone more sinister?

I didn't sleep that night, but as I tossed and turned and jumped at the slightest sound, I told myself that this would all seem better in the morning. Little did I know, things were about to get a lot worse.

TWELVE

I hadn't slept much because of the man at the window, but tried to focus on getting Sofia to school safely and without anything happening. I obviously didn't tell her about the face at the window, but walked her to school, telling her I needed the exercise before work, which she bought with much eye-rolling. Then, as I ran to work, because I was now late, I called the hospital who informed me that Nancy was still 'comfortable'.

While at work that day, I told Mr Woods what had happened.

His hand flew to his mouth in horror. 'Oh, Emily, I feel guilty because I still haven't fitted the CCTV, I will make it a priority,' he said, 'but sounds to me like it was old Ben. He's always peering into people's houses, but he's completely harmless.'

This gave me some vague comfort, and I wondered if perhaps old Ben was behind everything, the break-in, and the chocolate wrappers and strawberry milk. He was very childlike and I could imagine him crouched behind our tree eating his snacks and watching avidly.

Throughout all this, I was still worried about Nancy and

wondered if I should drive over to the hospital when I'd finished, but it wasn't fair to drag Sofia out at night, and leaving her behind was not an option. I could have asked Mr Woods to go and sit with her, but it was his wine club evening and I didn't want to deny him one of his great pleasures.

So I gave up on the idea and decided I would just call instead.

That evening, I arrived home from work to find Sofia in the kitchen.

'I'm cooking dinner,' she said, which was a pleasant surprise. Breakfast had been quite tense after last night and I hadn't been sure what to expect, so I took this as a good sign.

'Lovely, what are we having?' I asked, walking casually into the living room and checking the window, nothing. No one at the window, and no one standing under the street lamp, thank God!

'Veggie shepherd's pie,' she said, beaming.

I felt a rush of love and relief that she was okay, that *we* were okay, there was no one at the window, and she'd forgiven me, as I had her. I needed this return to normality, because when Sofia and I argued it coloured everything for me.

As Sofia cooked, I laid the table. We talked about our day and I probed slightly to see if all was okay in her world. Pink Girl was seemingly no longer around, but I still worried about the risks, the dangers to Sofia – dangers she didn't even know about.

'Is Ruby okay?' I asked.

'Yeah, why?'

'No reason, I haven't heard you mention her recently.' Ruby was a good, polite girl and this was such a positive friendship for Sofia, I was keen to encourage it.

'She's not going out much, too busy with Archie,' she added sourly.

And there it was. I knew my daughter so well, I realised there was something causing tension in her teenage world. The reason for Sofia's sudden change in attitude, her anger at what she saw as my desertion last night. Archie, the boy that Sofia had secretly liked for ages, was going out with her best friend. Poor Sofia had lost a friend and a potential boyfriend in one go.

'Oh they're spending time together?' I asked casually, like it meant nothing, in an attempt to put this into perspective for her.

'Yeah,' she murmured, but in that one word I heard all the hurt and I felt her pain. I ached for her, and this was just the beginning. As any mum knows, this was nothing in the great scheme of things, a tiny ripple in life's ocean, but when you're fifteen, it's *everything*, and suddenly my own heart felt as broken as hers. This wasn't something I could simply put a plaster on. 'I don't know what she sees in him,' she said casually, while aggressively mashing potato.

'I don't know what he sees in *her*,' I offered, aware this sounded bitchy, but I was overplaying it slightly in my keenness for her to know I was on her side.

She turned away from the kitchen counter and gave me a smile. 'Mum, she's beautiful, he's so punching.'

'I think *you're* prettier,' I said, stubbornly.

'Mum...' she groaned.

'What?'

'Nothing.' She rolled her eyes and went back to smashing the mashed potato with gusto. No wonder she seemed jealous and resentful of Nancy last night. She probably discovered this treacherous act of betrayal by so-called BFF Ruby yesterday. She must have felt hurt and vulnerable so when I didn't come home or tell her where I was, she had a meltdown. Being fifteen could be a very lonely place, and I felt for her.

I gave her some space to talk, asked a few questions about school, knowing if she needed to she could bring it back round to Ruby and Archie, but she didn't and eventually asked me about Nancy.

'Nothing new, but at least she's still with us. I'm so relieved, I really thought it might be the end...' I stopped myself, couldn't bear to think about what might have happened.

Sofia was sitting opposite me at the table, her arms folded in front of her. She had this look on her face that chilled me to the bone. In a terrifying moment, I wondered if it was like her father.

'Why are you being so weird about Nancy?' I asked.

'I'm not!' she replied, the impenetrable, unreachable stare looking back at me, the past catching up with the present.

'She did it to herself,' she snapped. 'She was drunk, she probably didn't even know what she was *doing*.'

'That's a mean thing to say. Taking an overdose was a cry for help, but that doesn't mean what she did wasn't valid. She deserves our support and understanding, she was clearly suffering. Just because someone drinks—'

'I don't want to talk about it, or *her*.'

'Is this about Nancy, or is it about Zoe?' I asked, calmly.

'It's about both of them, it's also about double standards.' Her face was red with fury. 'It's about you being a hypocrite and telling me who I can be friends with, when your own friends are trash!'

I gasped, realising in that horrible moment that my daughter was becoming her own person. In just a few months she'd changed and grown into someone who didn't just accept her mother's view of the world anymore. It was probably healthy, but I found it very unnerving.

'I guess you're right, but I'm older, I won't be drawn into Nancy's drinking sessions or get tangled up in her life. But Zoe was taking drugs, mixing with older people and getting into trouble; you're younger, you may have been influenced by peer pressure. I didn't want that for you.'

'I can make my own choices,' she snapped.

'Yes, to an *extent*. But you aren't yet old enough to make those choices for yourself without guidance.'

'*Control* you mean?'

I shook my head. 'No, that's not *true*. I'm your mum, I want you to be safe and happy and to make the best choices for yourself. I don't want to *control* you.' Sofia had never said anything like that before and it was hard to take.

'Well, sometimes it feels like you want to control me, stop me, you won't even let me be friends with people I like.'

My stomach dipped slightly; was she talking about Pink Girl?

'I'm sorry if it feels like that,' I responded calmly, trying not to turn this into another fight. She was beginning to see a bigger world, a world where perhaps her mother wasn't always right, and she was kicking against that. I worried if I didn't keep a grip, things might escalate. 'I'm only trying to *guide* you.'

'Who *guides* you then?' she said, a ribbon of sarcasm stitched into her words.

'What do you mean?'

'Last night, you got caught up in Nancy's shit, and last summer, when I had that sleepover you went out with her. I heard you on the phone to Ruby's mum, saying you'd drunk too much gin and she's a bad influence. You said Zoe was a bad influence... and... she died. And then you made me block Pink Girl. But you can carry on seeing *your* friend—'

'That's enough,' I said, raising my voice, astonished that Sofia had held on to all of this. 'I was joking to Ruby's mum, I didn't mean that Nancy's a bad influence,' I said, reminding myself I must be careful in future to check she wasn't listening to my telephone conversations. 'And Nancy didn't *make* me drink; I did it because I'm old enough to make my own decisions. You're fifteen years old, I'm forty-three which is quite a difference,' I replied angrily.

She shrugged, like what I said hadn't touched her.

'Zoe's death has nothing to do with any of this,' I said, shocked at the outburst and still puzzled at this sudden condemnation of my friend. 'You can't compare my friendships to yours, Sofia.'

'Why not?' She was frowning, challenging me.

I struggled for an answer, so just said, 'Because it's *different!*'

For some reason known only to herself, my daughter had taken against the woman who'd been in our life for years and who had only ever shown her kindness, but I knew I wouldn't get anywhere by pushing her.

'Hey, let's just calm it down, shall we? We still haven't done that baking for the church bake sale. The oven's on with the shepherd's pie in, if we get a batch ready, we can put it in as the pie comes out,' I said. She didn't answer me, so I added, 'I promised the vicar.'

Sofia now looked at me, still frowning. I thought she was going to just say no, but she said, 'I guess we'd better get started, or we won't go to heaven.'

Apparently she was as eager as I was to close the cavern threatening to open up between us. Within minutes, we were both wearing aprons and measuring and mixing.

'I look like Nigella in this apron,' I joked.

'More like Gordon Ramsay,' she deadpanned, which made me chuckle.

Throughout Sofia's childhood, we'd baked together. It was really bonding and something I'd done with my mum before she became ill. When she had died, I had only really considered my own and my little sister and brother's feelings, I'd been too young to realise my mother's loss. She never saw her children grow up, never met her granddaughter or enjoyed old age. She died in poverty, worrying herself to death about what might happen to the three of us. But since having Sofia, I'd thought about it a lot and just hoped nothing happened to me, because she'd have no one.

We put the two trays of fairy cakes and a large chocolate sponge in the oven and ate the shepherd's pie while we waited for the cakes to bake. The kitchen air was warm and sweet, and I looked at my daughter. Long shiny hair, clear skin, smiling, and I thought, *If I could bottle this moment, I would*, but even these golden moments always seemed to be tainted by the dread of something happening to smash our happiness. The fear was always there, but intensified at times like this. I knew how much I had to lose.

'I think we should ice the cakes tomorrow, it'll be too late tonight,' I said.

'Mum, no,' she whined.

I saw the little girl with stamping feet who never wanted to go to bed, who always tried to stay up with Mum even at the age of three or four.

'Sofia, we have work and school in the morning, we can't be up late. They have to cool and then we have to make the icing and—'

'Can't we just do one tray of fairy cakes, just one. *Please?*'

I knew this wasn't just about the icing, it was because she wanted to spend more time together and how could I deny her that.

'Okay, just one, but then bed.'

She made a little clapping motion with her fingertips. 'Yay!'

The tension that evening between us had disappeared into the billowing flour and frothing egg whites, but still, there'd been a shift. Sofia was growing up, and a new dynamic was emerging. I knew it would come, it was part of growing, but it was bittersweet. And as I watched her dropping cake mixture into flowery paper cases, I wondered how long we had left.

THIRTEEN

The morning after our cake-baking, Sofia and I rushed around the kitchen, she was making toast, while I made myself coffee. I'd called the hospital first thing and was told Nancy was 'much improved'. From what I could remember, that was the line that meant the patient was out of danger, which was great news.

'We need to finish off the rest of the cakes tonight,' Sofia commented, as she crunched on her toast. 'Let's do that thick fondant and put Christmas stuff on the chocolate cake?' she suggested.

'Great idea. I'll pick up some edible sparkles during my lunch hour,' I said.

Within minutes, we were marching along the seafront in coats and hats and scarves to meet our respective days. When we reached the part where we split up, we hugged and off she went in one direction, me in another up the high street. I had only just arrived at the shop, when my phone went. I was surprised but pleased to see it was Nancy.

'Hey, how are you, sweetie?' I asked, as soon as I picked up.

'I'm okay, but stuck here. They're going to discharge me,

just waiting for the doc to sign me off. Trouble is, I don't have a lift and really don't want to get a taxi.'

'No worries, I'll come and get you,' I replied, wondering if I could get the afternoon off to pick her up. By car, it was only half an hour to the hospital, but she sounded shaky and after taking her home, she might need me to stay with her for a little while.

Mr Woods came in about 11 a.m. He had a spring in his step. Christmas customers had surged to the online perfumery business he'd recently started, he explained. 'That's why I'm so late,' he said, taking his coat off. 'I turned on my computer at home and it's gone mad. I may work from home for a couple of days.'

'Yes, that makes sense,' I replied, pleased for him.

I didn't want to ask for the afternoon off straight away, so made him a cup of coffee before broaching it.

'You know my friend from the art shop, Nancy?' I said.

His face dropped slightly. I knew he wasn't keen on her and it seemed like he wasn't alone, her neighbour had described her as a drunk and my daughter seemed to feel the same.

'Thing is she's been really poorly,' I told him. I didn't feel it was for me to tell anyone about the reason for Nancy being in hospital, it was her business and up to her who she told. Mr Woods was old-school and mental health, non-binary sexuality and courgetti spaghetti were a total mystery. Today wasn't the day to enlighten him.

Having told him Nancy was in hospital, it was agreed I would work until 1 p.m. and then I'd head off to Exeter, on what Mr Woods referred to as 'your mercy mission, dear'. People in the town often referred to Mr Woods as 'grumpy', but I always defended him. He was eccentric, disappointed by life, lonely – and yes, at times a little irritated by people – but to me he'd always been kind. I'd watched him nurse Dorothy during her illness, and saw how caring he was with me and Sofia, I knew the real Mr Woods had a heart of gold.

Later that morning, I was serving customers when I looked up and there was Oliver. I felt my stomach jolt slightly at the sight of him. I didn't really *know* this man, so why did his presence have such an impact on me?

'I'll be with you shortly,' I said, smiling and wishing I'd worn a different top and taken more care over my make-up that morning.

He lifted his hand. 'No rush, I'm just looking, or should I say sniffing?' He smiled at the elderly ladies I was serving, who chuckled at his little joke. He could charm the birds off the trees.

'Are you looking for more gifts?' I asked from behind the counter, after the women had left. He was looking closely at a perfume bottle, it seemed like he'd forgotten where he was for a moment, then smiled at me.

'Yes.' He put the bottle back on the shelf and started walking towards the counter. He then stood a moment and leaned towards me. 'I'm not actually,' he said, conspiratorially.

'Oh?'

He shook his head. 'Actually,' he said, pausing a moment, 'I wanted to ask you something?'

'Okay,' I nodded slowly.

'I wondered if you'd like to go for coffee or lunch sometime?'

'Oh... yes, I'd love to,' I said, unable to hide my elation and too old to play hard to get.

He seemed almost surprised at my immediate affirmative response. 'Oh... er, okay, well no time like the present, what about lunch today?'

My heart leaped, then plummeted in the two seconds it

took for me to realise I wasn't free. 'I'm sorry, I can't. I'm going to meet a friend,' I said. There was no point in explaining to him that it was my friend, Nancy. He'd only met her a couple of times, and again it was no one else's business that she was in hospital.

'Oh that's a shame.' He looked so disappointed. He moved sideways and I had a horrible feeling he might just walk away, say goodbye and I'd never see him again.

I didn't want him to think I was making excuses. 'I'm free *tomorrow* lunchtime though?' I offered, trying not to sound desperate, but not succeeding, even I could hear the pleading in my own voice.

'I'm afraid I can't do tomorrow,' he said, and I wanted to curl up and die. Neither of us said anything for a few moments, and he suddenly spoke. 'I could do tomorrow *evening*?'

To me, that was a whole different ball game. That definitely felt like a date, more challenging for me emotionally, and on top of that, I had Sofia to think of. But here he was, this gorgeous man, asking me out to dinner. I thought of Nancy alone in her little cottage drifting in and out of consciousness, her life ebbing away. Sofia would be going to university in just three years, I'd be alone like Nancy, too young to give up, but too old to be a catch. Was that my future, alone?

'I'd love to,' I replied.

'Great, what time?'

'Do you mind if we don't meet at my flat? I think I mentioned I have a daughter and...' I was about to add that she might not approve of her mother dating but paused unsure how to broach it. I didn't need to worry, Oliver stepped into the silence.

'Of course, I understand. Shall we say about seven? I know a nice quiet little pub down the coast. Perhaps we could meet outside the hotel on the front, The Belmont I think it's called?'

'Yes, that would be perfect,' I replied, trying to hide my

delight and anxiety, knowing I had a lot of juggling to do. 'Could we swap numbers?' I asked. 'It's just that if ever I'm meeting someone it's good to be able to get in touch if plans change,' I said, thinking about Sofia.

'I do hope your plans don't change though, now you can call me and cancel?' he joked as we swapped numbers and smiled at each other. I think we both felt that from that moment we had a proper connection and it was more than just a random bumping into each other.

'No, I hope not. I just don't want to leave Sofia alone. She's only fifteen. I'm sure she can stay with one of her friends though, or my boss Mr Woods would sit with her.' Under normal circumstances, I might have asked Ruby's mum if she could stay the night there. But given the Ruby and Archie situation, that didn't feel like an option.

'I suppose you could bring her along?' he suggested.

'Thank you, but I'll sort something,' I said, impressed at his offer. It told me how genuine he was, and perhaps how keen he was to spend time with me?

We said goodbye and he left, waving through the window as he walked away, leaving me amazed and happy, if extremely nervous. But my sunny horizon was filled with clouds of dread. Sofia and I had just got back on track, and now wasn't the time for me to introduce the totally alien act of going on a date. I'd never had a relationship while I was bringing Sofia up, she always came first and would continue to do so. Then again, perhaps it was time to think about the future and how that would look without Sofia in it? At almost sixteen, it seemed that her life was expanding as mine was shrinking and I needed something, someone to come along and make me feel like I *had* a future at least.

I was excited about getting to know Oliver, but it was bitter-sweet because given Sofia's current insecurity around her own friendships, I didn't feel I could share it with her. It wouldn't be kind to share it with Nancy either, the last thing she wanted to hear was that her best friend had just been asked out by the good-looking customer who Nancy had clearly had her eye on. No, to save their feelings, I'd hold off telling either of them for the time being, which meant I was going to have to lie to them both, which I hated. Then again, I was good at lying, I'd been doing it for years. But what I didn't know then was that I wasn't the only one telling lies.

FOURTEEN

At lunch, I collected the car and set off for Exeter for Nancy.

Walking into the hospital, the familiar smell of bleach and stainless steel took me straight back to the wards, long days and nights, fluorescent lights twenty-four seven. I was reminded of the past, it was always there waiting, hiding, then grabbing me by the throat when I least expected it.

I found Nancy waiting for me in a corridor. Apparently she'd been discharged because her bed was needed. Just walking her to my car, it was clear she was very fragile and in my opinion not ready to be abandoned to her fate due to a bed shortage. She told me she had an appointment with a therapist a fortnight later, but she seemed so quiet and listless, I would have brought the appointment forward if I'd been in charge of her care.

'How do you feel?' I asked, rather lamely, as we drove along.

'Numb,' she murmured, staring ahead.

'You never said anything, we could have talked, love.'

'I didn't want to. I didn't feel I could.'

'I know you and I are private people, but I'm your friend.'

'I know, it's just I've had depression before, I'll have it again.

Sometimes it's just there for no reason, and other times...' she paused, 'it's triggered by something.'

Out of the corner of my eye, I could see her looking at me, like I might know what the trigger was.

'So this time, the reason was the new man. Was it him who texted you?' I ventured.

'Yeah, but let's not talk about it,' she replied, her voice cracking.

'Well, I'm here if you want to talk.'

'I would like to...' she hesitated, 'one day perhaps?'

I nodded, my eyes ahead on the road, so I couldn't see her face. But I couldn't help but feel she was keeping something back.

'Mr Woods gave me the afternoon off,' I said. 'We could go and get coffee if you like?' I was trying in my rather clumsy way to get everything back to how it had been. We always went to the same café, the one where we'd seen Oliver, and I thought she might like that, but it was quite the opposite.

'I don't want to go there, I don't want to go there, Emily. I might bump into someone I don't want to see.' She sounded like a frightened little girl.

'Okay, okay, I understand,' I said. How foolish I'd been to think a cup of coffee in our favourite café would help her to forget the trauma she'd clearly suffered. She'd tried to kill herself, her life had been interrupted and it wasn't going to be that easy for her to pick up the threads. 'I've got your keys, I locked up after the ambulance left. So shall I just take you home, love?' I asked gently.

'I can't go back there,' she said resolutely. She didn't suggest anywhere else, and we were only a few minutes away from town. 'I just feel so anxious, Em. I can't be alone,' she said. It occurred to me that, to my knowledge none of the mess had been cleaned up after the ambulance was called the night she'd overdosed. It wouldn't be a pleasant place for Nancy to go in her current state.

We were driving along the seafront now, so I pulled the car over and we sat looking out at the blustery grey waves as they came and went on a loop.

'I wish I knew how to help you feel better,' I said into the silence of the car. 'It's just that I don't know where to begin. I've known you for almost ten years now, and I'm ashamed to say I had no *idea* you suffered from depression.'

'Good, I'm glad. I didn't want anyone to know.'

'Have you... have you done this before?'

She nodded without looking at me. 'When I was younger. Over some guy, you know.'

'Yeah. I know.'

'I'm just finding it hard to live on my own and I look in the mirror and see myself getting older and having no one to be with. And then I meet someone and think he's the answer to everything—'

'Men are *never* the answer to everything,' I said, patting her knee, trying to reach her. 'Let's face it, most of the time they aren't the answer to *anything*,' I joked.

She didn't respond, her eyes were on the ocean ahead of us.

I felt like this was part of the problem; she wanted a relationship so badly, it almost didn't matter if she was happy or not. She put pressure on her partners to stay, and when they didn't, she beat herself up.

'It's a cliché, but you just have to take things easy,' I said. 'And if men are your trigger, perhaps it's time to get a hobby?'

She smiled at this, and I caught a glimmer of the old Nancy.

'This is hard,' I heard myself say. 'I just thought you were always happy, that nothing really touched you, that you could get through anything. All the time, you were just hiding your hurt. I feel like I neglected you.'

She was looking down, clutching a torn tissue in both

hands, ripping it into little shreds. 'I don't want people feeling sorry for me. I just can't cope with life, that's all. I shout: "I'm over here, everyone look at me," when the real me is somewhere else, hiding.'

We sat in silence for a while, rain and sea splashing on the windows, the bright red cliffs ahead growing fainter as a veil of grey mist rolled in. I eventually checked the time on my watch, it was 4 p.m. and Sofia would be home, so I immediately texted her to say I wouldn't be long.

Okay, Mum. What's for dinner?

I smiled, the clarion cry of all kids, whatever age.

That vegetable soup I made yesterday. I bought bread, nice bread, I added, as an apology for the rather meagre meal, but, as always, money was tight.

Okay, I'll start warming it through, she replied.

I read it and smiled, then remembered that Nancy still hadn't told me where to take her. Normally, I wouldn't have thought twice about asking her to stay with us, but my stomach dipped slightly at the thought of having to take her home to Sofia.

'Sofia's home now, so we'd better head off,' I said. 'Where would you like me to take you? I can drop you home, and you can call me any time, I'll be on the end of the phone?' I tried.

She didn't answer, just continued to stare ahead.

In the silence, I felt forced to state: 'Obviously, you're welcome to stay with us, but it's a bit difficult because we don't have a spare room and you—'

'Yes, yes, I'd like to come back with you, if that's okay?' She was looking at me with these big, sad eyes. What choice did I have?

'Of course.'

I started the engine and pulled away. Nancy was my friend,

and Sofia would have to respect that, but as I drove the last ten minutes, I wished I'd texted her first while we were parked up so at least she'd be prepared. It was hard to fathom Sofia's new-found jealousy for Nancy, but I hoped if she saw how fragile she was, it might bring out the kind girl I knew my daughter to be.

'She's only here while she gets herself together,' I whispered. Nancy had gone to have a lie-down on my bed and it gave me the chance to explain to Sofia, who seemed pretty pissed off about our house guest. She'd been sitting at the kitchen table, watching the soup and gazing at her phone when we'd arrived. When she'd looked up and spotted Nancy, the smile had faded, and her eyes had become unreachable. I don't think Nancy even realised, she was overcome with exhaustion and asked if she could rest, so I immediately took her to my room. I'd offered to take her to her own home after she'd had a nap, so she could grab some fresh clothes and a nightdress. 'It's okay, I'll borrow one of your nighties, I can't face that place right now,' she'd said. I'd nodded, but it wasn't like I had a lot of clothes, so that wasn't going to be easy. At least she'd collected her medication from the hospital pharmacy, so hopefully there would be no sudden relapses.

As Sofia and I had our soup, I tried to get to the bottom of her rather sudden dislike of Nancy. 'What is it about her that's getting to you?' I asked.

'Oh let's not, Mum, I don't want to talk about her.' She wafted her hand like she wanted to shoo Nancy away. It was all so out of character.

'You've never said anything before. I don't understand why you suddenly have a problem with her...' I started, but I could see by Sofia's face that Nancy had just walked into the room behind me.

'Hey, ladies,' she murmured and plonked herself down on the seat next to Sofia. Nancy looked at her and attempted a smile, but it was more of a grimace, and Sofia barely acknowledged her.

'I guess we aren't icing the cakes tonight?' she said to me, unsmiling.

'Yes, of course we will, I just need to—'

'It's okay, I have homework to do anyway,' she said.

'Sofia, I said yes, we'll do it.'

'It doesn't matter now,' she murmured and disappeared to her room.

'What's her problem?' Nancy asked, her lip slightly curled.

'Oh just a teenage thing, I guess.' But, in truth, I was embarrassed, I didn't understand it myself and didn't like the way Sofia had behaved. 'I'm sorry, I'm not sure being here in this maelstrom of hormones is exactly relaxing for you, perhaps some soup will help?' I offered.

Nancy shrugged, and while I warmed it up, she lay her head in her arms on the table. She was clearly still suffering.

I placed the bowl in front of her, but she just moved down the table slightly to avoid it.

'You have to eat,' I coaxed her.

'I could do with a drink, to be honest,' she said, looking up at me like a child asking her mother for something.

'Water, tea, coffee?' I asked, knowing full well that wasn't what she meant.

'I could do with something a little stronger, to take the edge off, you know?'

'Sorry, I don't have wine or anything in the house,' I said, which was the truth. I didn't drink alone, and couldn't afford luxuries like wine anyway. I saw her eyes fall to the floor. 'Perhaps eat the soup, eh?' I suggested, and she reluctantly picked up the spoon, dipped it in the bowl, then lifted it slowly to her mouth, making each mechanical movement painful to watch.

As she ate, I was distracted by the idea of Sofia voluntarily going to her room to do homework. Was she really being so conscientious, after all she was in Year 11 and her GCSE exams were coming up, or was she just texting her friends, complaining about me bringing 'a drunk' home to stay?

After Nancy had eaten, I suggested she sleep in my room. 'It's your first night out of hospital,' I said, 'you can't sleep on the sofa.'

'Thanks, I'm just glad to be out of there. They gave me this injection, I was sick everywhere and then I said, "Let me go home,"' she said, tears springing to her eyes.

I suddenly felt a huge weight of responsibility. Nancy was a mess, and I was concerned about her but not qualified to help her through this.

'Did a psychiatrist evaluate you?'

'I saw someone, yeah. She asked me a few questions about my medication and why I wanted to end my life.'

Hearing her actually say that was quite a jolt, until then we'd danced around it, but this was just a reminder of how serious this was.

'And what did you tell her?'

'I said I'd just overreacted to something.' She turned to me. 'I'm fine now.'

She clearly wasn't.

'So did she want to explore your overreaction?' I asked, genuinely interested in how she was treated, and at the same time intrigued to know just what she'd overreacted to.

'Not really.' She didn't meet my eyes, was that significant? 'I said I wouldn't do it again, and she said, "Okay, here's a prescription, don't come back, you drama queen."' Nancy looked at me expectantly then, waiting for me to smile at this, but it felt too serious. She was so fragile. 'I'm paraphrasing,' she added.

I acknowledged then that instead of looking at her feelings, she buried them with humour.

'Look, I'm your friend, and if you need to talk, you know I'm here, right?' I said, unsmiling and hopefully making the point that even if she wasn't taking this seriously, I was.

'Yeah, thanks, Em.' She sounded overcome, tearful, and I wasn't sure if I'd made things better or worse. I wasn't the person to be helping her through this, what advice could I give? My relationship with my daughter was in a bad place, she'd changed, and I couldn't put my finger on what it was. But deep down, I had a feeling I knew exactly why she was different, and my darkest fears were about to be realised.

FIFTEEN

It was late, and I was exhausted, but it seemed like Nancy wanted to stay up and talk. She was now discussing a former partner, who had treated her badly, and I tried to be a sympathetic listener, but just wanted to go to bed.

'Sorry to interrupt,' I said gently, just as she was getting to 2019 and her suspicions about another woman. 'But I have to get up for work tomorrow, shall I pop into the shop and let John know you're out of hospital? I presume you told him you'd been taken in, so wouldn't be at work?'

She pulled a sad face. 'No, I'm not going to tell him for a couple of days, let him think I'm still in hospital, he'll only want me back in. Just don't mention it. If he asks, say you haven't seen me.'

'Okay,' I said, standing up from the table, hoping she'd get the hint. I couldn't go to bed until she had because I was sleeping on the sofa. 'I'll let you get to bed,' I said not so subtly. 'I'll just pop into Sofia and check she's asleep before I settle down on the sofa.'

She looked slightly deflated at this, and I felt terribly guilty, but I couldn't sit up all night talking. She didn't have work the next morning, but I did.

As she slowly got up from the table, I headed for Sofia's room. It was now after eleven, and I assumed she'd be asleep so knocked softly a couple of times, then opened the door. She was on her bed looking at her phone, with her headphones in, and for a moment she didn't see me.

'Hey,' I said and waved at her, which caused her to suddenly look up and immediately turn her phone face down. It was then I noticed she was crying. 'Sweetie, are you okay?' I sat down on her bed and put my hand to her face, but she startled away.

'What the—? Mum, ever think of knocking?'

'Sorry, I did knock,' I said as she pulled off her headphones. 'Are you upset?'

She shook her head. 'No, I'm fine. Just tired and trying to get to sleep.'

'With your headphones on and your phone in your hand?' I asked, gently.

She shrugged.

'It's late, what are you doing on your phone?'

'Nothing.' She was flustered, holding on to her phone like her life depended on it.

I could see this wasn't just about me walking in, her reaction set my radar on high alert, she was definitely hiding something. I immediately thought of Pink Girl. 'Have you had more messages?' I asked.

'Yeah.' She looked me straight in the eye, almost like she was daring me to pursue this. Then she seemed to think better of it. 'I've had messages off Ruby if that's what you mean?'

'That isn't what I mean, and you know it,' I replied. 'Have you had any more messages from Pink Girl?'

'No. You made me block her, remember?' she huffed.

'Yes,' I said. 'Because it was creepy, you have to be careful.'

'I know, I know.' She put her phone on the bedside table. 'I'm going to sleep now,' she announced and, turning away from me, lay down, bringing the covers up near her face.

I leaned in and, putting my hand on her head, kissed her and whispered, 'Night, darling.'

She murmured something, and I left the room. What was going on with her? The answer of course was in her phone, and I wasn't convinced she'd been talking to Ruby.

As I walked into the empty kitchen, her password flickered through my head, inviting me to peep into my daughter's world. Should I take a look? The person who was being Pink Girl online could be anyone, and as her mother it was my job to make sure she was protected. On the other hand, it might be nothing. Nothing more had been mentioned about the message she'd received – *Your mother isn't who you think she is.* It might be meaningless. In my fear and paranoia, I may have taken it completely out of context, and it was simply a rhetorical question. If so, wouldn't it be better if I looked at Sofia's messages and put my mind at rest? I was concerned about who she was talking to and why she was blocking me out. If I could just read the messages, then I could rest easy.

When I was younger, I could never share my problems with Mum. She was poorly for most of my childhood and as the eldest of three, I grew up fast. When Mum died, as we all had different fathers, my sister and brother went to live with theirs. But no one seemed to know who mine was, I was never 'claimed' and ended up living with a very old aunt of my mother's who was good to me but too old and tired of life to have much input with a teenage girl. I always promised myself that if I ever had children they'd be my priority, whatever happened in my relationship, the children would always come first, and I kept that promise. Sofia and I just had each other, I'd moved mountains to keep her close, and sacrificed so much. That was why it hurt to think she was so upset, but suddenly felt she couldn't talk to me about it.

Sofia's tears that night and her coolness towards me could mean that Pink Girl was back – in some form. I shuddered at the thought and sat down at the table to steady myself. In the dim light and the thick silence, nothing moved, but the shadows appeared to be growing. I was fighting the past, it was always there, and like a tide I couldn't hold it back. But if I didn't, it might wash us both away, so I crept into Sofia's room, and after checking she was asleep, I quietly took her phone from the bedside table. Returning to the kitchen, I sat in the dark, her phone in my hands, feeling like a thief, a stalker intruding on my child's life.

She was growing up and, like any teenager, needed her space, her privacy, her secrets, and I wanted to respect that. But there were things she didn't understand, and the secrets she was keeping from me could put us both in danger. So, I clicked on her phone, and entered the password, holding my breath, knowing and not knowing what I might find, and dreading it.

The light from the screen shone in my face as I tried to navigate my way through her life. The photo on Sofia's screensaver was of her and Ruby on the beach last summer, my heart stung a little seeing their laughing faces. I was sad to think how things had changed between them since then; she rarely talked about Ruby now.

I moved to Instagram, a grid of photos, mostly of Sofia, some laughing, some pouting, some just being silly with friends. She kept telling me I should open an Instagram account, and looking at these photos, I thought perhaps I should because then I could see her photos. It was lovely glimpsing into my child's world, a superficial view, but still it was nice to get a feel for the person she presented to the world.

I checked her settings, relieved to see they were still on private, and there was no sign of Pink Girl, even in her direct messages. In truth, I felt grubby opening up the private messages, like I was wading through someone's bin. She was my daughter, but still I felt guilty about invading her privacy like that, but when I saw no messages from Pink Girl, I felt relieved. I had one last search for anyone called Pink Girl on Instagram, but I couldn't find one that fit so had to assume she'd deleted her account.

Then I remembered Facebook. Sofia told me she didn't go on there anymore because it was for 'old people' who were 'sad', which I took to mean people over thirty. But just in case, I clicked onto the app, walking blindly into another aspect of my daughter's life.

I had to smile when I saw the posts and pictures from just a few years before, how she'd changed so much in such a short time. It wasn't just the physical difference between an eleven-year-old and a fifteen-year-old, it was the *person* who'd changed. Younger Sofia posted poetry and pictures of kittens and singers in bands she would now laugh at because they were 'for babies'. It was clear she hadn't been on there for a long time, and having looked at these just for my own memories, I felt it was time to leave her alone, and hopefully close the door on this. Her recent behaviour was due to friendship issues, Pink Girl was gone and I didn't need to worry any more. But just before logging off, I was horrified to see yet more messages between my daughter and Pink Girl. I could feel myself shaking with fear. I'd believed I'd put a stop to this, that I'd locked the door to our lives and we were safe, but the door had been left open, and someone had come back in.

SIXTEEN

Looking through the messages between Sofia and Pink Girl, it seemed Sofia had delayed blocking her for several days, long enough for this person to find out more, keeping their foot dangerously in the door to our lives. I was scared, and scrolled quickly, desperate to see every word, searching for hidden meanings, subtexts that would mean nothing to Sofia, but *everything* to me. Sofia had told her she had to block her, that 'my mum says you're not a teenage girl, you might be a paedo.'

Pink Girl had responded to this by sending photos of a teenage girl, supposed to be herself – but of course it wasn't. The girl in the photos had a tattoo, and Sofia remarked how 'cool' it was and that she'd wanted a tattoo, but 'my mum said no, she hates tattoos.' This wasn't strictly true, I was all for self-expression and said that when she was old enough, she could choose to have a tattoo if she liked. What hurt about this was that our relationship was being misrepresented by my daughter, who in reality had little to rebel against. I could only imagine Pink Girl rubbing her hands together at the implied lack of empathy or understanding from me towards Sofia.

I tried not to overthink Sofia's messages, she thought she

was talking to a peer and it wasn't cool to say 'my mum's great, we have no issues.' I kept reminding myself this wasn't about me, she was just a kid trying to fit in with other kids, but I knew the façade she was presenting might have terrible implications for us. And I noticed that after Sofia had revealed that I wanted her to stop talking to Pink Girl and block her, the tone of the conversation changed, like Pink Girl knew she had to gain as much information as possible before she was blocked. Suddenly, she wasn't talking vaguely about boys and bands and RuPaul's 'sick' dresses, anymore. Now she was asking specific questions, like, 'Where do you live? Where's your dad? Where does your mum work?' and 'What's the name of your school?' Pink Girl, whoever she was, knew I was onto her and was desperately garnering as much information as she could. This scared the hell out of me, but Sofia, to her credit, had avoided giving her those details, saying, 'Sorry but I can't tell you stuff like that, Mum would freak out if she found out I was telling you, and she has my password.'

There was a short gap in the messages where Pink Girl obviously had to regroup because Sofia wasn't the easy target she'd hoped for. But then I saw it.

Pink Girl's final message on Instagram before Sofia blocked her made my stomach flip.

Don't believe what your mum tells you. Your mum tells lies.

This was like a punch in the face. Sofia may have blocked her as I'd requested, but was it already too late? Just as I'd thought, Pink Girl wasn't some teenage friend. Was it Chris, my ex, or someone much worse, someone who knew every-thing about me, and wanted revenge for what I'd done? My heart was in my mouth, but as Sofia had blocked her straight after this message, there was nothing more to go on. So I moved back to earlier conversations between them, desperately searching for proof, a sign that told me who it might be. I kept on reading, devouring each word, consuming and translating the hidden meanings that might be staring me in the face. Then, suddenly, I heard a creaking floorboard behind me.

I froze and, at first, couldn't move, but then I heard it again, and shivering in the thick silence, I turned around slowly. To my surprise, Nancy was standing behind me. She was just a few feet away, in the doorway, the lamp from the hallway was behind her, framing her in an eerie light.

'I thought you'd gone to bed,' I said quietly.

She didn't respond, but what scared me most was the look on her face. She was just staring through me, her eyes blank, like she didn't recognise me.

'How long have you been there?' I spoke again, hearing the break in my own voice. What the hell was she up to? When she didn't answer, I slipped the phone into my cardigan pocket. 'Are you okay, would you like another glass of water or...?' For a moment, I wondered if she was having a joke, but the look on her face told me this was real.

Still she didn't answer, her eyes were on me, but not making contact, like she couldn't *see*, but she kept looking through me. It was as if her ghost had climbed out of my bed and appeared in the doorway, leaving the real Nancy in bed asleep. I suddenly felt very vulnerable sitting in the chair, my back to her, my head turned around to see her as she bore down on me. I slowly stood up, and moved slightly away from her, putting the chair between us for protection. I felt scared and vulnerable, and didn't know what to do.

'You're being weird,' I said nervously, as she walked towards me, one step at a time.

I turned on the kitchen light and passing her in the doorway, walked towards my bedroom, hoping she'd follow me, but instead she continued to stand in the doorway, as if frozen.

Then suddenly, she spoke, but her voice sounded strange, cold.

'Em, I think I said too much, I hope you don't get hurt – I'm a bad friend.'

'What do you mean?' Now I was scared, what had she said and to whom?

'Shut up, shut *up*, Nancy,' she berated herself.

'I don't know what you're *talking* about,' I whispered anxiously. I was standing in the doorway, almost next to her, looking into her face, but it was strange, her eyes were on mine, but she seemed to be looking through me, beyond me, into the kitchen. 'Are you asleep?' I asked, vaguely remembering her telling me she sometimes walked and talked in her sleep if she was stressed. But it was really creepy and I felt so uncomfortable.

She didn't answer me and I didn't want to wake her, so I gently manoeuvred her back to my room, and helped her into bed. She didn't wake once, but as she put her head on the pillow, she murmured, 'I'm really sorry, Em, I didn't mean it...'

I wasn't sure what she meant or even if what she was saying meant anything or whether she was just dreaming. I stayed with her a moment, waiting for the 'ghost' to disappear, and when I was sure she was sleeping, I left the room, but I couldn't shake the unsettling feeling. It was now after midnight, and I was creeping down the hallway back to the kitchen when I heard Sofia calling me. We must have woken her, and remembering I had her phone in my pocket, I gently opened her door.

'Is everything okay?' she murmured from under the covers, still half asleep.

I walked towards the bed and, discreetly and reluctantly placing the phone back on the bedside table, I bent down and whispered that everything was fine. Then I kissed her head, said goodnight and tiptoed from the room. I'd been spooked by my best friend and my daughter, and lay down on the hard, narrow sofa, knowing sleep wouldn't come that night.

The following morning, it was as if the night before had never happened. Sofia and I moved organically around each other, weaving in and out like dancers who'd been expertly choreographed. We danced around the kitchen, eating toast, pouring cereal. In between, Sofia checked her phone, as I did mine, our life support systems providing us with everything we needed on our little screens. She was typing a message. I watched discreetly over the box of breakfast cereal.

'You messaging Ruby?' I asked.

She looked up, surprised. 'No. Why?'

'Oh no reason, I just wondered how things were with her. I thought you weren't really speaking?'

She shrugged. 'I have to, I sit next to her for most of our classes, walk in with her. It's hard to cut people out when you're at school.'

'Do you really want to cut her out?'

'Sometimes.'

I looked up from my breakfast. She tried to smile at me, but it emerged as a grimace.

I said, 'I'm sorry about Nancy being here, but I have no choice. She's my friend.'

'Mmm, I know.'

I stood up and took my dish to the sink. I had to be the grown-up, so I turned to face her. 'Look, it won't be long, she'll go back to her place in a day or two, but while she's here, please be kind.'

She dropped her toast onto her plate. 'Kind? Everyone's using that word these days, even *unkind* people.'

Was she implying it was me who wasn't kind? But before I

could pursue this, she stood up, grabbed her bag and walked to the doorway.

'Sofia, I'm sorry,' I said quietly, 'but what could I do? She didn't want to go to her place, and I wasn't going to turn her away.'

'You did what you had to do, Mum,' she said stonily.

At the shop that day, I couldn't concentrate on anything but the messages on Sofia's phone. I was still trying to work out if I was overreacting and creating a scenario that didn't exist when the bell jangled over the door. Oliver walked in, and I felt a slam in my chest and remembered. Our date.

'Hi,' he said, smiling as he closed the door behind him.

'Hi, I was about to call you.' I had no idea what I was going to say, just knew I had to cancel our plans for the evening.

'I just wanted to make sure you were still okay for tonight,' he said before I could continue. 'I'm not used to this, I haven't been out with anyone for dinner in a long time.' His eyes were smiling. 'I booked us a nice table at this cosy little pub by the sea. It's about ten miles from here.' He paused, 'I know you want to be discreet, with your daughter and everything, and this place, it's perfect.'

'Oh... *lovely*,' I heard myself say. How could I possibly say no to him? Apart from the fact I really, really liked him, he said he didn't do this very often and it was a big deal. He'd gone to the trouble of booking and I didn't want to disappoint him. Despite his charm and good looks, there seemed to be a refreshing vulnerability about Oliver. I liked the fact that he seemed as nervous as I was about going out on a date. Mind you, *his* nervousness was around the date, unlike mine, which was about leaving my depressed, alcoholic friend with my stroppy teenage daughter who may be talking to someone dangerous online.

'I'll see you later,' he said quietly and touched my arm, sending volts of electricity through my body. I knew in my head that I should have just told him I couldn't make it after all, but childcare issues for a fifteen-year-old sounded a bit lame. I knew some mums left their kids alone at night as teens, but I couldn't because of our situation. I could call him and cancel any time. But in truth I was stressed out with everything at home and a night spent with someone different would be a welcome break. It might make me see things more clearly, stop obsessing and overthinking things. So, I did some deep breathing and texted Sofia. She couldn't take calls in school, but they were allowed to check their phones at breaktime, and I wanted to forewarn her so my absence that evening wouldn't be a shock.

Sweetie, I just wanted to let you know in advance I have to work late tonight. I will pop home after 5, but have to come back to the shop later, we have an event on. Sorry I forgot to mention it. Xxx

An event?

Yes a Christmas one.

But I always come along to that. Can't I come?

No. It's not that one.

So I have to stay at home with her?

Just be kind. Okay?

Okay

I put down the phone. That was the first hurdle jumped, then I called Nancy, saying the same. She was less interested, didn't ask what I was doing at work so late, didn't even ask where Sofia would be until I mentioned it.

'Oh, Sofia's not going with you, she's going to be *here*?' she asked, sounding as enthusiastic about their night in together as my daughter did.

'Yeah, but she's fine, she'll probably just be in her room.'

More than once I almost cancelled Oliver, especially when I arrived home to find Sofia in the kitchen with too many questions.

'Why are you dressing up? I thought you were going to work?' she asked.

'I am, it's a corporate thing. Mr Woods has invited some perfumiers to show us their products.'

'I thought you said it was a Christmas thing?'

I walked to the kitchen counter, turned the kettle on. 'It is, it's their Christmas collections.'

'In mid-December?' It was like she *knew* I was lying to her, which made me feel even worse.

'Look, I bought these during my lunch hour,' I said and, ignoring her inquisition, I opened the fridge and produced two boxed meals – a chicken pasta and a macaroni cheese.

'Ugh, we never have those. Why did you buy those?'

'Because I haven't had time to shop or cook,' I replied, frustrated. I leaned against the counter, waiting for the kettle to boil. 'I'm sorry,' I murmured. 'Just eat one of those tonight and tomorrow I'll go to the supermarket and we'll eat like queens – healthy queens!' I tried to make a joke, but it landed splat on the kitchen floor.

She peered at the two boxes from a distance, like they might be contagious. 'I'm not having those.'

'There's one for you and one for Nancy.'

'Why aren't *you* eating?'

'God, Sofia, why so many questions?' I asked, exasperated. I put a teabag in a mug, hoping this might soothe me. I felt nervous and edgy about the date, but these emotions were swirling alongside the guilt of lying and leaving two people together who might not look after each other. To top it all, I felt guilty as hell about giving my daughter a plastic tray of overprocessed mush for dinner, while I went out on a secret date. But there wasn't time to do anything now.

Ten minutes later, I was rushing along the seafront in the wind and rain, my umbrella being bashed this way and that, not to mention my hair. But I finally reached the far end of the promenade and saw a pale blue car, a big shiny one, waiting outside the arch of The Belmont Hotel. I marched towards it as confidently as I could, and when I got there, Oliver was in the driver's seat, smiling.

I opened the passenger door and climbed in. It was warm and dry and smelt of sandalwood and leather, and I felt this warm rush of relief and escape flood through me. I was here, with a kind, smiling man who liked me, and already I felt far away from all the questions, the tension, the fear, and Nancy's sadness. And having made up my face and done my hair and worn my nicest dress, I ruined it all by bursting into tears.

SEVENTEEN

'I am *so* sorry,' I said, emerging from my hands, a vision in leaky mascara and mucus.

'Are you okay?' Oliver asked. 'If you'd rather not go out, I understand.'

'No, it isn't that. I don't know what happened,' I said. 'I just... I'm so embarrassed.'

'Don't be,' he said, smiling. Reaching into the back of his car, he handed me a box of tissues. 'I didn't realise this was such an ordeal for you, is it that bad going out with me?'

We both smiled at this.

I already felt better in his company and was determined to make the most of this evening. I hadn't made the best first impression on this date so far, but Oliver seemed unfazed and understanding and that was the reassurance I needed. 'Right, now that I've got that out of the way, shall we make a move?'

He looked over at me, eyes full of warmth, then he started the car, pulling away from the seafront and heading slowly down the coast.

'I have a few things going on at the moment,' I offered by way of explanation for my earlier outburst.

'I guessed that was the case. I had children myself,' he added, 'I know what it's like to live with teenagers.' He turned to me briefly and smiled.

'Yes, it's difficult – well, things between Sofia and I have always been good, but recently, I don't know.'

'What's been happening?'

'Well, she seems to have fallen out with her friend who seems to be with the boy she likes. And now she's talking to people online who I suspect aren't who they say they are.' I told him about how she'd changed and become secretive and for some reason had issues with Nancy. I said far more than I'd intended, and that was just on the drive to the restaurant, but he was so understanding and explained that he'd experienced something similar.

'I have a boy and a girl, and gender makes no difference. The lovely little child you cradled in your arms at four is not the same beast that's wandering your house when they hit their teens,' he said.

I found him so easy to talk to and by the time we'd reached the restaurant, I even thought that if things didn't work out romantically, we could be great friends. But walking into the candlelit dining room, and being quietly ushered to a table for two, I looked across at him and knew this was going to be so much more than friendship.

Over dinner, he told me about his life as a lawyer, how he was retired but still did some work with his old firm whilst he was here in Sidmouth. 'I knew I wanted somewhere quiet but with a sense of community.'

'It's a small place, but big enough to hide in,' I half-joked.

'What do you mean?' He was smiling quizzically.

'Well, the population of Sidmouth is about twelve thousand, so it's small but everyone doesn't know your business,' I replied, wishing I hadn't mentioned hiding. I picked up the menu, trying to put space between what I'd said. Luckily, Oliver didn't jump on what I'd said and instead asked what I was going to choose. I was thinking that, for the first time, here was someone I felt I could trust. I'd kept myself removed and secluded for so long, I found the idea of sharing my problems quite liberating. As I watched him order his dinner, and choose the wine, I wondered if this could ever be what I wanted it to be. But I knew the only way it could be was if I was honest, and in doing that I'd risk losing him anyway.

Before our food arrived, I popped to the bathroom to call Sofia, just to make sure everything was okay at home.

'Are you still at the shop?' she asked. I had this weird feeling she didn't believe me.

'Yes, I'm still here, it's been a long night. I will be another hour or so, these people don't know when to leave.' I hated lying to her, it never got any easier even when your whole life was a lie.

'Okay, bye,' she said. 'I'm going to bed now.' With that, her phone clicked off. I knew she wasn't going to sleep, she'd probably seen my absence as an opportunity to sit up in bed on her phone until she heard me coming in.

'Sofia's okay,' I told Oliver, sitting back down.

'I'd forgotten what it's like when they're young,' he said, his head to one side like he was remembering. 'You can never rest, can you?'

'No, you can't. Tell me, does it get easier – please say yes!'

He chuckled. 'No, I'm sorry to say it doesn't. I still worry about Charlotte even now; she's all grown, happily married. They're always your babies, aren't they?'

'And your son,' I asked. 'Do you still worry about him too or is it easier with boys?'

He suddenly had this look on his face I couldn't fathom. A sadness mixed with a kind of embarrassment, like he wanted to tell me something but couldn't. Eventually, he spoke.

'My son, he died.'

I was mortified. 'Oh, I'm so sorry.'

He brushed away my apologies with his hand, shaking his head, his eyes down on the table. 'Please don't apologise, I just *hate* to talk about it. Too painful.' He paused, then looked at me. 'Let's talk about something lighter—'

I nodded. 'Of course, I wouldn't have asked if—'

'No, of course you wouldn't.'

It was at this moment that our food arrived, and we both thanked the waiter gratefully, not just for the food, but for the interruption. There had been nowhere to go after that. I hoped that perhaps as we got to know each other he might open up to me. As a parent, I couldn't imagine the immense pain, the heartache he must have experienced. Sofia was my world, it was why I was so protective of her, I couldn't let anything happen to her, I *wouldn't*.

After dinner, we drank coffee, and I found myself telling Oliver about Sofia and Nancy and how there was an atmosphere at home.

'I feel bad for Nancy, but I don't know how to help,' I said.

'Some people don't want to be helped.' He raised his eyebrows, as he took a sip of coffee. He put his cup down. 'I don't know your friend, but sounds to me like she'd be better on her own; you might be enabling her?'

'That's a good point, she's only been there twenty-four hours, but already I'm cleaning up after her and making sure she eats,' I said with a smile.

'Exactly, and if you weren't there, she'd survive, she'd look after herself and heal.'

I stirred my coffee, playing with the foam. Was it that simple? Was I just making the situation worse for Nancy rather than better? It was so hard to know what to do. 'I suppose...'

'And being around that kind of person might not be the best thing for your daughter? She needs positive role models at this age, believe me I know. I often think if things had been different, my son...'

I nodded silently, hoping to give him the space to open up, but he remained quiet.

'Was it sudden, your son's death?' I asked gently.

'Yes, but we saw it coming, if you know what I mean. He was only twenty-one...'

'I can't imagine how you coped with that.'

Oliver sighed. 'He had the best of everything: good education, holidays, wanted for nothing – except the one thing he needed, his parents. We were both busy climbing the career ladder. His sister was made of stronger stuff, but he was more sensitive. I sometimes think he felt neglected, unloved even? It was the usual story, he got in with a bad crowd when he was about seventeen. We just thought he was a bit wild, that he would grow out of it. Then he got into trouble with the police, drugs, stealing, and I'm ashamed to say we were glad to pack him off to university. It was the biggest mistake we could have made. Once he was there, he was free to take as many drugs as he liked, and he did. We thought his constant requests for money for books and research trips were a sign he was embracing university life, settling down, making a fresh start. We just kept transferring money into his account...' He paused. 'You know, sometimes I think we were as guilty as the drug dealers who sold it to him.' He hung his head, and I reached out to touch his hand in a comforting gesture, but he gently pulled it away, he just was so wrapped up in his grief.

'He could have got hold of drugs anywhere,' I said. 'I know what it's like, a member of my family went through it, and if they're determined, then you can't stop them.'

Oliver was still caught up in the past, shaking his head. 'He left a note, blaming me and his mother.'

I didn't know what to say, I felt such sadness for this man and the weight he carried.

'My wife couldn't live with the guilt, she died last year, but really the woman I knew died the day our son died, and they say you can't die of a broken heart,' he scoffed.

We sat at the table in silence for a long time, two people lost in their own worlds of pain. Eventually, he looked at his watch and said, 'Well, I suppose you'll want to be getting home to that girl of yours?'

I was surprised at how considerate he was, I did want to get back to Sofia, and as lovely as it had been gazing at each other over candlelight all evening, the subject matter had brought us both down.

The drive back was quiet; I ached to say something, but there was nothing I could think of. He'd listened to me, but talking about his son had, quite understandably, changed the mood of the evening and when he pulled up outside The Belmont, I really thought all was lost. He kept the engine running, and I got the message that he *did* want the evening to end.

'Well, thanks for a lovely dinner,' I said.

'Thank *you*, it's been great,' he replied, without looking at me.

I waited a moment before getting out of the car. Did he want to say anything, like can I see you again, can I kiss you or – what are you doing for the rest of your life? Nothing. He was just smiling benignly and, as far as I could see, just sitting like a taxi driver waiting for his passenger to leave so he could go home to bed.

'Thanks again,' I said, opening the door and climbing out. 'I owe you dinner some time,' I added. But it was as if he didn't hear.

I shut the car door then and waved him off. I marched along the freezing cold seafront, little puffs of snow now landing on the pavement and on me. I didn't feel the cold, I was too busy thinking over what had happened during the evening. I was disappointed how things had ended, but perhaps Oliver's reaction wasn't about me, it was about his son. His grief had been plain to see, he carried it with him, and who could blame him for suddenly closing off, his terrible loss had clearly left scars. Whatever it was that had caused him to cool at the end of the evening, he clearly didn't feel comfortable enough to share it with me. My deep insecurity made me wonder if there was something about me that had put him off. Had I not reacted appropriately, adequately, to what he was telling me, and had he decided I wasn't who he thought I was after all? I couldn't handle the uncertainty of dating, and wanted to go home, hug Sofia and forget all about him. But just then, my phone pinged. I looked down, and saw he'd sent me a text, the first line was 'I'm so sorry, I think I may have been...' What? *Leading you on? Mistaken? Deluded to think you might be someone I would want to date?* I didn't want to open it.

I continued walking along the front against the wind. It was a metaphor for my life, constantly fighting and struggling alone, always pushing head on into the wind and rain. I'd never considered sharing this weight with anyone else, I'd never wanted to get involved again, it was all too complicated. But that night with Oliver, I'd actually considered something more, I'd opened a door and now I'd have to close it again. How stupid I was to think someone as sophisticated and worldly and handsome as him would be interested in me.

After struggling with this for a few minutes, I decided to open the text. I couldn't wait until I got home because I didn't want to read it and get upset in front of Sofia or Nancy, so I sheltered in a shop doorway and held my breath.

'I'm so sorry, I think I may have been less than sparkling tonight. I apologise for getting upset about my son, it happened a long time ago, but it's still very raw, and as a parent I hope you understand...' My heart sank, this was an *it's not you, it's me* text. But I read on: 'But I had a lovely time with you and I'd love to see you again, if only to show you I can be better company. I completely understand if you don't feel the same. No pressure. Xxx'

My chest fizzed with excitement, but I decided not to look too desperate by waiting until the following day to text him back so we could arrange another date. I wanted to run home now and tell Nancy all about it, but it was probably the last thing she needed to hear. No, sadly this was something I couldn't yet share with my best friend, or my daughter for that matter. It was proving hard enough for Sofia to accept Nancy in my life, she certainly wasn't going to welcome a complete stranger. So I walked home, holding this secret like a baby bird in my hands, I didn't want to expose it to the elements, I wanted to keep it safe and see if it could survive before sharing it with anyone. A tiny part of me wondered would this perhaps finally lead to my happy ending, or was I simply heading for more disappointment and heartache? If I'd known that night what the future held, I'd never have believed it.

EIGHTEEN

When I'd returned home from my date with Oliver the previous evening, it had been very quiet and the first thing I did was check on Sofia, who was fast asleep. She reminded me of when she was little, cocooned, safe from the outside world, but now I knew we were never safe. The outside world could still get in online and now the dangers felt more frequent, more real, but also more obscure, more threatening.

The following day, I woke up on the couch, a reminder that Nancy was still with us.

'Good morning, Mum,' Sofia called through into the living room.

'Morning, darling,' I replied, still a little dazed from sleep.

Within seconds she appeared at my side with a steaming cup of coffee. 'How was last night?'

'Last night?' I asked, immediately thinking of Oliver, forgetting for a moment that I'd lied about where I was.

'At the shop?'

'Yes, yes, it was a success,' I said. 'How was your evening? All okay with Nancy?'

She shrugged. 'Didn't really see her, thank God! She stayed in her room – well, *your* room.'

I pulled an awkward face. 'It's not easy, I know, we just have to give her a little more time and—'

'Yeah. Mum, you're not going to start working late every night, are you?'

'No, it was just a one-off,' I replied, lying once more by reassuring Sofia that it wasn't going to happen again, when Oliver had asked to see me again.

I threw off the duvet, climbed off the couch and looked around the living room at the mess. My clothes were folded, but in a small pile on the coffee table; the book I'd been reading on the floor with my reading glasses; my make-up bag and toiletries also in bags in the living room. This was all so I didn't have to go into my bedroom and disturb Nancy, who didn't wake up until later, after Sofia and I had left. I felt like Ben, the man who slept in gardens and on benches around Sidmouth, like I had no fixed abode. My life was as messy as this room, everything now seemed so complicated. But I told myself to ignore everything else for half an hour and have breakfast with my daughter, give her some time. And as Nancy had now started wearing my dressing gown, I wrapped a blanket around me to join her in the kitchen with my coffee, hoping as we were alone she might talk to me, be more open. But I'd just sat down at the table with my coffee, Sofia with her tea and toast, when Nancy wandered in, and plonked herself at the table.

I was irritated at the way she just assumed it was okay to join in our conversation. This was her second morning with us, and already she was behaving like she lived in our flat, was part of our family, and I could feel the simmering tension coming from Sofia. I was also thinking about what Oliver had said about me enabling her, that having Nancy stay with us was not only making life difficult for us, but if it went on too long it might prevent her from taking care of herself.

'You okay?' I asked, trying to use my kindest voice to smooth over the prickles I was feeling towards Nancy.

'Just about,' she replied, flopping her arms on the table.

'Coffee?' I asked, getting up.

She nodded.

'You look like shit,' Sofia said, which took my breath away.

'Sofia!' I raised my voice.

'Hey, it's cool, she's right. I *feel* like shit,' Nancy said.

Sofia giggled, it wasn't an affectionate giggle, but a mean one. This was so unlike her.

'I'd like to apologise for my daughter,' I said and gave her a warning look.

'No need to apologise for me, I'm off,' Sofia huffed and, with that, grabbed her stuff and almost ran out of the front door.

'She didn't eat her toast,' I murmured, although, in truth, that was the least of my concerns when it came to my daughter's current behaviour.

'Oh didn't she? I'll eat it.' Nancy snatched up the toast.

'Do you have any plans for today?' I asked, sounding like her mother.

She shrugged and kept on munching the toast.

I appreciated she was suffering, but I doubted being here with us was going to be the answer. I was just as concerned that at this difficult time, I was in danger of causing Sofia to feel neglected, like she was taking second place to my friend, which really wasn't the case. I already regretted inviting Nancy, but felt guilty about that, I was her friend and I should support her, try and help her. She'd been through so many break-ups in the time I'd known her, I wondered again why this one had cut so deep.

'I'm here if you need to talk,' I said.

She looked up from the toast. 'Cheers, mate.'

'Do you feel any better?' I asked.

She shrugged again and pushed the plate away, only the crusts remained.

'I'm worried that being here all day, not talking to anyone and not leaving the house isn't going to help you.'

'Have you had enough of me already?' Her voice was full of pretend hurt, but I felt a simmering anger underneath. She seemed to be under the impression that her care was my responsibility completely, and anything less than total devotion made her resentful. It was a lot of pressure.

'God no, I haven't had enough of you,' I lied. She was my friend, but this was beginning to feel like another responsibility and I knew the longer she stayed, the more I felt the pressure of this.

'I do worry about you being here alone all day though, I doubt it will help you get better; if anything, it may make you feel more cut off.'

'I'm fine, and if I could stay a few days longer, I'd be so grateful.' She looked at me hopefully.

'Okay, of course. That's fine.' It *wasn't* fine, I had backache from sleeping on the sofa, and though I didn't mind a couple more nights, I would like to know when I was getting my room back, but my concerns seemed petty and rather selfish after what Nancy had been through. 'Right, I have to go, we're having a stock delivery today,' I lied for the third time in quick succession. How quickly the lies left my mouth, but Nancy seemed almost relieved her nagging friend was leaving her in peace. And, in truth, I was glad to get out of there too.

As soon as I opened the front door, the bracing sea air hit me, it was always a surprise, and a pleasant one. I walked along the front to work as always, but today, I stopped and looked out at the crashing waves. I'd always wanted to live by the sea, and coming here had been a dream. It was the first place I'd thought of when I'd decided to leave my marriage. So I'd packed as much as I could carry and ran to the nearest train station. Mum had a sister who'd lived in Sidmouth and as children we'd had a couple of holidays here. They were some of the rare times when I was happy as a child. Mum's cancer was in remission, my brother and I played all day on the beach, and Mum and my aunt seemed to always be laughing. It was wonderful for Mum to be so carefree, and I wished we could live there with my aunt for ever. The closeness and caring between the sisters made me feel secure for the first time in my life, and when my baby sister was born a couple of years later, I was delighted. I was ten years older, and wanted to look after her as Mum's big sister had looked after her. But my sister was just two years old when Mum died, and her father was granted custody. I remember him coming to collect her to take her to her new home; my brother had already gone with *his* father. I lost my whole family in a matter of days, but it was losing my baby sister that hurt the most, and I cried so much when she went. It felt like she'd been stolen.

So that night, when my husband wanted me to give up my family again, I couldn't go through that pain, so I ran to the station and boarded the first train for the south-west. It seems like madness, a woman taking a three-year-old halfway across the country, travelling through the night, but I just wanted to escape, and go back to a time I'd been happiest, with Mum and her sister. What I didn't know, was that little Sofia was poorly with chicken pox. It came on so quickly, by the time we arrived in Sidmouth she had a terrible fever. I'd never been so scared in my life. Thank goodness I found the church, and the vicar and his wife. They called the doctor, and within a few hours her fever was down, and within days she was better. But sometimes I wonder if I *had* gone a little mad back then, to take a little one so far away, to escape and start a new life. I was driven, knowing what I had to do and why I had to do it. Such a lot had happened, I had to go, I was alone and couldn't trust anyone, least of all my husband. I was lucky to find good people in

Sidmouth, the vicar and his wife saved Emily, then Mr and Mrs Woods saved both of us. It was hard to find people to trust. The vicar and his wife died years before, and with Mrs Woods gone, the only person I felt I could rely on now was Mr Woods.

I dared to hope that perhaps I'd found someone I could trust in Oliver? He'd lost a child, he understood about being a parent, and if things worked out for us, perhaps he might one day be a father to Sofia. But I was getting ahead of myself, we had only had one date and that wasn't exactly perfect. Thinking about this, I stopped at the coffee shop on the way to work, ordered a flat white to take away and determined to text him back.

I played around with the words, going back and forth. My coffee had been waiting on the counter for a while by the time I worked out what exactly to say. He needed encouragement, but at the same time I didn't want to seem too keen and scare him off, and so I came up with something short and definite, that wouldn't be open to misinterpretation.

I had a great time last night, and I'd love to get together again. Call me.

I sent it and carried on to work, where Mr Woods wasn't himself. He seemed low and not as chatty as usual. Christmas was only a couple of weeks away, and I knew December could be a difficult time for him.

'I'll be in the back if you need me, Emily. I don't feel like customers today,' he said, before closing the door.

'That's okay, it's what I'm here for,' I called back, but he didn't respond, probably didn't hear me.

NINETEEN

Returning home after work, I thought about what Oliver had told me about his son, how no one had listened to him, and I was determined that wasn't going to happen with Sofia. We'd been drifting away from each other and I had to pull things back before they went too far. Nancy was in my room and I wanted to take the opportunity of it just being the two of us to open up the lines of communication with Sofia, so as I cooked dinner, I asked, 'Hey, I wondered if you fancied going to the cinema tonight?'

The look on her face told me what she thought of that idea.

'Okay, so that's a firm no?' I said with a chuckle. 'Not cool to be at the cinema with your mum?'

'Kind of lame to be honest,' she murmured, picking up her phone.

Children were so much easier when they were younger. Only a year before, her sheer delight at a trip to the cinema with Mum would have been overwhelming. So we stayed home, ate dinner together and talked about her day.

'I got an A for that essay on *King Lear*,' she said.

'Oh wow, Sofia, that's brilliant.'

'I love English, I've decided to do that at uni.'

'Great, have they talked to you yet about your A-level options?' I asked. I desperately wanted her to go to uni, but at the back of my mind was always the fear that I couldn't protect her when she was away.

'Yes, I have the list of timetables and you have to choose what you want but also what fits in with the lessons!'

'Oh, let's have a look.'

She was about to get up and head to her room for it, when the door to my bedroom slammed and Nancy came into the kitchen. I felt my heart drop.

'What's that smell?' she asked.

'We just had lentil stew. There's some in the pan if you'd like to warm it through.' I smiled brightly.

'Ugh, no thanks, I might order a pizza.' She plonked herself down on a chair at the table. I saw Sofia recoil.

'Good that you've got your appetite back,' I remarked.

'I guess.' She was now scrolling her phone for pizzas.

I felt torn between staying and listening to her and looking at Sofia's A-level options. But remembering Oliver's regret at not being there for his son, I said: 'Sofia and I are just going to look at some school stuff, so we'll take it in the living room and leave you in peace.'

'I can eat my pizza in there with you. Unless of course you'd rather I didn't?'

Since she'd been staying, I noticed she always seemed to end her demands on this note. She managed to sound reasonable, while making me feel guilty, which forced me to agree to whatever she wanted.

'No, that's fine,' I said.

'I've got homework anyway, so let's do it another night,' Sofia replied, putting our plates in the sink.

'You're a good girl,' Nancy remarked, which sounded vaguely patronising, and Sofia clearly took it that way because she rolled her eyes at me behind Nancy's back. After washing our plates, she almost threw the tea towel on the side and left. Nancy looked at me. 'What's wrong with her?'

'Nothing, I think she's tired, she has her mock exams in February, she's under pressure.'

'Aren't we all?' Nancy groaned.

As much as I wanted to be there for my friend, I knew we couldn't go on like this. The mood in the flat was constantly gloomy and Sofia was becoming more alienated. 'Nancy, I wonder if perhaps being here isn't good for you. Sofia and I are both a bit stressed. I checked her phone the other day and she's still talking to that stranger.' I tried to approach this sensitively, because I had to be careful and considerate given Nancy's psychological vulnerability right now.

'Oh God, Emily, you need to chill out,' she said. 'She's a teenager, she's online, she doesn't have to tell you everything.'

'I'm not saying she *does*,' I replied, frustrated at her dismissive response. 'But Sofia aside, I don't want us to have a detrimental effect on your recovery.' Again, I tried to make this feel like I was considering her too, not just Sofia and I.

'But I *like* being here.' She looked up from her phone.

'Yes, but you can't stay forever, you need to start making plans, you've been here a few days now and—'

'I don't have anywhere else to go, I can't face going back to my place yet.' Her chin started wobbling and tears landed on the table.

'I'm not throwing you out,' I said. 'I just don't think this will work long term, for any of us.'

'It won't be long term, just a few more days, a couple of weeks. God, Emily, how many times do I have to say thank you!'

'You don't,' I said, puzzled, 'that's not what this conversation is about. I don't expect you to be constantly grateful.'

'Oh but you do! You think you're some kind of angel

because you saved me. Well, I wish you hadn't.' She stood up abruptly and walked off into *my* bedroom, slamming the door.

I took a deep breath. I knew she was struggling, but this was tough for all of us and I felt winded by Nancy's reaction.

But before I had a chance to dwell on it, she was standing in the doorway, fully clothed, which was unusual because she'd been wearing my dressing gown all day every day – and night. I rather naively thought she was about to apologise to me, but instead she said, 'I'm going to stay with a friend tonight, can't take any more, I need a break from the drama!'

I was almost speechless, but anger bloomed in my chest. '*You* need a break from the drama? You brought the bloody drama, Nancy!' I snapped.

'If you think trying to kill myself is drama, then you've got a lot to learn.'

'I don't mean that, I just... We didn't have any drama before you came.'

'Rubbish, don't blame me for your troubles, you had enough of them before I moved in. I'm not sticking around to be patronised, nagged at by you and made to feel like shit by your daughter,' she hissed and stormed out of the flat.

It struck me then that I really didn't know Nancy at all, and in the aftermath of that extraordinary encounter, I marvelled at how you could be friends with someone for years and yet not know the real person. I wanted to cry, and the only reason I didn't burst into tears and wallow in self-pity and rage was because the doorbell rang.

I walked up the hall, seeing a shadowy figure standing the other side of the door. 'Who is it?' I asked from behind the door, but they couldn't hear me, the sea was rough and roaring that night. 'What do you want?' I pressed, an unsettling feeling growing in me.

'Slippery Giuseppe?' the voice said, questioningly.

I opened the door to see Nancy's bloody pizza sitting on the doorstep as the delivery guy walked away. I picked it up, carried it through to the kitchen and flung it onto the counter.

'What's going on, Mum?' Sofia was standing in the doorway. 'Has she gone? I heard the door go.'

'She's gone for tonight, but before she went she ordered pizza.'

'Yes!' Sofia ran to the table and we fought over the biggest slice, and sat together munching on large triangles of lukewarm pizza. And despite still stinging from my row with Nancy, it was almost worth it to have this rare moment alone with my daughter.

'This is probably the unhealthiest thing ever to eat pizza after 9 p.m. on a school night,' I said, through a mouthful of pepperoni and stringy cheese.

'Yeah, but it tastes better *because* it's after 9 p.m. on a school night,' she said with a giggle.

I nodded in agreement, my mouth too full to speak.

'And it tastes even better because it's Nancy's.' She gave a cheeky smile, and I chuckled.

'You're very naughty, Sofia.'

'No, *she* is!' she said.

With a little help from me, we finished off Nancy's supper and for a short while it had felt like old times, just Sofia and I against the world.

When Sofia had gone to bed, I made a cup of coffee and put something mind-numbing on the TV. Despite the fact I now had my room back, I didn't want to go to bed yet, I still felt unsettled about the way Nancy had left. It wasn't in my nature to be confrontational, even if Nancy had been fiery. She was recovering from an attempted overdose, and in my anger I'd forgotten that. So I texted her and asked if she was okay, and within seconds, she texted back: 'Sorry, you're right, I bring the drama. See you tomorrow?'

I was glad she was okay, but the 'see you tomorrow,' was an

indication she was coming back, and hadn't returned to her own place yet. I decided to turn in for the night, and worry about all that the next day.

On my way to bed, I knocked softly on Sofia's door, and when there was no answer, I crept into her room. She was fast asleep, and I went to pull the bed covers over her shoulders, kissing her gently, so as not to wake her. Then I leaned to turn off the lamp and saw her phone sitting there. I stopped for a moment, then picked it up and crept from her room. I sometimes ask myself if I did more damage by checking Sofia's phone, and whether I should have just left well alone. By reading her private messages that night, did I set off a runaway train that became impossible to control?

Whatever I think now, it's an easy question in retrospect, but leaving Sofia's room with the phone in my cardigan pocket, I genuinely felt I was doing the right thing. I didn't *want* to look at Sofia's messages, I was filled with trepidation at what I might find. But as a parent, I had to look.

So, I clicked on the lamp in the living room and curled up on the sofa, clutching the phone. I waited a few seconds to listen for any movement, a sign that Sofia might be awake, and when I was satisfied, I fed Sofia's password onto the screen and opened up my own Pandora's box.

I went straight to her private Instagram messages, I scrolled through them more slowly this time to see if perhaps I had over-reacted and it *could* be innocent exchanges between two girls. Reading through, I wasn't surprised my daughter enjoyed talking to Pink Girl, she seemed bright and bubbly, constantly asking questions. To Sofia that probably felt like someone was showing a genuine interest in her. Perhaps they were, or perhaps it was something else?

I then looked at her posts on Facebook. I wasn't online at all. I'd kept a very low profile, but it meant I didn't really understand social media, and I felt that as long as Sofia didn't give personal information to strangers, that she would be safe. But it was far more complicated than that, and it seemed friends of friends might be able to see her posts and photos. This sent me down a rabbit hole of Sofia's friends' lives, their parents' lives, so much information – holidays, careers, marriages, deaths. You could even see what someone's mother had for dinner, or how she felt about the latest Netflix offering. There was so much useless stuff about so many people, it scared me, everyone's lives was laid there on a platter for anyone to see.

Pink Girl already knew Sofia lived in Devon because of previous messages, now she only had to click onto her Facebook to find out *where* in Devon. If Pink Girl was a danger and had made friends with any of Sofia's friends who'd liked her posts, she could see photographs of her in school uniform and identify the school she attended. The photo with Ruby on the beach showed the telltale red cliffs of Sidmouth behind her. Coffee bars, the front door of our flat, were all easily identifiable. My heart jolted – what if Pink Girl was already here?

Going back to the Instagram chats, I could see how the rather limited information Sofia had given was like a jigsaw identification. If you put the Instagram information together with the Facebook material, the pieces all fit together to create a full picture of my daughter's life. Anyone with just a little knowledge would be able to find us if they wanted to.

The Instagram chats reminded me that there was also private messaging on Facebook, so I went back there to the icon on top of the page. I clicked on it, not expecting to see anything, just curious – but there it was, a whole thread of messages beginning from the date Sofia had blocked her on Instagram. So Sofia had blocked her on Instagram, but they were apparently still friends on Facebook – she'd kept remarking that she didn't use Facebook, so never expected me to check here. I felt like crying, but now wasn't the time, I had to brace myself and read through the past few weeks, and find out exactly what was going on. She had no idea of the harm she'd done. By doing this, she'd put us both in danger, and who knew what the outcome of this might be? She was constantly telling me how 'uncool' Facebook was, and I'd been so brainwashed by this and the fact she hadn't posted anything on there for months, it never occurred to me that the communication had continued. I don't know what worried me more, the fact Sofia had lied or the fact that their last chat was merely thirty-four minutes before. And these messages were different. Tears stung my eyes as I started to read them, it was like overhearing a conversation about yourself – it cut so deep.

> *Your mum is so controlling, it's like she doesn't want you to have friends. If she tried to block you from talking to me, I mean, who knows what happened to Zoe. OMG! You don't think your mum killed her do you?*

This was followed by laughing emojis.
'LOL!' was all Sofia said.

I wouldn't put it past her, she hates you being with anyone but her. Controlling much?

I can't do anything. And now her friend Nancy is living with us, and you know what she's like.

Yeah, a bitch. I've seen her Facebook, always with a different guy, always drinking. You're not going to block me on here are you?

> *No, I had to block you on Instagram cos I know that's where she'll look. But she won't look here, she thinks I don't go on Facebook. She doesn't understand any of it anyway.*

Too old.

Sofia hadn't responded to this, but she told Pink Girl all about Ruby seeing Archie and Pink Girl was encouraging her to confront Ruby. 'Tell her she's hurt you, that she's a nasty cow who didn't deserve you and you've got someone else now who's dead fit.'

She was being manipulated to say stuff that wasn't in her vocabulary, let alone her thoughts.

I moved on to more recent exchanges. I held my breath, scared of what I might see.

Mum's working late tonight; I don't want to be stuck in the house with Nancy.

Your mum isn't working late.

Yes she is, there's a thing at the shop where she works.

Nah. She's out with a bloke.

No she's not. She doesn't go out with blokes.

She is tonight, follow her.

No. She has to work late, she told me.

Not true.

Mum wouldn't lie to me.

She would.

I was barely able to get my breath, how did Pink Girl know all this?

I scrolled on, and found messages from just minutes earlier...

Can't believe That's why she wanted you to block me, because I know stuff about her.

Like what?

Stuff. Like why she tries to control you.

'She just worries about me,' Sofia had replied.

She only worries about herself and that pisshead friend she's moved in.

She hides vodka bottles under Mum's bed, then shoves them in the bin when she goes outside for a vape. She lets Mum wait on her but when no one's here she's at the Tesco Express buying vodka.

Drunken cow.

Yeah. I'm going to sleep now.

Just then, I saw the three little dots flashing to tell me that Pink Girl was typing.

You back Sofia? Thought you'd gone to sleep?

She must have seen that Sofia's account was active.

I waited, my heart was in my mouth, did I risk responding? This was too good an opportunity to find out more.

'Yes, I'm here.' I wrote, my fingers shaking as I typed out each letter.

I was breathless, my heart pounding as I typed again.

Who are you?

I waited what seemed like minutes, but was probably only seconds for her response.

I'm Pink Girl of course.

I'm blocking you.

Don't block me. I've got something to tell you.

What?

You remember I told you your mum isn't who you think she is?

Yes.

Do you wanna know who she is?

Again an eternity of waiting, holding my breath, nausea rising in my gullet.

NO!

I clicked on block and sat with the phone in my hands, pushing back the urge to run outside and hurl it into the sea. But that wouldn't erase it, the message was there, and even if I knew how to delete it, Pink Girl would find Sofia again. This wasn't my ex-husband, it was someone even more dangerous than him, and the only way I could keep us safe was to find the person who had haunted my life for so long, and who wanted revenge. I had to find Pink Girl.

TWENTY

The last time I saw Cerys Morton, she'd told me she wished I was dead. I googled her name now, and when nothing came up, I added Manchester and criminal proceedings to the search, but to no avail. Torn between needing to know where she was and what she was up to and being terrified of what I might find, I searched for different permutations of her name. After a lot of searching, her name came up as a match for someone on Facebook, but even if it was her, there was no way of knowing because she'd have privacy settings on. But something was telling me to do it anyway. I clicked onto Facebook, put in the name and held my breath, and there it was, my daughter was friends with the woman who wanted me dead.

When I finally saw her photo, I could have passed her in the street, because at first glance, I didn't see the nineteen-year-old girl I'd once known. She'd be thirty-three now, but looked older, her face was filled out more, with dark shadows under her eyes. She had a cigarette in one hand, a pint of beer in the other, and was standing in a bar. I didn't recognise the surroundings, but it was years since I'd been in Manchester, so it could be somewhere new.

How the hell had Cerys managed to wheedle her way into my daughter's life? I began to shake, my whole body was pumping blood so fast, I felt like I was going to pass out. I had to go to the sink and splash cold water on my face.

Was *Cerys* Pink Girl? Or was she someone doing Cerys's bidding? I picked up the phone again and clicked on Cerys's friends list – and there she was, Pink Girl. No real name, no identity as such, just the one that Cerys seemed to have made for her. Just how much had Sofia told Cerys? But, more worryingly, what had Cerys told Sofia? That message referring to my secret was Cerys playing with her, teasing Sofia, beckoning her in, perhaps even hoping I'd follow? I couldn't work out what to do. Why hadn't Sofia listened to me? I felt like she'd betrayed me, because if Pink Girl was really Cerys, not only had she been talking to this woman for weeks, she'd handed her the weapons to destroy me, and I knew Cerys Morton well enough to know she'd probably been dreaming of this for twelve long years.

I was exhausted, both physically and emotionally, and I couldn't think straight, so I decided to come back to it the following morning. I picked up the phone, turned off the light and quietly slipped into Sofia's. It was dark, but the light from the hallway gave me enough visibility to walk to the side of the bed, and I placed the phone carefully down.

I was about to creep out of the room, when I stopped to hear her breathing. I'd done it all the time when she was little, and sometimes even now, I'd pop my head round her door just to hear her. But after standing there for a few seconds, I heard nothing, and I suddenly felt very uneasy. At the risk of waking her, I turned on the bedside lamp as quietly as I could and turned to see her bed was empty. I assumed she must be in the bathroom, so checked there, but the door was open and there was no sign of her. After everything I'd discovered that evening, my first thought was that Cerys had paid someone to kidnap her, or had even turned up herself and lured her out of the house.

I didn't know what to do, I was desperate. I ran back into her room and checked under the bed, in the wardrobe, lifted the duvet again, like she might be hiding. But she wasn't there. Was I going mad, had I missed something? I willed myself to stay calm and sat on her bed, trying to work out where she might be. She couldn't have passed me in the hall because the kitchen door was open. The front door was heavy and if she'd gone out, I'd have heard her and felt the inevitable blast of freezing cold air straight from the sea as I had when Nancy had stomped off earlier.

The only place I hadn't looked was my own bedroom, so before I called the police, I decided to check. I opened the door. Nancy had left the lamp on and the bed in a mess. And then I saw her, a hunched figure in the corner of the room, sitting in front of my open wardrobe. Around her were some mementoes, a shoebox of birthday cards, a small jewellery box and an old biscuit tin of photos. The lid was off the tin, and the few photographs it had contained were now spread out on the floor.

Sofia was sitting cross-legged, holding a photograph album to her chest, the look on her face was shock and anger.

I couldn't speak, I had no words. I had tried so long to protect Sofia from the past, to keep our little family of two intact, but now it was all coming crashing down. I walked towards her, reaching out my hand, but she pulled away from me. Then she turned around and looking directly at me, her eyes on fire.

'All this stuff, I've *never* seen it before,' she said. 'Wedding pictures of you and Dad, birthday cards for me when I was one! You said you left everything behind the night you left Dad, which is why I had no toys, no photos, *nothing* before I was three. So why is it all here, hidden in the back of your bloody wardrobe?'

'What were you doing snooping in my wardrobe?' I asked, in a feeble attempt to stall for time, gather my thoughts. I couldn't believe this was happening. I'd tried so hard to conceal the past.

'What were you doing snooping in my phone!' she yelled, and I saw the anger, the resentment in her eyes. 'I woke up, my phone was gone and you were sat totally engrossed in my business, so it must be okay for me to push my nose into yours. After all, you're the one with the secrets!'

'I'm not... I didn't mean for this to happen...' I faltered.

'Mum, you made me block someone because they know something about you!' Her voice was raised, she'd been holding on to this resentment and now it was flooding out. 'I'm not bloody stupid, I knew Pink Girl was telling me the truth, and for some reason you didn't want me to know.'

'It's not like that, I wanted to tell you, but—'

I carefully sat down next to her, not knowing what to say, or how to say it.

'I brought that little tin of photos with us because I wanted you to have them one day,' I replied weakly, aware I wasn't really answering her question.

'But why would you keep them from me, why lie and say you don't have any pictures of me as a baby?' She looked down at her past, lying on the floor. 'All the time they're *here*, it doesn't make sense...' She was staring at the photos like they were a jigsaw and if she placed them together, somehow her questions would be answered. And *still* I didn't know what to say. I'd dreaded this moment for years but always imagined it would be up to me when I decided to tell her; I never expected this. I felt trapped, ambushed, with nothing or no one to help me.

'Who's this?' Without looking at me, she pushed a dog-eared photo along the carpet of a baby in a cot, standing, smiling at the photographer through the bars.

'It's you,' I said.

She studied it more closely, then put it to one side before shuffling through the dozen or so pictures on the floor like she was searching for something, suddenly stopping, her head still down. Then she said, 'Where are you and Dad? Who are these people I'm with?' Finally she looked up at me, her eyes narrow.

I should have told her sooner, I should have told her years before, but I didn't. 'Look, I know you didn't totally block Pink Girl, and you're still messaging her.'

'Mum, what are you talking about?' She seemed shaky, unnerved. 'Don't start having a go at me about that. She's got *nothing* to do with this.'

'Just listen to me, and try to stay calm.' I touched her shoulder, but she flinched. I wanted to cry but knew I had to continue on. 'Pink Girl isn't a teenage girl... I think she's your mother.'

Sofia flushed. 'What? I don't get it, you mean *you're* Pink Girl? You've been catfishing me? Mum that's even more messed up than bloody Narnia here.' She threw her hands up at the wardrobe.

Oh God, I was making this worse, if that was possible. I paused and then tried again. 'I'm not your biological mum, darling.'

Her mouth fell open, and she stared into my face like she was searching for clues.

'Pink Girl seems to know that, and apart from the social worker who arranged the adoption and my ex-husband, your real mother is the only other person who knows.'

The colour drained from her face. 'Is this a joke? You're joking me, right?'

I shook my head slowly, tears filling my eyes. I picked up a photo I'd taken of Sofia when she was first born, Cerys holding her in her arms, looking down at her lovingly. What the photo didn't reveal was that, five minutes later, I was bottle-feeding

Sofia while Cerys was having a cigarette outside. 'This is your biological mother; her name is Cerys.' I handed her the photo. 'She was seventeen and struggling. She couldn't keep you.'

'So you and—' She couldn't finish her sentence, she was in shock.

'So Chris and I... we adopted you,' I cut in gently. 'Cerys sent the early photos through the social worker, she wanted you to have them,' I lied. I had to be very careful or I might trip up.

'I'd never even... I can't... I don't know what to say.'

'I'm so sorry, love, I didn't want you to find out this way.'

'Did she *want* to give me up – my mum?'

I sighed, and tried to explain as carefully as I could. 'No, she didn't. But she was young and couldn't cope. She loved you though,' I added. This whole scenario felt surreal, I hadn't planned to have this conversation late one night on the floor of my bedroom, but this was how it was. 'I should have told you, and so many times I nearly did. I should have told you when you were little so it wasn't such a big thing, but there was never a right time. I knew I'd have to tell you one day, but the longer I left it, the more difficult I knew it would be for you to hear and the harder for me to say. It was selfish of me, but if I'm honest, I didn't want to lose you.'

'But how could you live with me every day and just *lie* to me?'

I shook my head, tears fell down my cheeks, horrified and guilty at my daughter's bewilderment and anger.

'I've been an idiot, putting my head in the sand thinking if I loved you enough that it didn't matter, that we could carry on with our lives. My aim was to keep you safe, and have a happy life—'

'A happy life? How could I be happy when I don't know who I *am*?'

'You're still you, you're Sofia...'

'No, no.' She was shaking her head vigorously. 'You don't

get it, I have another *family*, another *identity*.' She was on the verge of tears.

'I don't see it like that—'

'Well I do!' Her eyes were moving in her head like it was so full, there was no room to take any more in.

'Just ask me, ask me what you need to know, we can do this bit by bit. I want you to know what you need to know, anything that will help you come to terms with this.'

'I'll never come to terms with this, my world has just changed, Mum... or not Mum. Whoever you are!' she hissed.

I didn't respond, we were both hurting, but it was the guilt that hurt me most. I'd caused this, the horrible revelation that I wasn't her mother, she wasn't who she thought she was. It was all my fault.

'My real father...?' Her eyes were wide, desperate to know everything and anything.

'He was with your mum for a while; they weren't together by the time you were born.'

'How old was I when you adopted me?'

'You were three, but... I found you when you were two years old, wandering the streets.'

'Oh God.' She put her hand to her mouth in horror.

'Your mum had left the back door open, and you'd wandered out. I happened to be walking down the road and saw you. I couldn't believe it, that someone could let their precious little child—'

'Did *she* know I was out there?'

'No.' I hesitated, this was so hard to say and I didn't want to break her heart. 'It's very sad, your mum... she had issues with drugs.'

'Shit.' She shook her head, more tears emerged, so I leaned over and gave her a hug. This time, to my great relief, she didn't pull away.

'I'm *so, so* sorry, darling,' I whispered into her hair.

She hugged me back, and we clung to each other for some time. I recalled the way I was hit by a tsunami of feelings for this child from the moment she was born.

Eventually, I pulled away. 'I know I was wrong not to tell you any of this, but I just didn't want to burst the bubble. Seeing you there that day, all alone, neglected, it was like a sign,' I said, my mind wandering back to that spring day and Sofia sitting on the pavement in a dirty yellow dress crying. I knew then that it was time. 'I think perhaps Cerys now wants to make contact with you, but she'd have to go to court, so I think she is choosing a different way. I've always worried that she might try to find you.'

'But why would she do that, I was legally adopted, she isn't allowed to, is she?'

'Until you're eighteen, she isn't *legally* allowed. But when you live that kind of life, the law is meaningless.'

'Did you know my mum?'

'Not really.'

'Do you know where she is?'

'No, but you might?'

'How?'

'She's your friend on Facebook.'

'No!' I thought she might faint.

'Cerys Morton,' I said, and she checked her Facebook account on her phone.

'I think Pink Girl *is* Cerys,' I said, spelling it out.

'She *can't* be.'

'I didn't want to say this, but Cerys is... She probably would pretend to be someone else. The social worker dealing with your case said Cerys and her partner had both been in trouble with the police. I don't think she is to be trusted,' I added gently.

'Pink Girl said her dad was dead; that was something we'd bonded over, the fact we didn't have dads.'

Just like Zoe, I thought.

'I understand, but I didn't have a father either, and I turned out okay,' I lied.

'Yeah, I know, but I just wish...'

'I know, love, but Cerys also knew, and she realised your weak spot. I suspect Cerys tailor-made Pink Girl just for you, so she could lure you in.'

'Oh God!' Sofia put her hands to her face in a gesture of self-comfort.

'I knew Cerys couldn't be trusted. There was the option of keeping the lines of communication open,' I said, 'but I was genuinely worried that if she had contact, she might try to take you.'

'So she *wanted* to keep me?' She looked almost hopeful at this, and why wouldn't she? No one wanted to believe they weren't wanted by their mother. I longed to make Sofia feel better by confirming that her mother loved her but couldn't risk painting a warm and caring picture.

'I'm sure she loved you in her way, but she wasn't equipped on any level to care for a child.'

'I'd like to meet her,' Sofia murmured, which just about cracked my heart in two.

'Look, I'm sure you're curious, of course you want to know where you came from, but you can't see her until you're eighteen.'

She shrugged. 'I need time to think anyway, I don't even know who I am anymore.'

'I think you're wise to want some time but know that whatever happens, I love you, and I feel like your mum as much as if I'd given birth to you myself.'

She reached out her hand and held mine. 'You're still my *mum*, aren't you?'

'Of course, and I always will be.'

'I don't want them to come and get me, Mum, I want to stay with you.'

Those words were like music to my ears but I knew Cerys wouldn't give up, she would fight to the bitter end to get her child back. But it wasn't out of love, it was revenge, and if she couldn't physically force Sofia to be with her, then she'd target my relationship with her. In fact, she'd already started.

'Mum, look,' Sofia was saying, she was holding the photo of herself as a baby in her cot. 'Can you see the mobile over my cot?'

I screwed up my eyes to get a better look.

'Do you remember me asking about a toy cow... or a real one? That's it, I remember it now, the cow was on the mobile.'

'Yes, and that mobile wasn't moved, even when you grew too old for a baby mobile, that's why you remember it.' I sighed, thinking about the squalid little room that Cerys laughingly referred to as the nursery.

It had been bittersweet, I'd come clean to my daughter about her parentage, which had weighed heavily on me for years. But now she knew, I felt exposed, like we'd left a door unlocked and someone might come inside.

TWENTY-ONE

The next morning, everything felt different. Sofia was rifling through the kitchen drawer when I got up. 'Where's that plastic, you know the crescent-shaped piece that they left after the break-in?'

'Why?' I asked.

'I've been looking at the photos, and that mobile, over my cot, when I was a baby...'

'Yeah?'

'I think that's where it came from, it's the moon, from "Hey Diddle, Diddle." You know, the cow jumped over—'

'Oh, God, I reckon you're right.'

We both looked at each other.

'Do you think Cerys left it?' she asked.

I nodded slowly, feeling really uneasy. I went to my room and found the piece of plastic in the bag at the back of the wardrobe where I'd stashed it, took it through to the kitchen and handed it to Sofia.

'It *is*!' she said. 'It's the crescent moon from the cot mobile!'

She was strangely delighted at this, like she had found a jigsaw piece she'd been looking for all her life. I hoped, in time, she'd be able to accept that she was adopted. I'd been an idiot not telling her, but I had my reasons. Besides, a part of me felt that if I didn't say it out loud, and she continued to believe I was her birth mother, then why rock the boat? But a couple of times that morning, I caught her taking sidelong glances at me. I wondered how much this knowledge was going to affect our relationship, it was bound to, it was so fundamental to who we were to each other. And more than that, Sofia now had to discover who she was, and I wanted that for her, but at the same time, I didn't want her to delve too deep.

Given the lateness of the previous evening, and the huge emotional conversations we'd had, we were both a little late, and a little tired that morning, so I drove her to school. I dropped her off feeling strangely bereft, and it seemed her feelings still echoed mine, as they often had.

'Would you pick me up later, Mum?' she asked quietly.

'Yes, of course. I'm not going into work today. I'll be here at 3.30, and we can talk some more, eh?'

She nodded, and before she climbed from the car, she gave me a hug. 'Love you,' she said, as she opened the door.

'Love you more,' I called back, watching her walk away. I didn't leave until she was safely in school, I couldn't.

I called Mr Woods to tell him I was poorly. I never took sick days so he was concerned. 'Can I bring you anything, I hate to think of you alone, not able to get to the shops, Emily, and what about Sofia, will she be okay?'

I assured him we'd be fine, that we'd had a bit of an emotional couple of days, but I'd tell him when I saw him.

'Is everything okay, Emily?' he asked, concerned.

'Yes, I think we're going to be okay.'

'You know I'm here, remember my promise to Dorothy,' he replied.

'Yes, and you've kept that promise. I appreciate everything you do for Sofia and I. You've always looked after us.' It was good to have someone batting for me, I hadn't had that kind of support before in my life.

I was just wondering how to spend the next few hours before collecting Sofia, when my phone pinged, it was a text from Oliver.

Just wondered if you were free for lunch today? I'm twiddling my thumbs.

It just so happens, I am too! I'd love to meet, but I phoned in sick and I don't want Mr Woods to see me.

My boss was a lovely kind man, and I'm sure he'd have been happy to know I was seeing someone, but that was for another time. And having lunch within a short distance of the shop when I'd called in sick was, I felt, taking advantage of his good nature.

Okay, we can drive somewhere? he texted right back. He was certainly keen, which was encouraging, and two hours later, I was climbing into his car.

'Are you okay?' he asked.

'Not really.' I held it together this time. I didn't want me bursting into tears every time I got in his car to be a regular fixture.

He pulled away and kept glancing over at me, concerned as we headed off up the coast.

'Sorry, I'm not always like this, it's been a difficult few weeks.'

'You don't have to explain yourself to me,' he replied, his eyes on the road.

I glanced over at him, he was wearing driving glasses, he probably had his car serviced regularly, had money in the bank for a rainy day and left nothing to chance. He drove slowly, carefully, he didn't jump lights or take risks, and suddenly I realised that this was what Sofia and I needed in our lives, someone we could rely on, who'd look after us.

I'd always had this feeling that Mum sent Mr and Mrs Woods to me when I needed them, and now I wondered if she'd sent Oliver now, when I needed *him*. I don't believe in angels or magic, but when you lose your mother young, you have to cling to some hope, and I always have. I'd been waiting for Prince Charming all my life; I'd always been the carer in a relationship, I seemed to attract people who needed to be cared for. From my mother, to my siblings, to my husband, I was always the person who nurtured, mediated, smoothed over any problems. But Oliver was different, he'd also known loss, we were both broken, and I dared to hope we could heal together.

Once inside the café, we sat down at a quiet table in the corner and ordered sandwiches and coffee.

'I'm so glad you asked me for lunch, I could do with a friend today,' I said.

'Oh?' He put the plastic menus back in their stand.

I decided to tell him. I'd kept it a secret from Sofia, but now she knew, I was free to tell those close to us. So I explained about how Sofia was adopted, and that I'd just told her.

'Oh wow,' he said. 'How did she take it?'

His lack of judgement and his concern for Sofia made me like him even more.

'She was upset obviously, but she took it all on board with her usual maturity and grace.'

'She sounds like a good girl, you must be proud.'

'I am, but I know this is just the beginning, and by teatime she could be feeling angry and hurt; it's such a huge thing.'

'It is, especially at her age; she's old enough to understand, but a little young to deal with the emotions involved.'

'Absolutely,' I replied. 'It's clear you understand children.' I could only imagine what a wonderful father he must be. 'And thanks for not asking "why on earth didn't you tell her years ago?"'

'I'm sure you have good reasons, I wouldn't judge anyone when it comes to raising kids.'

'No, I don't think you would,' I said, looking up at him and we both smiled warmly at each other. In spite of everything, I had this wonderful feeling of hope blossoming inside me. 'I knew the day would come when I had to tell her, but I was forced into it.'

'*Forced?*'

'Oh, she discovered some photos in my wardrobe, and someone online seemed to know about it.'

'What?'

I took a breath. 'Sofia thought she had a new best friend – but all the time, whoever it was just wanted information about her. I think it might be someone I knew way back, who was aware Sofia's adopted.'

'That's concerning. It's your business. Who on earth would get involved like that?'

'I think it's her biological mother,' I said, then corrected myself, 'I *know* it is. I think the woman is trying to get revenge on me.'

'What on earth for?'

'The adoption was fast-tracked, I knew the social worker, and Cerys Morton – that's the biological mother's name – was deemed unfit. She was furious about it at the time, said I'd framed her, that I'd lied about her. She pushed notes through my door, threatening to kidnap Sofia and kill me, the woman mixed with some bad people. I was terrified just taking Sofia to the park, and recently I've felt the same, like she might come back for her... I wonder if it was Cerys Morton or one of her friends who broke into our flat a few months ago.'

'You've really been through hell, haven't you? Did you go to the police back then?'

I shrugged. 'No, I didn't want to make more trouble. Besides, I had problems at home too. My husband, who'd agreed to the adoption suddenly changed his mind and said I should have Sofia taken into care because he didn't want the responsibility.' I sighed, remembering how awful it was. 'It felt like there was no way out, and I moved here. I thought, rather naively, that Cerys might have moved on by now, and accepted that even if she didn't want the adoption, it was the right thing for Sofia. But it looks like she's been waiting all these years to find me, and now she has...' I couldn't finish the sentence, it was too horrific to contemplate.

'This woman sounds *dangerous*. I really think you should go to the police and tell them everything, Emily.'

That was the last thing I wanted, it would raise her like a phoenix from the ashes. The accusations, the death threats would all start again and this time it wouldn't be her word against mine. Chris, my ex, had been prepared to join forces with her, and after I walked out on him I was sure he'd be happy to back her up. He could have said so much, and as a teacher he'd have more credence than her, they could destroy me and she could take Sofia. God knows what would happen to me.

'I will go to the police if I feel there's a real threat to Sofia,' I said vaguely. 'But now she's finally blocked her, I'm hoping that's the last we've heard of her.'

He shrugged. 'I hope you're right. But if she's holding on to some grudge, who knows what she might do? I'd go to the police and tell them everything. Would you like me to come with you, we could go now? Obviously, given my background, I could help explain?'

'That's so kind of you, but for now I'll just let sleeping dogs lie. No point in winding her up and setting her off again.' I rolled my eyes.

'But you're vulnerable, you have to think of your daughter, and the police would keep an eye out for you. I mean, even if it's just to log your concerns, I can't stress enough how important it is that you report this person to the police.'

I understood his reaction, and he was obviously concerned about us, but no way was I opening that hornets' nest. 'I just need to wait. I want it to go away, and if Sofia doesn't speak to her any more, it might.'

He raised his eyebrows like an anxious father. 'Well, it's your call,' he said.

At this point, the waitress brought our sandwiches, giving me a chance to change the subject.

'How are things with you?' I asked, cutting my chicken sandwich in half.

'Very boring compared to your bombshells. I've been looking at places in the area, thinking of making the move.'

'Oh that's great news,' I said, delighted.

'Nothing concrete, just a few viewings in and around Sidmouth.' He took a sip of his coffee. 'How's your friend by the way?'

'Oh Nancy? She's the same, still very down. She stormed off last night. And apparently she's drinking vodka and hiding it under my bed.'

'Your bed?' he asked, puzzled, before taking a bite of his cheese sandwich.

'I'm on the couch while she recovers,' I explained.

'None of my business,' he stirred his coffee, 'but I think you're probably too kind for your own good.'

'Perhaps I am.'

'If it were me, I would ask her to leave. She seems somewhat problematic, your daughter's unhappy, and right now she needs some stability in her life. But what do I know?'

'I can tell you were a lawyer, you sum up very well,' I said, smiling at him.

He smiled back. 'It never leaves you. M'lord.'

'I appreciate you taking an interest, I like that you care.'

'My wife used to say I was bossy,' he said with a smile.

I took a long breath. 'Not at all, just good with advice. And I agree with everything you say about Nancy, but she's with me because she tried to kill herself, and I'm worried if I ask her to leave, she might do something stupid.'

He looked genuinely shocked. 'Oh I had no idea, forgive me for—'

'No, you weren't to know, I probably shouldn't have said anything.'

'That's so sad. Obviously I feel for anyone who's going through that. Do you know *why* she did it?' He pushed his half-finished sandwich away.

'She won't really talk about it. I *think* it was some man.'

'Ah.' He sipped on his coffee. 'Well, however bad things are for her, I hope she comes through.'

'Yes, me too.'

'But, and I'm going to sound bossy again, she isn't your responsibility. You have enough to cope with; don't let others add to your problems.'

'I know my life seems pretty complicated, but I promise you that most of the time I live a simple life, just looking after my daughter.' I looked at my watch. 'Which reminds me, I said I'd pick Sofia up from school today, and given everything...'

'Of course, of course.' He stood up, and held my coat out for me. I know some women, my daughter included, wouldn't approve of this. But I'm old-fashioned, and so was he, and as I slipped into my coat, I felt cared for, cherished in a way I never had before.

We walked from the café and into the little car park, I was tempted to grab his hand, but before I could, he'd taken his keys out of his pocket and was holding them. We got to the car, and I climbed in, feeling safe and secure, the sandalwood and leather interior like a warm, scented bath. He went to put his keys in the ignition, and I reached out and touched his arm.

'Thank you for listening,' I said. 'I hope you know I'm not always like this, I'm a happy person really.'

'I can see that.' He gave me the warmest, loveliest smile and put his hand on mine, which I saw as a sign that something was about to happen. So I leaned across, and went to put my mouth to his lips, waiting for him to meet them, but to my horror he moved his face, and I ended up kissing him on the cheek. I was mortified, but pretended that's exactly what I'd meant to do, by saying, 'Thanks for listening.'

All the way back to Sidmouth, we said very little. He drove back as he'd driven there, safely, within the speed limit, but what I'd seen as reliable and safe on the outward journey seemed almost too careful now. I doubted he ever took any risks, or did anything spontaneous, and wondered if perhaps his risk-averse personality extended to kissing women he dated? Then again, I might have just been pissed off because he hadn't kissed me back when I'd tried to kiss him. I couldn't work it out, I just wanted to get out of the car and lick my wounds. But the journey seemed to take *forever*, and I kept going over and over in my head my clumsy attempt at kissing him. Just thinking about it brought the blood to my face. I understood he was shy, and probably hadn't been with anyone since his wife had died, but I was in a similar position and wasn't exactly a stranger. How many 'dates' did we need to go on before things moved forward? We'd talked a lot, shared life stories, been out on an evening date and now one more, some women might expect sex on a third date, so a kiss wasn't exactly rampant. I told myself not to be embarrassed; he was the one who'd done all the running, he was the one who'd asked me out. Perhaps I'd misread this whole situation, and he wasn't interested in anything but friendship? But I didn't want another friend. I wanted more.

TWENTY-TWO

Oliver pulled up outside the hotel on the front and, clicking his engine off, turned to me as if he wanted to talk. But we'd arrived back in Sidmouth later than I'd expected and I had to get off and collect Sofia, so I explained my hurry and opened the door to get out of the car. I didn't want to be late for her on that day; I needed to be *there* for her in every sense. I was also keen to put some distance between me and Oliver after the failed kiss, and reluctant to prolong my embarrassment.

'I love spending time with you,' he started, but I was worried about meeting Sofia on time and didn't want to have this conversation now. I also felt like this was his way of apologising for not responding to my kiss, but the moment had passed, I was embarrassed, and late for my daughter. 'Let's get together soon?' he called after me as I shut the passenger door and waved.

Without looking back, I began marching along the seafront to my car, which was parked outside our flat. But when I got into the car, the damned thing wouldn't start! It was a very old banger, and because of the rain and cold, it must have been damp, so after trying several more times, I texted Sofia explaining about the car. And in an attempt to make it up to her, said, 'Hey, why don't we both start walking and meet at Mocha's,' her favourite coffee shop. I would worry about the car another day; today I had to be with Sofia.

I arrived at Mocha's ten minutes later, soaked through and freezing cold. I ordered her hot chocolate and my coffee, aware I was spending money like I didn't have a care in the world, and took a seat by the window to wait for her. When after fifteen minutes, she hadn't arrived, I called her, but there was no answer. I texted her, 'Where are you? Your hot chocolate is getting cold!' Still no answer.

Almost an hour after I had first texted her, she hadn't responded and there was no sign of her. I didn't know what to do, I was feeling really anxious. I'd watched all the kids in her school uniform pass the window, the last stragglers were now wandering past. Perhaps she'd been kept late and wasn't allowed to use her phone?

I waited and waited. I called Nancy and for once I was pleased she was at the flat, she'd obviously let herself in with the spare key I'd given her.

'Is Sofia there?' I asked. 'I'm supposed to be meeting her at Mocha's, but she hasn't arrived.' I was shaking now, tapping my fingers on the table, anxiety levels through the roof.

'No, she's not here.'

'Is she in her room?'

'I don't know.'

'Would you please check?' I snapped. She sounded to me like she'd emptied another bottle that afternoon, how had I not realised this?

She took her phone with her, and I could hear knocking on the door, Nancy calling her name.

'She's not coming to the door.'

'Open it, push it if you have to!' I almost yelled down the phone.

But Sofia wasn't home, nor was she at Ruby's when I called her mum, and she wasn't at Archie's either. When, at 7 p.m., the waitress told me I had to leave because they were closing, I called the police, who said they'd send someone to the flat, so I grabbed my coat and ran all the way.

I walked in and Nancy was in the kitchen. She put her arms out to hug me, and I hugged her back, but it was awkward.

'Has she turned up yet?' she asked.

'No. The police are on their way.'

'You must be out of your mind with worry.' She picked up the kettle and filled it with water. 'Do you think she might have... run away?'

'No, I *don't*,' I frowned, sitting down at the kitchen table, resting my head in my hands.

Nancy made some coffee, put a steaming mug in front of me, and sat opposite. 'Have you called her friends?'

This irritated me. 'Of *course* I have.'

'Okay, okay, I just—'

'Look, I wasn't going to tell you yet, I wanted Sofia to accept it first, but I told her last night that she's adopted.'

'What? I had no idea.'

'I never told anyone.'

'Wow, Em! What the hell? How did she take it? I mean, to spring something like that on her, wow!' She'd obviously had a drink, but I wished she'd stop saying wow. Given what I was going through, I found it annoying listening to her talk in small sentences strung together, like her mind could only come up with three or four words at a time. I was relieved to hear the doorbell ring so I could escape her, and I answered it to two police officers, one male, one female.

They came in, sat down, took some details and were both very sensitive and sympathetic, both concerned, until I said:

'I told her last night that she was adopted.' I knew how it

sounded: she'd had this monumental news, and I could see why it looked like she'd run away. But I didn't believe that.

'Was she upset when you told her?' the female officer asked.

'Of course, it wasn't easy for her, but she seemed to take it as well as she could. She was shocked, but—'

'Perhaps she had time to think about it, after you'd taken her to school, and she got upset then?' Nancy suggested. She'd been sitting at the kitchen table when I invited the police in, and I'd hoped she would perhaps discreetly disappear. But not only was she staying, she clearly planned to take part in the discussion, which was really none of her business.

'She might have,' I murmured.

'She might have been so upset she decided to just leave school and not wait for you?' Nancy added.

I really didn't appreciate her saying this, the implication being that Sofia had gone off of her own accord. I didn't want the police to think for a minute that she'd run away because it might make their search less urgent.

'Sofia *hasn't* run away,' I said firmly.

'But this news was a shock to her, and if she was upset...' the officer picked up where Nancy had left off.

'Of course it was a shock, but we have a good relationship, we talk, I explained everything. Look, I don't want to be rude, but I *know* what you're all thinking, and you're wrong! When I dropped her off at school she was fine – perhaps feeling a bit wobbly understandably, but better than I'd hoped.'

'But you told me on the phone, you were supposed to pick her up and you didn't,' Nancy said, and both officers turned to look at me. What the hell was Nancy playing at?

Of course, the officer immediately jumped on this. 'So you said you'd be there and you weren't? Given what you had told her, do you think that might have upset her and she decided to go somewhere, hide somewhere to make you realise—'

'No! Well, of course there's a possibility,' I muttered, feeling attacked. I was a good mother, but they were making me question myself and my actions – but mostly my assumptions. I'd assumed Sofia had taken the news well, but was she simply covering up her real emotions?

'Could she have just wandered off when you didn't turn up?' the female officer asked.

'No, and even if she did it wouldn't explain where the hell she is now,' I snapped, and standing up, I started pacing. I was angry that they were asking me endless questions but not *doing* anything. 'I'm sorry, I'm just anxious,' I murmured.

'That's perfectly understandable, and it's not easy, but if we can just go over the order of what happened,' the female officer said. 'So, you texted her...?'

'Yes, I explained I was held up so I wouldn't be able to meet her at school and suggested we meet at Mocha's.'

'And she replied?' the female officer asked.

'No, she didn't. She hasn't responded to any of my calls and texts. It's like she has just disappeared.' I started to cry. I felt helpless, like whatever I said, no one believed that Sofia had just gone. In fact, the more I told them, the more they seemed convinced that she'd run away because of what I'd told her. I was running out of options, but there was one thing I knew would get their attention. 'There is something else,' I said, and told them about the messages from Pink Girl.

'Do you believe this person isn't a young girl?' the male officer asked.

'I think it's someone who knows us, knows me. I think it's someone from my past, Sofia's birth mother.'

'Oh, I see,' he said, and I almost detected the catch of excitement in his voice.

'It might not be,' I added. On the off chance that it wasn't her, I didn't want her being contacted by the police which would just serve to remind her of her hatred for me and raise the devil again. But, of course, the police were keen to know more, they wanted names and addresses, and I didn't have them. 'I know the mother is called Cerys,' I said. 'I think her surname was Morton. I have no idea of the father's name. I don't know anything about him.'

'Okay, okay, and they are in Manchester?'

'As far as I know.' But now they could be anywhere, even here. It was what I had dreaded for so long.

'Do you have a recent photograph of your daughter?'

'Probably on my phone.' I wasn't sure when I'd last taken her picture.

'Or her Instagram,' Nancy suggested, which was probably the first helpful thing she'd said. 'There'll be one there, probably *full* of selfies,' she added and smiled, like she was hosting a bloody tea party, not trying to find my missing daughter.

The police asked me a million questions and I tried to answer them, but Nancy kept butting in. She really wasn't the friend I needed right now, I just wished she'd go to my room and keep quiet, especially when the female police officer asked me why I was held up.

'I'm sorry?' I said, pretending not to hear, stalling for time.

'You were late meeting your daughter from school. You said you were held up?' She was sitting, pen poised over her notebook, waiting for my reply.

I'd never been asked questions by a police officer before, and I worried I might be coming over as non co-operative, or odd even. But I didn't really want to share my afternoon's activities in front of Nancy. 'I went for a coffee, and then the car wouldn't start so I couldn't collect Sofia.' I knew as soon as I said it that they would want me to detail my afternoon. I was beginning to feel like they thought I was hiding something significant, so I just came clean. 'A friend met with me, we went for a drive along the coast, we had coffee,' I said. From the corner of my eye, I saw Nancy turn to look at me, the police noticed it too. 'We were a little late back, then my car wouldn't start.'

'And your friend, would you mind giving us her name?'

'I don't mind at all, but it just isn't relevant to Sofia going missing,' I stressed, but their expectant silence told me different.

'His name's Oliver, Oliver Foster,' I said firmly and clearly.

I heard an audible breath from Nancy at the side of me, no doubt angry because I hadn't shared this with her. The officers couldn't have missed it, but fortunately they didn't press me.

'Do you have an address for Mr Foster?'

'No, I don't. He's planning to buy somewhere around here, but I don't... I don't know him that well.' I'd been reluctant to even *mention* Oliver, I didn't want them to think he was more than just a friend and drag him in on this. 'Look, I just need you to concentrate on finding Sofia,' I pleaded.

They tried to reassure me and said they would head back to the station and a search would soon be underway. *Soon?* Why couldn't they set it in motion now?

They got up to leave and I was grateful that they might finally start looking for her.

'As far as you know, does Sofia have her phone with her?' the male officer asked, and I nodded.

'She always has it with her,' I said, walking them to the door. As I opened it, a blast of cold hit me. It was pitch black outside and I shuddered at the thought of Sofia out there somewhere alone – or not. 'I don't blame you for thinking Sofia might have run away,' I said, shivering on the doorstep, 'but honestly she wouldn't. I just can't imagine where she could be, there's nowhere open out of season at this time in the evening, and she's too young to be in a pub – not that she would,' I added quickly before they got any ideas. 'So, wherever she is, she's out there in the cold and the dark, and she's only fifteen and I'm scared, please find her.'

I closed the door, rising panic surging through me. Where was she? Was she in danger? Was somebody hurting her? Did it have something to do with our conversation last night? Had I deluded myself that she'd accepted the news so readily?

I went back into the flat, exhausted, tearful and extremely anxious. Nancy made me another coffee and as we sat silently at the kitchen table, I nursed my mug, racking my brains, but it was getting me nowhere and I was desperate to do something.

'I have to go out there and look for her,' I said.

'But what if she comes back and you're not here?'

'You call me and let me know.'

'It won't do any good.' She sipped from her mug, as if we were just two friends enjoying a coffee and chat.

'Is sitting here doing any good? I can't stand it, I just keep going over and over everything in my head.'

'You never told me about Sofia being adopted,' she suddenly said. 'Why didn't you tell me?'

I was surprised at this, even from Nancy it was rich – how could she turn Sofia missing into an event where she was the victim?

'I don't tell people everything, even my friends,' I said, checking Sofia's Instagram on my phone. Nothing, she hadn't posted anything, she wasn't online or active. Where had she gone? I couldn't wait any longer. I got up and grabbed my coat. 'Call me if she turns up, or if the police come back,' I said to Nancy, heading to the front door. I couldn't sit there and do nothing, but walking along the seafront, I wondered if Nancy had been right. Should I have stayed at home?

I didn't know what to do, where to go, and slowed down to look out at the blackened sea, foaming and roaring. My heart hurt at the thought that Sofia may have had some kind of accident, a car, someone chasing her – and as always there was the sea, waiting like a hungry giant. Only a couple of weeks before, a man had drowned saving his dog. It was treacherous in weather like this. One gust of wind, one misplaced step, one push and you could topple in and at this time of year the water would be dangerously cold.

I turned away and marched over to the other side of the road, unable to bear the thought of her caught up in those huge waves, being pulled under, struggling to get out. I kept walking, the volume on my phone was on high in case she called, but still as I walked along, I kept checking. The wind was becoming stronger, the rain harder, but I felt nothing because the pain of losing my child was more than any physical pain or discomfort.

I walked into the town, down the little back alleys, up through the high street, then left past Mr Woods' perfume shop. The light was on; he must have been working late. I checked my watch – it was almost 10 p.m. Sofia had been missing for more than six hours. At the top of the street was the church where we came that first night. I looked at it and wondered if I should pray. I'm not religious, but at times like that you'd do anything.

I wandered the grounds; it was dark and cold and creepy, but again, my fear for Sofia was more than any childhood fear around churches and graveyards. But I didn't find any solace there amongst the shadows and gravestones.

I decided to walk back, passing the perfume shop again, just as Mr Woods was leaving. I crossed over the road to catch him.

'Emily,' he said with a smile. 'What are you doing out this late, I thought you were poorly?'

'Oh, I am. I was... I'm feeling better now,' I faltered, having completely forgotten my earlier lie.

'Good.' He started locking the door.

'I'm looking for Sofia, she hasn't come home.'

He knew her like I did, and showed genuine sympathy, and concern.

'Oh? Oh dear, and you don't know where she is?'

I shook my head.

The look of concern on his face made me want to cry on his shoulder.

'Come on, let's walk together and take a proper look, see if we can see her,' he said kindly. As we walked, he asked me if I had any idea where she might be, and I told him everything, all about the adoption and how I'd thought she'd coped well with the news, but now I was worried.

'Emily, I had no idea.' He seemed disorientated, and stood for a moment in a shop doorway, leaning against the door like he might collapse.

'I'm sorry...'

'It's just such a shock.'

'I know, and I should have told you sooner, I should have told *Sofia* sooner, but I didn't and I've made it so much worse.

'You think she may have been upset and run away after all?' he asked.

'I don't know.' I started to cry, and he was sensitive enough not to ask me any more, and composing himself, stumbled slightly as he moved from the doorway.

'Come on, dear, let's keep walking, we won't find her if we don't look – try not to worry, let's be positive.'

I nodded uncertainly. 'Thank you,' I said, gratefully, reassured by his words. 'So... shall we go down here?' I suggested, pointing to a small alleyway. I felt so much more brave with Mr Woods.

He led the way, checking doorways, peering over fences.

'Good job I'm on foot today,' he said.

'I'm so worried I feel sick,' I admitted.

'I'm sure she'll be fine, try not to think too much. Your mind will take you to all kinds of places if you let it.'

He was right, but it was hard not to imagine the worst.

We trawled the whole town. It was only small, but still we investigated every nook and cranny. Some of the shops were closed for the winter, so many buildings were locked up. All I kept thinking was, *What if someone connected with Cerys has kidnapped her and she's inside?* No one would know.

We continued to walk together through the streets, but there was no sign of Sofia and it was clear this was nothing but a wild goose chase. It was tortuous, and I realised that I wasn't achieving anything, and my inner compass was leading me home.

'I think I'd better go back, see if there's any news,' I said, defeated.

'I'll walk with you.' Mr Woods lived about half a mile from me, further down the coast.

'That's kind, but I don't want you to go out of your way.' Mr Woods would be seventy-six soon and had bad knees, I didn't expect him to walk further at the end of a busy day, in the cold and dark.

He was insisting that he walk with me when my phone rang. It was Nancy. I picked up straight away to hear her voice.

'Emily, she's here, Sofia's home.'

TWENTY-THREE

By the time I reached the flat, I was breathless, and my legs were shaking, not just from the running but the very real fear. I'd never known a feeling quite like it.

I banged on the front door, almost falling in when Nancy finally answered it, and pushed past her into the kitchen. But Sofia wasn't there. I ran through into the living room, but she wasn't there either, and returning to the kitchen, I had a horrible feeling I'd imagined the call.

'Where is she?'

'In her room.' Nancy stood there clutching her mug.

'Is she okay?' I said, heading for Sofia's room without waiting for an answer. I didn't even knock on the door, I just walked in. 'Sofia, where have you been?'

She was sitting on her bed with her laptop, and slammed it shut the moment I went in.

'I called the police, they're looking for you. I've been walking the streets,' I cried, moving towards her with my arms out. I was so relieved. I bent down to hug her and heard myself sobbing. I had both my arms around her, my face in her neck, rocking her backwards and forwards. 'I was so worried.' I pulled away, vaguely aware she hadn't reciprocated my hug. 'Darling, what happened? You didn't meet me.'

'You didn't turn up at school.'

My heart sank, I felt like such a bad mother. 'I'm sorry about that, the car wouldn't start. But I texted, then called and left a message, and you didn't respond, I've been out of my mind. I thought you'd been kidnapped or assaulted or...' I could feel my chin wobbling, I was about to start crying again.

I waited for her to say something, but she just stared ahead.

'What is it? Has someone hurt you?'

'No, stop making a fuss.'

This felt like a slap in the face. 'I thought something had happened to you. It's after 10 p.m., you always phone and let me know if you're doing something and going to be late. I called Ruby's mum and Archie's—'

'Oh my God. How embarrassing.'

I was riled by her reaction; why couldn't she understand how worrying it had been for me and why was she acting so thoughtless now? 'I'm sorry if I've embarrassed you, but if you'd let me know you were okay, I wouldn't have needed to call anyone. Where the hell have you been, Sofia?'

She breathed out loudly, I saw the eye roll. She was making out this was all so tiresome she could barely be bothered to answer. 'I was with a friend.'

My heart plummeted, had she met with Cerys? 'Who?'

'You don't know them.' She shrugged.

'Is it something to do with Cerys Morton?' I pressed.

She sighed. 'It's just a friend, you don't need to know. After all, I don't know all your friends.' She looked at me fiercely then.

I sat down on the end of the bed. 'Sofia, I don't understand what you're saying. Talk to me.'

'I don't feel like talking, I'm tired.' She was shutting me out, pushing me away.

Was *this* why I hadn't told her she was adopted? I knew in

my heart that if I wasn't her mother, she wouldn't respect me, love me even? But we'd always been so close, surely it didn't have to be this way.

'Is this about being adopted? I know it was a shock, and I may not have handled it in the best way, but is there a right time to tell someone? Perhaps I should have told you when you were younger, but I didn't and maybe I was wrong not to.'

'Yes, you were wrong. And you were wrong because you lied to me for years, and you're still wrong because you lied to me about being at work the other night when you were out with some bloke. And you were wrong for not coming to meet me today when I needed you, because you were out with him *again*!'

This felt like yet another slap in the face, only much harder than last time. I wasn't even sure how she knew this – had Nancy told her? Was she getting her own back for me going out with Oliver when she had been interested him. I pushed the thought away; it didn't matter now.

'I'm sorry,' I said. 'I should have told you I was with a friend.'

'A *friend*?' she scoffed. 'I'm not five years old, you're seeing some guy, and you never told me, and then you lied about the car not starting when all the time you were with him. You'd obviously rather be with him than me.'

'Sofia, no – no, that's not true! And when I say he's a friend, that's all he is, that's why I never mentioned it to you, because he isn't anything more. And the car *didn't* start!' I insisted.

She turned away. 'I just don't want to talk anymore.'

'I do,' I said. 'I want to know where you were tonight?'

'I told you I was with a friend.' She practically spat the words out. 'I've got a practice paper for my English mocks tomorrow and I don't want to fail because of you. At least if I get decent exam results, I can go to a uni far away from here and get away from *you*!'

I gasped. I wanted to say something, reassure her, find a way to reconnect, but she turned out her lamp before I had a chance. In the sudden dark silence, I could see from the sliver of moonlight through her curtains that she'd pulled her covers over her head. She couldn't make it any clearer, but I couldn't leave like this.

'I just want you to know that whatever you think, and however you feel, I love you, and I know I got it wrong.' I waited in the dark for her to answer, and when she didn't, I repeated, 'I love you, Sofia, and whatever happens, I always will.'

I stood for a little while as my eyes got used to the darkness, but she stayed covered up and still. I watched her, and returned to that place that was embedded in my mind, the filthy room, the dank, musty smell of neglect. I trembled inwardly remembering the baby wrapped in filthy blankets, abandoned, unloved and destined for the same kind of life as her mother.

I pushed the vision away, left Sofia's room and walked into the kitchen and sat down. My relief at her being home felt like a distant memory already. God, I felt so wretched. I'd made such a hash of everything, and where was I now? I'd given up my marriage, my career and I was living in a small town, with a small job and a child who hated me, and that was the worst thing of all. If Sofia and I were okay, I could live with anything else.

I heard Nancy shuffling around in my room, reminding me I didn't even have a bed at the moment. I picked up mine and Nancy's mugs from the table – as usual, she hadn't bothered to wash them, even if hers only had water in. I took them to the sink, but before I poured Nancy's away, I had a little taste. It was vodka.

'Hey, I heard you guys.' Nancy came up behind me.

'Heard us?'

'Arguing. She came in like nothing had happened. I told her you were worried, but she just swept past me into her room.'

'I let her down.'

'I didn't know you were seeing *Oliver*,' she said, her concern for Sofia short-lived.

'I'm not *seeing* him,' I answered. I'd no idea what I was doing with Oliver, and at that point I didn't even care, I was too upset about Sofia.

I watched Nancy wander over to the sink and pick up her now empty mug. I noticed her shoulders tense. She was obviously pissed off that I'd just emptied half a pint of vodka down the sink, but she couldn't complain because she thought she'd fooled me and that I had no idea she was drinking alcohol from a mug. Quite honestly, I hadn't noticed until Sofia had told me, but did she really think she would get away with it? And did she even care that she was deceiving me?

Oliver was right, it really wasn't wise to have someone like Nancy around Sofia, especially now with everything being so chaotic. Come to think of it, all the problems seemed to have started since Nancy came to live with us. What had once been a happy home with two of us was a mess with three of us. Nancy's question about Oliver came back to me then.

'Did you tell Sofia I was *seeing* Oliver?'

She spun round. 'No!' She frowned. 'I didn't know, but even if I did, why would I?'

'I don't know,' I murmured, as she washed her mug thoroughly, so there were no traces of alcohol left. Then she padded off to my room, leaving me to call the police to let them know Sofia was home.

I made a cup of herbal tea and headed into the living room. There was nothing I'd have loved more that night than to crawl into my own bed and sleep. Instead, I was half on and half off a cheap couch that was never meant for sleeping. My clothes were half in the living room and half in the bedroom and the whole situation was getting to me. I lay on the hard couch looking up at the ceiling, going over and over the terrible day. I knew the adoption news was a huge deal, and there would inevitably be a slightly bumpy road ahead, but I had made it worse by being late for Sofia and not telling her about Oliver. I should have told her, I should have told her she was adopted, I should have told her about Oliver, instead of allowing Cerys to come back into our lives and opening this can of worms.

I heard footsteps in the hall then and I jumped.

'Hello?' I called quietly.

Nancy was suddenly in the room.

'What are you doing?' I asked.

'Just getting some water, babe,' she replied and walked towards the sink.

I lay there watching her through the open door of the living room, which led straight into the kitchen. The moonlight from the window lit her face as she took a mug from the cupboard, turned on the tap and without putting the mug under, turned it off again. Then she popped her head into the living room.

'Night, night,' she whispered and lifted the empty mug.

'Goodnight,' I said, as she left the room. Not only was Nancy a drinker, she was a liar too. This whole situation was toxic and here I was stuck right in the middle.

TWENTY-FOUR

The following morning, I went in to wake Sofia with a cup of tea.

'How are you feeling?' I asked.

'I'm fine.' She sat up and took the tea from my hand.

'I know it will take more than a cup of tea for you to accept everything and to forgive me, but it's a start.'

She looked down into her mug. 'It isn't just that. I feel like there's obviously other stuff you've not told me.'

'You're right,' I said, 'and from now on I'm going to be honest with you. But will you be honest with me too?'

She nodded.

'So I'll tell you about Oliver, the friend I've been meeting, if you tell me who told you about him.'

She shifted uncomfortably in her bed. 'It was Pink Girl.'

My stomach flipped at this. 'How on earth did she know? And I thought you'd blocked her?' I didn't want to break her trust so soon by acknowledging that I knew, because I'd discovered this when I'd accessed her phone.

'I did.'

'So, how did she talk to you?'

She looked really uncomfortable now. 'I'm not telling you because you'll freak out.'

'Tell me, I won't.' But inside I was panicking.

She looked up at me with those same eyes that looked up at me when she was five and she'd eaten all the icing off the cake I'd baked for her friend's birthday. Guilt all over her face. 'She called me on my phone yesterday.'

'You gave her your *number*?' I was horrified but tried to control my voice. I had to seem calm or she wouldn't tell me and now more than ever we needed to be open with each other. 'What did she say?'

'She wanted me to meet her.'

Again, I had to fight to rein in my fear. 'You didn't... did you?'

She looked away from me, which meant she had, and it was impossible not to react then.

'Do you realise how dangerous that is? I can't believe you'd do that. I told you it isn't Pink Girl, it's Cerys and she's dangerous.'

'Mum, you're wrong, Pink Girl isn't Cerys. She was who she said she was.'

'Really? So she's a girl your age that you've never met, who spies on your mother? That sounds like a good healthy friendship.'

She rolled her eyes. 'It's not like that.'

I was confused and angry. 'This doesn't add up. Someone's lying—'

'Yeah, well, we know who *that* is.' She threw her covers off and climbed out of bed.

'So did you meet her after school?'

'Yeah. I'd told her you were meeting me so I couldn't see her, but she turned up and you didn't. Then she said you were out with some guy and that's why you were late. You'd promised you'd be there, so I believed her.' She shrugged.

'And didn't you ask her how she knew I was with a man?'

'No, she just told me, and I believed her.'

'And you decided to go off with a total stranger, rather than wait for me.'

'She was *there*, you *weren't*. I don't know who to believe any more,' she cried, and burst into tears, and my anger evaporated.

I put my arms around her. 'I'm so, so sorry. I know it's all my fault and I want to put it right with you.'

She just continued to cry, and I felt like crying too, but wanted to be strong for her. I'd really messed up, but I knew something wasn't adding up – who the hell was this girl who seemed to know so much about me? She had to have something to do with Cerys.

Eventually, Sofia stopped crying, and I asked her gently what the girl's name was.

'She didn't say, she calls herself Pink Girl.'

'And that's who you were with last night?'

'Yeah.'

'Where did you go?'

'We hung around the park.'

'Christ, with all the kids who take drugs.'

'No, we weren't with them.'

'Did she say anything – about Cerys... or me?'

'No!'

'How do you know she wasn't there on behalf of Cerys? Or anyone else wanting to use her to get to you?'

'She *wasn't*!' She frowned at me.

It just didn't add up. 'Sofia, please promise me you won't do that again. If she turns up at school, call me.'

'No, that would be weird, my friend comes to meet me and I say, "Just got to call mum and let her know you're here."' She rolled her eyes.

'No weirder than her knowing where I was and who with yesterday,' I pointed out.

Sofia suddenly looked a little sheepish. 'She didn't say you were definitely with a guy – she said, "I bet your mum is out with some guy, she's not bothered about you."'

'Well, that was nasty and completely untrue.' Who was this girl and why was she being so malicious?

'Mum, I have to get to school,' she said. 'I need to get dressed.'

'Okay, well, just so we're clear. I still don't want you seeing this girl without me. If you do, I'm sorry, but I'll go to the police and tell them I'm worried she's dangerous, and part of a paedophile ring.'

'What?' She was open-mouthed at this. 'But that's not true!'

'How do you know, she could be anyone?'

I had no intention of going back to the police, I just wanted to shock Sofia into doing as I said.

She didn't say anything else, just started to get ready. I hoped I'd got my message across; there was no way I wanted Sofia hanging around with this girl, whoever she was.

Half an hour later, we silently put on our warm coats and walked together as always, splitting up on the seafront. Just before we parted, I reminded Sofia I would be checking her phone. 'So please don't think you can pull the wool over my eyes,' I added. 'Just remember, I'm doing this because I love you.' With that, I forced a hug on her while she rolled her eyes. 'Love you,' I said. 'Call by the shop on your way home so I know you're safe.' I'd been tempted to meet Sofia at the school gates that afternoon, but couldn't abandon the shop, mid-afternoon just before Christmas. Besides I felt bad for letting down Mr Woods the previous day, especially after he had gone out of his way to help search for Sofia the night before.

'Okay,' she said in a voice that suggested this was an extremely tiresome request. I was just relieved she agreed.

When I arrived at work, Mr Woods was delighted Sofia was safe and well, and quite righty scolded me for not letting him know.

'I'm *so* sorry, I called the police and it was so late, I forgot to tell anyone else,' I said.

'I knew she was back after the girl from next door called you,' he said, referring to Nancy's call the previous evening, 'but I didn't sleep for worrying she'd been hurt, but I forgive you,' he replied. 'At least the little one is safe.'

'She is, and not so little anymore,' I pointed out.

He was looking at me like he wanted to say something and suddenly seemed a little awkward. Eventually, he spoke, 'Emily, I think someone wants to cause trouble for you.'

'What do you mean?' I held my breath in readiness of what was about to come.

'Well, yesterday, you phoned and told me you couldn't work because you were sick...'

I could feel myself blushing.

'Someone phoned the shop, said you weren't sick and that you'd been out with a gentleman friend.'

What the hell? This had to be Cerys, but how did she *know*. Had she paid someone in Sidmouth to follow us? I wouldn't put it past her, she knew some very shady people. Perhaps Pink Girl did exist, perhaps she was a teenager, vulnerable and lost, like many teenagers, and Cerys had found her on social media and manipulated her, or paid her to befriend Sofia and get information about us?

'Did this person give their name?' I asked.

'No, but it was a female voice. I just wanted you to know.'

'Someone's obviously spreading lies,' I lied. The irony wasn't lost on me, I'd been lying for most of my life and my biggest lie had now meant I had to sprout smaller ones.

'I thought as much, and I told them so. But I think you have to be careful, Emily, so many snakes.'

'Yes there are, and you're right, I think someone *is* causing trouble for me.' I explained about Cerys being Sofia's birth mother. 'This woman is dangerous,' I said.

'And now I think she's come back to claim her and it was probably her on the phone to you.'

'Goodness, it's all very dark, isn't it, dear?'

I took a deep breath. 'Yes, it is, *very* dark.'

Later that day, I received a text from Oliver asking if I wanted to meet for lunch.

Sorry, I'm not having a lunch hour today, as I took yesterday off. Let's catch up soon!

He texted back immediately. 'It's actually illegal not to take a lunch break. I know these things. So, on legal grounds, I'm going to have to insist that you meet me at the coffee shop in the square, at 1 p.m.'

His message made me smile and after everything that had happened, I needed some respite. Obviously he knew nothing about Sofia not coming home last night, and the fact that Cerys had seemingly now taken her revenge up a notch. She'd made sure both my daughter and my employer knew where I'd been the previous day, which must have felt like a betrayal to both of them. All because I had adopted her daughter, she was trying to turn my closest family and friends against me. And now I *knew* someone was watching me, which made me wary when I eventually headed out just before one.

I intended to meet, have a quick coffee with Oliver and leave. A lunch with 'a gentleman friend', as Mr Woods referred to him, would no doubt be reported to my nearest and dearest and made to look like something else. But I ended up telling him all about what had been going on, and as always, he listened as I told him how Sofia had gone missing.

'Oh, Emily, that must have been dreadful for you. I wish you'd called me, I'd have driven over and helped you look for her.'

His kindness and sympathy were nearly too much. 'That's kind of you, but it's a small town, and by the time I'd covered most of it, along with Mr Woods, she was back.'

'Where was she? You must have been out of your mind.'

I explained that I thought she was with Cerys, then told him about the phone call to Mr Woods. He looked genuinely shocked, and I worried this was all becoming a bit sordid for a nice retired solicitor. Even to me, my life now seemed like one endless drama.

'Don't worry. I explained it wasn't some afternoon tryst, and no one knows who you are anyway.'

'I wasn't even thinking about me in all this,' he said.

'No, but I don't want you to think you might be dragged into this.'

'I'm more concerned about you. Like you say, this is a small town, and it's just tittle-tattle, but it seems someone tried to affect your employment.'

'Exactly. I think Sofia's birth mother is definitely out to destroy me.'

'But how does she know who you were with? I thought you said she lives up north?'

'Yes, Manchester, as far as I know, but she could have got someone else involved, could have paid someone. Or perhaps it isn't even her behind all this, perhaps it's my ex-husband, or even Sofia's biological father?' It was all just so confusing and right now I didn't know what to think.

'But she was legally adopted, wasn't she?' Oliver asked gently.

'Yes, I have all the papers. At the time, Sofia was taken from her birth mother because she was deemed unfit. Apparently there was drug paraphernalia everywhere, Sofia was wandering the streets, Social Services had no choice but to remove her. Cerys kicked up a fuss at the time, but it died down, and everyone continued with their lives.'

'Until now?'

'Yes. That's what I don't understand, why *now*,' I murmured to myself.

I had barely touched my salad; there was so much going round in my head. And when Oliver asked if I'd like to meet up again, I suggested we leave it for a couple of weeks. After everything, it felt like I needed to put ideas of romance on the backburner for a while.

'I feel that I need to be around for Sofia at the moment,' I started.

'Absolutely, of course you do,' he said. I didn't need to explain; as a father, he understood. 'Stay in touch in the meantime and look after yourself.' He hugged me, and I leaned into him, breathing him in, feeling invigorated, stronger. Whatever this was between us, I sincerely hoped we could pick back up and pursue it later. But for now I had to concentrate on my daughter.

Walking back to work, I wondered again about Cerys. She had never wanted a baby, she had told me she cried for days when she had found out she was pregnant. After Sofia was born, I remember saying to Chris, 'What an irony, here we are in a happy marriage, with a lovely house, and we can't have children. And there they are with a perfect little girl neither of them want.' Little did I know that that baby would become mine one day, and I'd love her more than I thought possible, with every sinew of my body, every breath in my body. She gave me purpose and love. That's why I was prepared to do whatever I had to do to keep her. *No one* was *ever* taking her from me. Not even her mother. Especially not her mother. Cerys's maternal love might still flicker, but she didn't know how strong mine was – I would do anything to keep her from Sofia. *Anything.*

TWENTY-FIVE

Sofia and I talked a lot in the following days, usually when Nancy was holed up in my bedroom to avoid her joining in, this wasn't a spectator sport. Sofia's whole identity had been stripped like a skin with the news that she was adopted, and I ached for her. Each day she'd think of something else, an odd query, a sudden realisation of how this affected different aspects of her life, and who she was. I wanted her to feel comfortable talking about it and encouraged her to ask random questions as they occurred. By day three, she'd covered everything and anything, from the obvious, 'I wonder who I take after?' to the more considered, 'What if, in my birth family, there's a messed-up gene?'

I couldn't answer all of her questions, but we talked them through, and I googled teen counsellors, to see if there was anyone she could talk to. But for now, I just wanted her to feel free to talk to me. There were things I couldn't tell her, things I didn't want to share, but in our chats, I was as honest as I possibly could be.

'Is that why I've never seen my birth certificate?' she asked one evening after we'd eaten dinner. 'It's why I don't have a passport, isn't it, and why I could never go on holiday with the school?'

'Well, you *could* have a passport, and we will go on a foreign holiday one day, we've just never been able to afford trips abroad,' I replied, which was true, but I *had* to keep Sofia's birth certificate from her because that would have given everything away. In an attempt to make her feel better, and to distract her somewhat, I talked to her about the good times after I'd adopted her. I added a little flourish here and there, the bare truth is often too much to take, so I made her history as sweet a story as I could. She particularly liked my fairy-tale version of the day we met.

'When I saw you in the street, I walked up to you and you lifted your arms up to me. My heart melted.'

She smiled, she seemed to enjoy this.

'But my concern was that you'd have done that to anyone who happened to be passing. I can't even bear to think about you being in the wrong hands.' I shuddered. 'It made me realise how vulnerable you were. So I took your hand and walked with you down the road.'

'Where to, your house?'

'No, I took you to the local library, and from there the librarian called the police who contacted Social Services. That week I was in the newspaper, as "The Good Samaritan". Your social worker said she wished there were more like me. But, having found you like that, the authorities were now involved, they realised you were neglected, in danger and your mother wasn't capable of looking after you. So it was decided to remove you from Cerys and place you in temporary foster care.'

'So I was meant to go back to Cerys?'

'Well, that was the plan. Cerys had been told if she stopped taking drugs and basically cleaned up her life, there was a chance she might get you back. But each time the social worker visited, she was still using, and the house was filthy. It just wasn't a safe or healthy environment for a child to be. So it was deemed better to leave you in foster care until they could find a more permanent solution.'

'And that was you?'

'Yes. Having found you that day, I wanted to stay in touch with you, I felt a bond there that I can't explain. I'd pass on gifts for you to your social worker, we became friendly and she asked if I'd ever considered adopting. She said they were finding it hard to place you, given your lack of care in the early years, and the problem with drugs in the family. But I was a nurse, I knew I could cope with whatever was thrown at me, and Chris was a teacher, so the social worker supported and championed our application.'

'But he wasn't happy; you said that's why we left. Was that my fault, had I been difficult?'

'No, not at all. It was *his* fault, we couldn't have children and he'd accepted that. He didn't have the all-consuming *need* for a child like I did. But eventually he agreed to adopt. Once you came to live with us, however, I think he felt pushed out. He didn't understand the strength of our mother-daughter relationship.'

'Didn't he *like* me?' I could see the vulnerability in her face.

'Of *course* he did, it was just the changed dynamic he didn't like. But from day one, to me you were my daughter and that was it.'

She smiled at this, and I hoped I was restoring her emotional security and sense of self, even if it had been shattered by the recent revelation.

'It's funny that we both even look a bit alike,' she said.

'Yes, and when strangers commented on how alike we were, I realised it was meant to be. It was like I'd given birth to you myself.'

'Weirdo,' she said, with a chuckle.

'That's me, I'm a great big weirdo,' I chuckled.

And right then, I felt that as long as we could still laugh together, we could get through this, but things were about to take a sinister turn.

While Sofia and I seemed to be getting back on track, there was still the issue of Nancy. Now more than ever, Sofia and I needed space, a chance to reconnect and grow, and she still wasn't comfortable with Nancy in our home, so I decided to try to tackle the issue.

'How are you feeling?' I asked Nancy one Saturday morning close to Christmas when Sofia had gone out shopping with a couple of friends. I hadn't seen much of Nancy over the previous few days, but the mugs constantly left for washing were a reminder she was still around. I hadn't had the time or motivation to approach her over this; Sofia was my priority. But I was concerned that there seemed to be no follow-up from the hospital and no mention of any more counselling. This couldn't go on, there was no progress, no evidence of healing, and as for the drinking, Nancy was in complete denial, but I worried it was getting worse.

'I feel empty, like I have no future. I'm scared to leave the flat Em.'

'Oh, Nancy,' I said. I knew this wasn't strictly true; she'd been out overnight when she had stormed out, and only the previous day I'd seen her staggering out of the Tesco Express with what looked like a bag full of bottles, but what could I say? 'Look, I know you're still hurting, but I wonder if you should see your doctor, see if you can get some support, perhaps think about going home? There's so much drama going on here at the moment, I'm sure it can't be good for you.'

'I'm better here,' she replied firmly. 'If I go home, I'll probably spiral back into depression – and God knows...' She didn't finish her sentence, just let it hang over me like a threatening cloud.

'But it's been more than a week now and I don't think being here is helping you get better,' I offered as gently as I could.

Nancy's eyes shot to mine. 'You were a nurse, surely you know this kind of thing doesn't just *get better* overnight?' She was quick to anger these days, hated to be challenged on the smallest issue. The woman who'd once seemed easy-going and fun was now brittle and edgy. I knew the constant alcohol consumption couldn't be helping, and I had to tread carefully with her.

'No. It doesn't, Nancy,' I said, 'it's a long haul, and you need proper help, that's why I was suggesting you think about where you stay next. I think you need to be somewhere where you're supported by professionals.'

'No *way*,' she raised her voice, 'I've done it before, and it doesn't *work*. I won't be locked in an institution with zonked-out patients and overzealous helpers pushing sedatives and forcing me to make crocheted hats!' she snapped.

'Okay, okay, I wasn't suggesting anything as extreme as that. But perhaps you could think about going home?' I suggested calmly.

She shook her head and folded her arms, like a surly child.

I paused, and took a breath. 'Thing is, Nancy, I'll be honest, I'm not just thinking of you. I'm exhausted from sleeping on the couch, I need my bed back,' I said, hoping my blunt request would reach her vodka-misted mind.

She looked up from her sulk. 'Oh, why didn't you say?'

I smiled with relief. 'I didn't want to upset you, but I think it's for the best.'

'Yeah, yeah, I'm sorry, I've been selfish, didn't even think about you stuck on that hard old couch every night.'

'Oh I'm so glad you understand. I can help you move.'

'I can move *myself*,' she said. 'I'll move my stuff tomorrow. I can sleep on the couch, no problem. And you can have your room back.'

My heart dropped. No wonder she had been so agreeable; she thought I just wanted my bed back, but I needed my home back, and my life, I needed my daughter back too. Perhaps it was a coincidence that everything had started to fall apart at the seams when Nancy had moved in, but it couldn't be a worse time for her to stay now. I was desperate for her to leave, so tried a more firm approach.

'Look, Nancy, I'm struggling financially,' I said, truthfully. 'I can't afford for the heating and hot water to be on all day and night, and I know it's really cold, but you like to be in a warm place and—'

'I'm sorry, you must be so fed up of me being here, I know I'm a burden.' I could see her shoulders drop, her eyes welling up. But I was only too aware that this was her way, she manipulated me into feeling guilty and this time I needed to be strong.

'No, you're not a *burden*,' I lied, 'I just think—'

'Okay, you're absolutely right, this arrangement isn't fair,' she said, and my spirit dared to lift a little. 'So when I get some money, I'll give it to you to put towards the heating. This flat can be really cold, and it affects my depression when I'm cold.'

'It isn't nice for anyone to be cold,' I murmured, deflated once more, 'but I can't afford it, Nancy.'

'No worries,' she patted my arm. 'I'll give you something as soon I can. I'm just really grateful for you letting me stay.' She seemed so upbeat at the prospect and I was all out of ideas. So, it didn't look like Nancy was leaving any time soon. It seemed our flat, with meals cooked and washing done – all for nothing – suited her. I hated myself for being mean, but I was struggling emotionally, as well as financially, and I was worried about my daughter. Nonetheless, I tried to have kind, calm thoughts. I knew Nancy was going through a tough time and her behaviour had been a cry for help. I didn't want to let her down, I actually missed my friend, the one I met once a week for lunch, or a chat over coffee. We could talk for hours, really laugh, and then just walk away and say 'see you soon,' which suited me. I didn't want a 'best friend' who lived in my house and knew all my business, but it seemed for now I was stuck.

'I thought you were supposed to be kicking her out?' Sofia said the following day, when Nancy had left her dirty crockery in the sink as usual, despite me asking her to wash it. I wasn't quite sure how she spent her time during the day, but a bit of washing-up wouldn't have been too much to expect.

'I suggested alternatives, but she isn't ready,' I said, aware this sounded weak. 'You had to be there, she really lays it on thick, and ties me in knots,' I whispered.

'She is so manipulative, you just need to give it to her straight,' Sofia hissed back as she ran each piece of dirty crockery under the tap, then banged it on the draining board in temper.

'I tried, I really did – don't worry, I'll sort it,' I said.

'You'd better,' she replied in a loud voice, 'because if *she* stays here much longer, I'm going!'

'Sofia, keep your voice down.' My eyes moved in the direction of the bathroom, where Nancy was taking her daily bath.

'I won't keep my voice down,' she yelled. 'It's *our* home!'

'*Sofia*, just calm down, will you?' I hissed back.

With that, she banged the final cup on the draining board, wiped her hands with a tea towel and stormed out of the kitchen, slamming her bedroom door.

I'd handled it badly again. It didn't seem I was able to get anything right at the moment. Sofia was going through a lot, and I knew Nancy's presence was making it worse. I'd just have to be even more blunt with her, stop asking, just *tell* her to leave. Tough love would have to be the way forward.

I decided to give Sofia ten minutes, then take her a cup of tea. So I put the kettle on. But before the kettle had boiled, I heard Sofia's bedroom door open and close. I turned as she stormed down the hall, and just as I ran out to stop her, the front door was slammed hard. I looked at my watch, it was 9 p.m., where the *hell* was she going at this time? Nothing had been mentioned of Pink Girl since we'd spoken about her and I was hoping that was all in the past, but there were other dangers out there for a fifteen-year-old girl out at night, alone.

I was terrified. It was dark and she'd left in a temper, and anything could happen. I needed to find her, but I couldn't go in the car because, with everything going on, I hadn't got round to getting it fixed. So I raced down the hall, got my coat and scarf. I noticed that her keys had gone from the dish we kept them in.

Outside, I ran along the seafront and headed for the park area, which was where she'd gone before. I had no clue if I'd find her there, but I just kept walking in that direction. When I arrived, I didn't go in, just hung around nearby to see if I could see her. After about ten minutes, I heard voices. It was an unusually clear night, no clouds, no rain, just biting cold, but it was good for acoustics.

'Come to ours,' the voice was saying, and for a moment I wondered if it was Ruby, but I reminded myself that Ruby wouldn't hang around the park. It was only a certain group of kids who did that, and until recently Sofia wasn't one of them. But now I wondered: nature or nurture? I always believed that there was no such thing as a bad person, someone who was born to be mean and selfish and destructive.

Cerys had had a difficult upbringing with her dad, and before she had Sofia, she'd been in trouble with the police for stabbing someone. I'd also seen a report online in *The Manchester Evening News* about how Cerys Morton, of no fixed abode, had emptied the bank account of an elderly lady she used to visit. This led to a court case, where other offences were taken into consideration, and she ended up with three years in prison. I hadn't googled her for a while, but when I had, I couldn't find her, which made me think she might have changed her name, or married – until I had found her recently on the Facebook page.

Now I wondered about genes and behaviour, was Sofia destined to be like her? If so, could she be saved not only from her mother, but her destiny? And I wondered was it already too late?

I thought of her friend, Zoe. My stomach dropped, had that been the beginning, a flirtation with the dark side, a compulsion fixed in her DNA to take risks, rebel? In that dark little corner of the park, among the used condoms, the hopelessness and the stink of weed, had Sofia recognised her tribe? Was that still my Sofia, or was it Cerys's daughter? Was this where she felt she belonged, in a park with other lost children driven by what they were rather than who? And was everything I'd tried to do for Sofia in vain? Was it already too late when I saw her on the pavement at three years old? But no, I couldn't give up on her now, not after all I'd done to save her, to keep her.

A few minutes later as I waited behind the trees, I saw them emerge from the park, Sofia and another girl. They walked in step, quite quickly, and as they passed under a street lamp, I could see the girl looked very thin. She was wearing a denim jacket and must have been freezing. She also had *pink* hair – it was Pink Girl. It seemed as if she was everything Sofia had believed her to be, a teenager she'd met online. But how did this teenager know that my friend drank too much? And how did Pink Girl know when I'd been out with Oliver, when I hadn't told Sofia? I'd assumed she was Cerys, but perhaps Pink Girl had no connection to Cerys? She lived here, Cerys lived in Manchester, how could they be connected – had I got this all wrong? But if it wasn't Cerys who'd been trying to scare us and ruin our lives, who was it?

TWENTY-SIX

I continued to follow Sofia and Pink Girl down the back roads, aware that if they saw me, I'd have some questions to answer, so I stayed well in the shadows. They walked over the bridge where water from the overflowing ford roared down the lane like a strong river. Then down the roads, turning corners. They were obviously heading somewhere, and it seemed Pink Girl was leading the way.

Eventually, they slowed down, and I loitered on the opposite side of the road a few hundred yards away. It was a tree-lined street, and I was able to stand behind a tree trunk and look out onto the large Victorian terraced houses, the kind of family houses with several kids, a dog and a piano. It wasn't the kind of area I'd expected this girl to live, but that was my prejudice, I guess. Perhaps she wasn't at all what I thought she was. But if she lived here, and was a couple of years younger than Sofia, then why wasn't she at her school? The only thing I could think was that she went to the private school. It was becoming more and more confusing, and when the girl opened the front door, let herself in and Sofia followed, I felt sick.

My instinct was to bang on the door and scream at her to get out. But what if it *was* innocent? What if Sofia had just stormed out of our flat and simply called her friend? I couldn't just walk away, though, and leave her in a stranger's house. So I settled in by the tree trunk on the opposite side of the road, a perfect vantage point in the freezing cold where I would wait, hoping she'd emerge at some point.

As time went on, one or two people wandered back home, presumably from the pub or the local cinema and I realised I looked like a stalker. So I had to keep moving and seem less suspicious, and less conspicuous. But it clearly didn't work because someone tapped me on the shoulder. I leaped so high, I almost stumbled, and turning around, I saw an elderly lady.

'Are you okay, love?' she asked.

'I'm fine, just waiting for my daughter. She's at her friend's.'

'Oh, I was going to say, I live on this road. If you need to call a taxi or anything, I can help, can't be much fun standing out here in the freezing cold.'

'No, it's not the best night for my daughter to ask me to pick her up,' I said with a smile. 'Do you know them?' I asked, nodding in the vague direction of the house.

She screwed up her eyes and looked. 'That used to be the Richardsons' house,' she said, 'but I think they've moved. I used to know all the neighbours round here, it was a nice community, but since Covid, we've had an influx from London...'

'So you don't know who lives there now?' I asked, interrupting her as politely as I possibly could.

'No, I've seen a couple with a teenage daughter, haven't met them, just see him coming home from work. Is that where your daughter is, number 22?'

'Yes.'

'You could knock?' she suggested, like I hadn't thought of this.

'Oh, you know what teenagers are like. She asked me to text and wait outside.'

'So you're an embarrassing mother, eh?' she chuckled at this.

I immediately felt defensive. 'No, I'm not the—'

'I was *always* the embarrassing mother,' she said with a giggle.

I smiled in acknowledgement, while wishing she'd go now. I was concerned that Sofia would come out of the house while she was talking, and I'd miss her, or worse still, Sofia would hear her and see me.

But the lady was on a roll now. 'Yes, I was a huge embarrassment to my sons. They're both married now, and live miles away. They've got their own families, their own lives,' she paused. 'My husband died last year. I'm on my own now, rattling around that big house – funny how one minute you're in the middle of your life and your family, then suddenly everyone's gone. I don't get out much, went to the cinema tonight with my friend, her husband picked her up,' she added sadly.

'I'm sorry about your husband,' I said, 'it must be very difficult.'

'It is, I get very lonely in that house. Would you like to come in and have a cup of tea?'

'That's so kind, but my daughter will be out in a minute.'

'Oh, not to worry.'

I felt a little guilty then at the disappointment in her eyes, but I couldn't afford to miss Sofia leaving. 'Please don't stand here, you'll catch your death, it's freezing.'

'I live at number 43, just across the road from 22, we could sit in the front room and you could watch for her out of the window? It would be so much warmer than standing out here,' she offered.

I politely declined and thanked her again, moving slightly away, hoping my body language would end her conversation. Sadly it didn't and she just kept on talking, oblivious to my anxiety. My eyes kept darting across the street to the house as she talked, and suddenly, I saw something happening. The door of the house was opening, a shaft of light from inside making a long rectangle on the doorstep.

'Oh,' I said quietly and plucked my phone from my pocket. 'She's just texted me. I've got the wrong street!'

'Oh, you silly,' she said, laughing.

'I'll get off then,' I said. 'Lovely to chat.' I headed off down the road, my head down, desperate to see but not *be seen*. As I came closer to the house, I lifted my head. Sofia was standing on the doorstep talking. It wasn't easy to see the two people standing inside the hallway, but as she stepped away, they followed her down the path to the front gate. They all hugged, and that's when I saw her – and heard her laughter, a tinkling sound that chilled my bones. Cerys. She was behind this after all, she'd been there for years loitering in the shadows of my life – she'd always been there, just waiting for the right time. And now here she was. Somehow she'd wormed her way into my daughter's life.

It was twelve years since I last saw her, but having seen the Facebook photo, I knew it was her, even with the slightly chunkier build. She stood the way she'd always stood, her whole demeanour laid-back, but she was always ready for a fight. She was wearing a hoodie, just like that stranger a few weeks ago who had been leaning on the lamp post outside our flat and staring in. Coincidence? I didn't think so, and my chest filled with a dull, unmoveable ache, as she now hugged my daughter at the gate. I had to stop myself from crying out, 'Get off her!'

So Cerys had finally tracked us down, and she'd been here a while, turning my sanctuary into a place where I was frightened to walk down the street. She hadn't come for Sofia, she didn't care about her child. No, Cerys was here for me, to take her revenge. It seemed that Pink Girl was merely bait to get to Sofia. Absolute fear thrummed through my veins.

Sofia started to walk home, and staying at a distance behind her, I followed, not knowing what to do next, my mind whirring. Why now, after all this time? And how on earth had Cerys managed to *move* here? She'd never had a job, or ambition or money, and you needed at least one of those things to move house halfway across the country. And a big Victorian house like that would cost a fortune. The old lady I spoke with said she'd seen a couple and a teenage girl, perhaps Cerys had married someone with money?

I managed to keep myself out of sight all the way, while making sure Sofia got home safely. Once she was inside, I waited about fifteen minutes, then went in. She was in the kitchen looking at her phone.

'You're *here*?' I said gently, with what I hoped seemed like a surprised and relieved smile.

She looked up. 'Where've *you* been?' she responded abruptly.

'Looking for *you*.' I sat down opposite her at the table.

She continued to gaze into her phone.

'Sofia, are you going to at least tell me where you've been?' I asked.

'You don't tell me where *you've* been.'

'I thought we'd agreed to tell each other where we were going and who with.'

'I don't remember that.' Then she looked up from her phone, and I saw Cerys's green eyes staring at me. Cold, cruel eyes that took my breath away, and I wondered again if she was already lost.

'We did, we promised,' I replied, feeling frustrated but mostly flustered as the piercing green eyes bore into mine.

She closed them like she couldn't even look at me, then went back to her phone.

'Where have you been tonight?' I asked firmly, reminding myself that I was still the guardian here.

'With a friend,' she muttered.

'Anyone I know?'

She shook her head without taking her eyes from her phone.

'Would you like to tell me?'

Again, she shook her head without making any eye contact.

I stood up from the table, I wasn't playing any more games. 'I just hope you aren't playing with fire,' I replied, walking into the living room and closing the door. Then I remembered that Nancy was supposed to move out of my room that day, but as all my stuff was still in there, with no sign of hers, I had another night on the couch to look forward to.

I couldn't sleep worrying about Sofia, resenting Nancy, fearing Cerys and wishing I could see Oliver. I finally abandoned the idea of sleep and got up and dressed at 6 a.m. and pottered around quietly until 7.30 when Sofia wandered into the kitchen. As she put her bread in the toaster, I made a point of saying good morning, and she mumbled something back.

'I'm going to talk to Nancy today,' I said.

'Good.' She took a bite of toast, but seemed disinterested.

'I tried the other day but got nowhere,' I murmured, turning on the radio, putting it on a music station, then turning up the volume. High.

'Mum, what are you doing?' Sofia asked. 'You always tell me off if I make a noise because it will wake them upstairs,' she complained.

'Well, I'm fed up of worrying about other people's feelings,' I replied, pouring my cereal into a bowl.

Sofia was rushing her toast and about to leave when Nancy appeared in the doorway, her hair on end. 'What the bloody hell's going on? That racket woke me up,' she grumbled.

'You were lucky to *get* to sleep,' I said. 'That's a luxury I don't have on the couch.'

'Okay, okay, I'll move my stuff, I said you could have your room back,' she mumbled, like she was doing me a favour.

'Yesterday, yesterday you were supposed to move your stuff.'

'I'm going for a vape,' she said, like I was boring her with my silly demands, and putting her coat on over her pyjamas she headed for the door. I heard it open, but didn't hear it close, just another annoying habit of hers. Keeping the door open meant all the heat left the house, to be replaced by the sea wind, that whooshed into the hall.

'Inconsiderate,' I muttered.

Sofia tightened her lips and looked at me in the way my mother used to, a warning look – *you'd better do this or else* – if I hadn't cleaned out the fire grate properly or washed the pots.

The front door slammed and Nancy came thundering down the hall. She was holding an envelope. 'The post just came,' she said, putting it down on the table in front of me.

I opened the envelope. 'What is it?' I murmured, holding up the transparent bag inside.

'Is it a bomb?' Nancy was freaking out.

'No, of course not,' I said gently, as Sofia got up from her chair for a closer look.

I carefully put one hand into the bag, while holding it flat with my other hand, and brought out a piece of plastic in the shape of a cow.

'What the hell is that?' Nancy asked.

Sofia gasped. 'Mum, that's from the mobile above my cot, in the photo. You remember?'

I nodded slowly, I knew exactly what it was as I turned it around in my hands. But I didn't know what it meant, why I'd been sent it.

'There's a note too,' Nancy said.

'Oh no,' I moaned, as I delved inside the bag, and brought it out. 'Shit,' I muttered, gazing at the note, 'this is really messed up. What's wrong with her, why can't she just leave us alone to live our lives?'

Sofia leaned in to look more closely, then picked up the note, and read it out loud. 'Hey, diddle, diddle, The cat and the fiddle, The cow jumped over the moon; the little dog laughed, to see such fun, and the dish ran away with the spoon. What the hell *is* that?' she asked, looking at me.

'I've no idea,' I shrugged, 'but I think I know who sent it... and I bet I know who the little dog who laughed is. I bet she's laughing right now.'

TWENTY-SEVEN

I was still sitting at the table, aware of Sofia standing next to me, on the verge of tears. 'Don't take any notice of this,' I tried to reassure her. 'It's just some nonsense.'

'Is it about *me*, Mum?'

'No, of course not, darling.'

She continued to stand stiffly beside me, her face deathly white, guilt and fear etched into it. My heart was breaking for her.

'It's got something to do with me,' she said quietly.

'Why would you say that?' I looked from her to Nancy, who stared at us both.

'I *met* her.' Sofia spoke so quietly I had to strain to hear her. 'I met Cerys. Last night. I told her I'd found photos of my cot, she remembered the mobile, told me about the house where we'd lived... and I told her about how I loved the little mobile, and the plastic cow was my favourite. I think it might be her way of saying she has it, she has the mobile and—'

'And therefore has you?' I suggested, my heart dropping at the idea of Cerys and Sofia having this cosy, intimate chat.

She shrugged.

'The dish ran away with the spoon! Sofia, you're the spoon and your real mother's the dish, she's going to run away with you!' Nancy yelled, like she'd just cracked the enigma code.

'Shit,' Sofia murmured.

'Calm down,' I said to both of them. 'First of all, Cerys is not Sofia's *real* mother, she's her *birth* mother,' I said, putting her straight.

'Yeah,' Sofia echoed, sitting down next to me in an act of unity.

Nancy shrugged, watching us both, one hand protectively around her waist, her other hand clutching her mug of God knows what.

'And secondly, *no one* is running away with you, Sofia,' I asserted, giving Nancy a warning look. She'd clearly scared Sofia with her crazy interpretation of a nursery rhyme. I turned to Sofia. 'So, how did you meet Cerys? She's in Manchester, it's miles away?' I asked, feigning confusion.

'No, she's here in Sidmouth.' Sofia looked flustered. 'She only wanted to meet up with me, find out if I was okay, and—'

'Why didn't you tell me, we'd agreed...'

'But, Mum, she was really nice. She has a little dog called Dylan.' Tears were forming ion pools in the bottom of her eyes. I wanted to hug her, but that would make it okay, and it wasn't okay.

'But why didn't you talk to *me* about it *first*?' The hurt and disappointment still burned through me from the previous evening. Even though I knew, it felt like a fresh betrayal.

'I don't know, I just thought you'd be upset and I didn't want to hurt you.'

'But you *have*, you've hurt me because you did this without *telling* me. When you're old enough to handle it, then it's up to you, Sofia, but I told you, Cerys is a dangerous person.'

'She told me about the drugs, said she was all mixed up

when I was adopted, said the social worker pushed her into it. She says she's regretted it ever since.'

'I'm sure she has, who wouldn't regret giving you up? You're a wonderful kid, but trust me, your life would have been very different if you'd stayed with her.'

'I know,' she replied. 'But it was the drugs that made her like that, and she hasn't taken drugs for years, she—'

'That's what *all* addicts say,' I pointed out, trying not to look at Nancy. I hoped my daughter would see the connection between the addict we currently lived with, who she seemed to hate, and the addict who was her mother.

'But she *did* change, she went to college,' Sofia said. She seemed hell-bent on defending the woman who would have gladly exchanged her for a few wraps of weed twelve years before.

I shrugged, tears of hurt and frustration filled my eyes; my daughter wasn't hearing me, she was hearing her biological mother instead. Had she already gone, was this the end for Sofia and me?

'So how did she find you?' I asked.

'Through Pink Girl.'

Nancy sat down. 'The internet's so bloody dangerous,' she interjected, unnecessarily.

'I warned you, Sofia,' I said, ignoring Nancy, wishing she'd leave us alone now. 'I told you there are some scary people out there manipulating youngsters online. And one of those scary people is your mother! The fact she used another teenager to bait you— I'm appalled!'

'But, Mum, Pink Girl isn't bait, she's my *sister*.'

My mouth opened in shock.

'She's Cerys's daughter,' Sofia paused. 'Her name's Jody.'

It had never occurred to me that Cerys had more children. 'Wow. I can't believe she was allowed to keep another child, she was on the Social Services' radar for years after you.'

Sofia shrugged.

Cerys must have been pregnant when I found Sofia. I shivered at the memory of her drug taking while pregnant, I just hoped the child was born healthy. But even if she was physically fine, I couldn't imagine how Cerys cared for a child this second time alone with no support.

Nancy was now perched on the edge opposite us, clearly settled and enjoying the show.

'So, it looks like this,' I said, touching the bag with the plastic cow inside, 'is Cerys letting us know she's back in charge. And you might be right, Nancy... the dish ran away with the spoon, could be her threatening to take you, love,' I said to Sofia.

'No, she wouldn't do that – would she?' I could finally see some doubt in Sofia's eyes; it bothered me that she thought she could trust Cerys.

'Who knows how her twisted mind works?' I replied, with a sigh. 'That's why we had left Manchester and moved hundreds of miles away, I couldn't risk her finding you.'

Sofia now looked chastened. 'I've messed everything up, haven't I?'

'It's not your fault,' I reassured her.

'I won't see her again.'

I was relieved to hear this. 'I know this is hard for you, but she's disturbed, love, and for her it's about revenge and settling the score as much as anything. For some drug-addled reason, she genuinely believes that I stole you from her. And now, I suspect, she wants to "steal" you back.'

'She can't "steal" me though, can she?' I could hear the uncertainty in her voice.

'No, I'm your mother by law, but I need you to be careful.' I glanced at the note, 'Stuff like this shows how dangerous she is and by meeting up with her, you're putting us both,' I looked up at Nancy, 'well, *all* of us, in danger.'

Nancy shuddered, as I gestured towards the plastic cow.

'How could anyone use something from a nursery rhyme as a threat to a mother and her daughter,' I murmured.

'That's so creepy,' Nancy muttered, she now had both her arms wrapped around herself.

'I'm sorry, Mum, I never realised, I thought she was nice, and kind and—' she paused. 'You don't think she'll try to hurt you or kidnap me, do you?'

'Darling, trust me, no one is taking you anywhere you don't want to go.' I stood up and gave her a big hug.

'I'm calling the police,' Nancy said.

I pulled away slightly from Sofia, who was now in tears. I wanted to cry with her, I hated when she was upset.

'Nancy, we won't call the police just yet. There's nothing I'd love more than to call them now, but this is Sofia's birth mother, and it isn't fair on Sofia.' I looked at my daughter.

'But this woman's a bloody lunatic, she could kill us in our beds,' Nancy was yelling now.

I shook my head; Nancy's words were far from helpful. 'She wouldn't kill us in our beds.' I took a breath. 'I just think we need to be more vigilant.'

'Shit. I can't sleep on the couch now, I'll be sleeping in the front room, they'll see me through the window and get to me first,' Nancy hissed.

She was getting carried away, but I was glad she was taking this seriously and hoped that Sofia would too. 'You'll be fine in the living room,' I said. 'We just have to make sure we keep all the doors and windows locked, and keep an eye out for anyone hanging around.'

'She sounds like a bloody psycho,' Nancy muttered to herself, almost whimpering with fear.

Sofia and I both ignored this, but I did appreciate the confirmation of what Cerys was.

'So, last night, while I was walking around town in the freezing cold, desperately searching for you, you were with

Cerys and Jody?' I felt bad that I wasn't being completely honest with Sofia, because I'd known exactly where she was and who with – but I had to hammer the danger home to her.

She looked ashamed, and bowed her head.

'Where is she living?'

'Acorn Road, it's about a mile from here.'

'So she knows exactly where you live because she presumably walked you home?'

'No, she didn't, she didn't walk me home,' she replied, keen to make me realise she'd not, even inadvertently, given our address away.

'Hang on,' I said. 'So it was after eleven, pitch black, middle of winter, and you're telling me your biological mother let you walk home alone?'

She slowly lifted her head, and nodded. I think she took my point.

TWENTY-EIGHT

Over the next few days, I felt like I'd finally got through to Sofia, and she was beginning to understand the implications of what she'd done. Then, one evening, we were eating dinner, and Nancy said she heard someone at the door.

'Can you get it, Nancy,' I said. I was clearing the plates and she was nearest to the door.

'No way, it might be *her*,' she said.

Sofia huffed and rose from her seat, saying, 'For God's sake, Nancy, she isn't a murderer!'

Nancy looked at me. 'I wouldn't want to bet on that,' she murmured.

This seemed to wind Sofia up even more. 'That's my mother you're talking about!' she hissed, and in that moment, I realised that, for Sofia, blood really was thicker than water. Even a plastic mobile toy with a creepy cryptic message about kidnapping her hadn't really changed that.

'I'll get the door,' I said, gently pushing past Sofia. 'Whoever it is, they shouldn't be visiting at this time, it's after eight.' I walked down the hallway holding my breath, braced for a confrontation with my daughter's mother, a dull thud in my chest, a sick feeling in the pit of my stomach that I had carried around ever since seeing my daughter walk out of Cerys's house. The last few days I'd felt as if I was in the middle of a nightmare, constantly looking over my shoulder, waiting for Cerys to make her next move, keeping Sofia as close as possible, and I wondered now if this was it, the moment my past caught up with me.

I reached out and began to unlock the door, knowing this could be the beginning of something horrible. When I opened it, I looked both ways, stepped out onto the pavement, and saw nothing. I even hung around a few minutes outside, checked the vicinity. But nothing. I just had this feeling though, but I couldn't put my finger on it, something ominous and unsettling, and I quickly shut the door and locked it.

'Find any kids' toys with creepy notes?' Nancy asked nonchalantly as I walked back in.

I shook my head. 'No, thank God, there was no one there.'

'There was definitely *someone* there,' she said. 'Before I heard the knock, I saw someone walk past the front window.'

I looked to where she was pointing. Given Nancy's own issues and the fact she was so clearly rattled by everything that was going on, I wondered if she was imagining things. I didn't want her to scare Sofia, but I also now knew that if there was a dangerous situation, she wouldn't be there for her. So later, when she'd gone for a shower, I warned Sofia, 'If I'm not here, don't rely on Nancy. She won't look out for you.'

'Gosh, really, Mum?' she replied, sarcastically.

It was my turn to roll my eyes. 'Look, all I'm saying is, if I'm not here and anything happens, call me, or run. Don't wait for her to advise you, she'll be the first one out of this flat.'

'Er, yes of course she will. I wish she was as quick to be out of the flat full stop. I thought you were going to tell her to leave?'

'She will,' I replied. 'I reckon Cerys's little gift has already made her think twice about being here.' And after a few nights trying to sleep on the couch, perhaps she'd also start to think about returning to her own bed.

'Let's hope so. I'm going to bed,' Sofia said, her voice cold.

I watched her leave without coming to hug me, or say goodnight, or just smile. I wondered if, in spite of the plastic mobile toy and the threat veiled in a nursery rhyme, she still had some trust left for Cerys.

So, the following day, I told Mr Woods I had some concerns about Sofia and needed to go home early. He agreed immediately. 'Is there anything I can do?' he asked, but I said I'd call him if I needed any help. I meant it too, he'd been such a great support, sometimes I felt like he was the only person on my side.

Sofia was at school and I knew Nancy had a doctor's appointment. I'd suggested she see her doctor because she didn't seem to be getting any better, and in my opinion, a lot of her problems were being exacerbated with a daily cocktail of antidepressants and alcohol.

As I opened the door to the flat, I felt that familiar pull towards my daughter's room. This time, I didn't even try to fight it, telling myself that this was necessary for her own good, and walked down the hall and straight to her bedroom. Once inside, I checked some of her drawers, looked under her bed and ran my hands along the top of her bookshelves. I felt guilty, I hated invading her privacy like that, but in the eyes of the law, she was still a child – *my* child – and it was up to me to look after her. It seemed to me that Cerys's influence was beginning to come through in her attitude, the way she spoke to me, her total dismissal of Nancy. Was Sofia just being informed by Cerys, or was it something more fundamental, something in her DNA? I wasn't sure either way, but I wanted my daughter back.

I didn't know what I was looking for in Sofia's room, but it was clear I was wasting my time with drawers and shelves – the place where Sofia's secrets lived was in the laptop. Until recently she'd left her laptop lying around the flat, but now it was always safely put away under her bed, to avoid prying eyes – mine.

I took it out from its hiding place and sat on the bed. I opened it up and signed in with the usual password, pressed return and waited. 'Incorrect password' came on the screen, so I assumed I must have mistyped it, so I put it in again. The same message appeared on the screen and this time I knew I'd inputted it correctly.

I only had one more go, and after that I'd lock myself out for a few hours, I'd also lock Sofia out and I didn't want her to know I'd looked, or been spying, as she would see it. So, I racked my brain as to what her new password might be. The answer niggled at me and I found it hard to even contemplate it, but time was running out, so I went for it. CERYS, I typed – and there it was, my daughter's online world, via her birth mother's name. My heart dropped; it was just a password, but it was so much more. *Was I already too late to save my daughter?*

I went straight to Facebook, where I saw private messages now between Sofia and Cerys, she was calling herself Green Girl, emulating her daughter Jody's moniker. They thought I was so stupid, I wouldn't have a clue, but the very fact that I guessed her new password was proof I knew my daughter well.

'So great to meet you last night,' was the opening message from Cerys. The rest was basically Sofia saying how 'cool' she was, how 'awesome' it felt that her mother had travelled so far to find her. The words cut into me like a knife – 'I'm so happy to have a sister, a family. I even have a dog!' she wrote, which tore me apart. As we rented a small flat, pets weren't allowed. It was something I'd never been able to give to Sofia.

Then, as I scrolled down, I saw Sofia's most recent comments: 'That plastic cow? Not cool.'

Green Girl: 'What do you mean?'

Sofia: 'You know exactly what I mean. My mum is really upset, and so am I. Why did you do that?'

Green Girl: 'I have no idea what you're talking about, please let's meet up, Sofia. Why don't you call by on your way home from school today?'

Sofia: 'No.'

Green Girl: 'We need to talk, you're obviously being poisoned against me. It's just her lies. I'm so upset, have you forgotten already that I'm your real mother?'

Sofia: 'See how I feel later.'

I was so angry at this. I wanted to march to Acorn Road and bang on her door, how dare she use emotional blackmail on my daughter. After twelve years, she thought she could stroll back into Sofia's life and cause this kind of carnage. I was tempted to send a message myself, but of course I couldn't. Eventually, I closed the laptop, put it away and crept from the room.

I thought about going to school to meet Sofia to stop her from meeting with Cerys. I hoped to God she wouldn't be taken in so easily, but she was fifteen and her life had been turned upside down overnight. Of course, she was going to be confused, uncertain, and I wasn't sure whether to give her space to find her own way back to me or to pull rank and lay down the law. I found it all so stressful and I had no one to talk to, and I suddenly thought of Oliver; he was a father who'd been through difficulties, he was wise and thoughtful and I needed someone. I hadn't seen him for a few days because I had to be around for Sofia, which he understood, so I texted him now, asking if he was free to meet for coffee. He agreed and, half an hour later, I met up with him.

I hadn't seen him for a few days, and as we drank coffee, I told him about Sofia meeting her birth mother. It felt reassuring to have another parent to speak to. Of course, our situations were different, but there was something so kind and genuine about him and it was clear that he was a doting father. I felt safe and comfortable opening up to him.

'That must have been very difficult for you,' he said.

'I was hurt, and I feel for Sofia too – but she's a child in all this and I can't help but feel she's believing a fairy-tale version of her mother. The truth is quite different.'

I didn't mention that I'd secretly followed my daughter to Cerys's house. I didn't want him to think *I* was the psycho. So I told him about the plastic cow and the note. 'It was from Cerys,' I said.

'*What?* Threatening nursery rhymes, that's like something from a movie.' He looked horrified.

'I know, it isn't pretty,' I said. 'But I guess you've seen stuff like that in your career?'

'No, not really. I dealt in far more boring aspects of law – property.'

'Oh, I see.' I hadn't considered his speciality and felt rather foolish.

'So what did the police say?' he asked expectantly.

I hesitated. 'We didn't call them.'

'You *have* to, this is harassment now,' he insisted.

'I didn't want to upset Sofia – after all, it was her mother that sent it. And Sofia seems smitten, I couldn't do it to my daughter.'

'But you *know* that it was her who sent it?'

'Well, she didn't *sign* the note, but she was the one with the cot mobile – who else would have it? I saw an exchange between her and Sofia, she – Green Girl, or Cerys – claimed not to know what Sofia was referring to, but of course that's what she'd say.'

He nodded in agreement.

'I'm worried about the effect of all this on Sofia,' I admitted.

'I can imagine.' He was frowning. 'She must be scared to death.'

'Yes, and she's so low. She had a difficult time last summer when she made friends with a girl who was troubled, and then she died, so that was hard. But since then Sofia went back to being an A student, always reading, always studying, and loved school. But most of all she was happy, and it didn't take a lot for her to be happy – I mean, garlic bread with dinner would send her into paroxysms of delight. There's been such a change in her, she doesn't place the same value on her studies, on learning; she's miserable, and I know it's down to all this online intrusion, the sudden relationship with her birth mother. She's ruined our lives.'

'That's so sad,' he commiserated, then he paused, like he wasn't quite sure how to broach what he wanted to say.

'Forgive me for playing devil's advocate, but it must have been such a shock for your daughter when she found out you weren't her mother? Perhaps she isn't sure *who* to believe?'

'Yes, you're right, of course you are. The trust was broken by me first because I never told her she was adopted.'

He shrugged. 'I suppose you just have to keep reassuring her.'

'Yes, but, meanwhile, God knows what that woman is saying to her, and it hurts that Sofia believes her lies because of this invisible mother-daughter bio bond she obviously feels. But what's a mother? The one who plastered her grazed knee, who sat up with her all night with chickenpox, who taught her to read and to spell and to care about the world. Or is it the one who suddenly turns up when she's fifteen and wants to play?'

'But if this *is* her mother...?' he said gently, without finishing the sentence.

'I know, I know. I get that she needs to work this through, perhaps even get to know Cerys, if only to realise how bad she is. But I don't know if I can risk that.'

'I've said it before, you can't fight this on your own, you should get the police involved.'

'I... I will,' I lied, unable and unwilling to explain.

The past had been stalking me all these years and was now reaching out and dragging me back there. I was ashamed of what I'd done, and believed that by running away I could erase it. But I didn't leave it behind, I carried that shame, and it was a cloud that hung over me. The only other person who knew my truth was Cerys, and now she'd found me. I had to stop her, because if I didn't, I'd lose my daughter, and that wasn't going to happen; I would kill first.

TWENTY-NINE

I left Oliver with vague plans to meet later in the week, and walked home along the seafront trying to work out my feelings. Talking to him was so good for me, he made me question myself, made me really think about my own reaction to what was happening. I just wish he didn't keep telling me to go to the police. I could see why he and Nancy felt I should get them involved, but I knew it would create more trouble for me than it would solve.

I had this recurring dream that Sofia had run from our house straight into the sea. It was night-time, the sea was rough, the wind was howling, and I ran into the water, grabbing her by the hand. I held on so tight, and kept calling her name, but she was oblivious to me, just pushing forward into the waves as I tried to hold her back. It always ended the same, her hand slipping from mine, as the waves sucked her under, and in the crashing of the waves, I could hear Cerys's laughter. I woke in tears every time.

As I walked along the seafront now, I considered the journey I'd made from an industrial town up north to this place with its promenade, and genteel façade. It was as different from

Manchester as anywhere else in the world, and as far away as I could get. I not only ran away from my husband, but from the letters pushed through my door promising to kill me, and threatening to kidnap Sofia and return her to her 'real' mother. But what is a 'real' mother? Someone who loves their child and cares for her, sacrifices everything to keep her safe. Or the woman who gave birth to her?

I arrived home to a rare moment alone in my sanctuary and sat in silence, just me and my thoughts. And my mind wandered, as it always did, to that awful house, where Cerys had lived with Sofia. She was struggling alone, her boyfriend had long gone and she was holding on to anger and hurt. There was rubbish in the garden, cardboard at the windows, and then there was the attic she referred to as 'the nursery'. Old, creaking stairs led to the room at the top of the house, a room where a crying baby couldn't be heard, and therefore wouldn't disturb. No décor or soft bedding in pretty pink for baby Sofia, just damp walls and sour air, acrid with mould and the stench of used nappies. The only clue that suggested a toddler slept in there was the teddy bear in the corner, and the battered nursery rhyme mobile hanging over a rickety old cot. Just thinking back to that godforsaken place confirmed for me that whatever wrong I'd done, I'd done right by Sofia.

I could never stay there for too long in my head, it was the worst place I'd ever been, the room was so dark, and so far away from anyone. I once commented to Cerys that if Sofia cried, she wouldn't be able to hear her.

'That's the idea,' she'd said and went on to tell me how she too had a bedroom in the attic when she was little, and when she was naughty, she'd be locked in there for days. I couldn't hide my horror at this and tried to offer some sympathy, but she had been so hardened by the cruelty of her past, she was beyond help. My biggest fear was that the pattern was being repeated with her own child.

I was caught up in the memory of her revelations, and as always, had to push them away, lock them in a box in my head. In the thick silence of the afternoon, I suddenly heard a noise coming from the front room. As quietly as I could, I picked up a kitchen knife and, holding it down by my side, gently pushed open the adjoining door to the living room. It was dark, but out of the corner of my eye, I saw something move on the couch. I couldn't make it out but went silently towards it, my knife ready, my heart now thudding in my ears.

'Em, what the fuck are you doing?' Nancy was almost falling off the couch.

'Oh I'm sorry, I thought someone had broken in.'

'Honestly, my nerves are shredded,' she moaned. 'All I wanted was a little sleep, and you come in with a bloody knife.'

'I thought you were someone else.'

'It's too much, Em, I'm going to have a heart attack.'

'Look, I'll make us a cup of tea,' I said. I went back to the kitchen, made us both a cup of tea and we sat together.

'Bloody hell, as if it's not bad enough with creepy cows turning up in the post, and weirdos knocking on the door and running. I try to have an afternoon nap and wake up with you standing over me brandishing a bloody knife!'

We both ended up giggling, partly with relief, but I also felt the threads of our old friendship. In the intense atmosphere of the flat, and everything that had happened, I'd forgotten why Nancy and I were friends. This moment was a reminder of what we used to have. Nancy had never asked too many questions and accepted me for who I was, our friendship had been easy – until she'd moved in.

'Anyway, I thought you'd gone to the doctor's?' I said.

'The doctor can't help me, she'll only tell me to stop drinking and clean up my act, I can do that.'

'Yeah? By sitting alone in the dark with the curtains closed all afternoon?'

'I realise it's not the way you would deal with a drink problem, because you're Miss Goody Two Shoes, you'd just turn round three times and stay "stop now" and that would be that.'

She really seemed to think I'd had life easy, and that I was in control, if only she knew. I was about to address this with her, and explain that I understood only too well about addiction, when the door slammed and Sofia stomped up the hallway.

'Hello, darling, we're in here,' I called to her.

She didn't respond immediately, and I was about to call her again when she appeared in the doorway. She wandered into the kitchen and Nancy began talking about recent events, rather than continue talking about her drinking in front of Sofia.

'I'm sure last night I heard someone rustling around outside,' she said. 'I couldn't sleep, I really think we should call the police, it's scary, and that woman's unhinged, we don't know what she might do.'

'We don't know it's Cerys,' I offered weakly, aware of Sofia's feelings.

'Who the hell else would do shit like that?' Nancy was as blunt as ever.

Sofia slammed the fridge door, and from across the room, she glared at her. '*Who else?* I wouldn't be surprised if you did shit like that after a couple of bottles of vodka!' Sofia said, raising her voice. 'You probably did it cos you're pissed off Mum's got a boyfriend and you haven't.'

Nancy was stopped in her tracks, as was I. Nancy looked like she'd been hit, and after the initial shock, her face sank into sadness. 'I'm calling the police. Why are we listening to a kid who hasn't got a clue about people and life. You're letting her dictate to us. Our personal safety is at risk, a madwoman is on the loose and all you two keep saying is, "It's Sofia's mum, we can't," or "How do we know it's her?" For God's sake, I wake up every night thinking I see her face at the window. And one night it will be!'

'Then go back home!' Sofia yelled back. 'None of this has anything to do with you. No one wants you here, you take up too much space and fill the air with your negativity and vape fumes... and... alcohol breath!'

'Sofia!' I gasped, taken aback by her outburst.

'You've changed, you used to be a sweet kid, but now you're one nasty piece of work!' Nancy spat. 'Just like your birth mother!'

Sofia didn't flinch, just stared her down, her face flushed with anger, her mouth tight. I'd never seen her so angry.

'And don't worry I won't be breathing my alcohol breath in here a minute longer!' Nancy added.

'Good!' Sofia responded. But I heard the wobble of anger and tears in her voice.

'I'm going, I can't spend another minute in this place.' She spun around and said to me, 'I should never have come here; your daughter verbally abuses me and you threaten me with knives,' she spat. 'It's a madhouse!'

With that, she stormed into the living room, while Sofia flounced off to her bedroom. I stood in the kitchen helplessly watching the fall out. I knew it was best for all of us if she left, but still it all felt horrible and I wished it hadn't happened like this.

Once she'd packed her few possessions, she walked back into the kitchen, and stared at me, like she was waiting for me to apologise. So I did.

'I'm sorry, Nancy, and I apologise for Sofia too, I'm sure she didn't mean what she said.'

'I'm sure she *did*!'

'I think this whole mess is getting to all of us, and as much as I don't want you to leave like this – I think it's probably for the best.'

'I agree. Your daughter's nastier by the minute. Meanwhile, you're being strung along by some weirdo older guy who has commitment issues; it'll never go any further, so forget it. Your life's a mess.'

'Wow!' I said. 'Where did that come from?' It seemed Sofia was right, Nancy was jealous of me seeing Oliver.

She began to walk down the hallway, but stopped at the door, her back to me, and said, '*Why* won't you call the police?'

'I told you why.'

'Is it *really* because you don't want to upset Sofia by blaming her mother for the weird post?' She turned around and was now scrutinising my face. 'Or is there another reason?'

'Like what?'

'To protect the person who *really* sent it?'

'Cerys sent it,' I murmured, my heart starting to thump.

'I'm not talking about Cerys,' she said, opening the front door, and looking me in the eye.

'I'm talking about Sofia.'

THIRTY

The atmosphere in the flat once Nancy had left felt much better, despite the anger of her parting words. I even started to believe that Nancy's presence had caused more problems than we realised and said so to Sofia.

'Do you think Nancy sent the cow?' she asked.

'No, love, there's only one place that came from. Nancy wouldn't understand the significance, and besides, *the dish ran away with the spoon*, it's got Cerys's pawmarks all over it. For some reason Cerys believes I adopted you under false pretences, that I somehow was the reason you were taken off her. She can't accept responsibility for her child being removed from her home for their own safety.'

Sofia didn't respond, she just looked sad and serious, she'd been through so much recently. But now Nancy had gone, I hoped that she and I could slip back into our mutually supportive roles, and in time she would be able to move forward.

For a few days, everything seemed to be returning to an even keel. I, of course, kept my eye on Sofia's messages, and it seemed she'd stopped talking to Cerys and Pink Girl – or her half-sister, Jody, as Cerys had told her. I think the message with the plastic cow had freaked her out as much as it had Nancy, and despite Cerys's denials, Sofia seemed to be genuinely scared of what else she might do.

Then one evening, we were watching TV and Sofia suddenly said, 'I think she's going back to Manchester.'

I knew who she meant straight away. 'Oh, is she selling the house here?' I hid my absolute elation at this news, mindful of Sofia's feelings.

'No, they only rented it, they still have their own house up north.'

I wanted to cry with relief, the very idea that my nemesis was living less than a mile away had been tortuous for me, but maybe now it was over. Cerys had tried her best to get to Sofia, to me, but she hadn't succeeded, and perhaps now our lives could go back to normal.

'I can't say I'm sorry. Having her here was difficult, my heart was in my mouth every time the shop door opened or someone walked past the window outside here. I kept thinking, is it her?'

Sofia nodded. 'Bit sad though.'

I accepted that for Sofia this was something to grieve, not to celebrate. 'I understand. You've only just met her, and now she's leaving. She has her own life and you have yours. I think in the long run it's better for everyone, especially you.'

'Yeah, I guess,' she mumbled.

'And whatever she told you, take it with a pinch of salt, and please don't let it poison *our* relationship. It's easier for her to deal with putting you up for adoption if she creates some kind of scenario where I was the baddie.'

'I know. And I'm not glad I'm adopted, but I'm glad I know, if that makes sense.'

'Of course, and I feel like a weight's been lifted, to be honest. I never wanted to keep it from you, life just got in the way.'

'I don't want to live in Manchester. I want to stay here with you.' She looked at me pleadingly then.

'Oh, has she asked you to go with her?' I hadn't even realised this was something Cerys would try.

'Not in so many words, but she said if I wanted to, I could go with them.'

It would be illegal for her to take Sofia, and also a cold day in hell if I sat back and let it happen. 'You're not going anywhere,' I assured Sofia and she seemed to relax at this.

I felt like we'd come through a terrible storm, survived it, and were now even stronger. I was exhausted by the uncertainty, not always knowing where Sofia was, not knowing what Cerys was saying to her, and not knowing what the outcome would be. As an adoptive mother, you feel the same unconditional, death-defying love as a birth parent, but always in the back of your mind is the agony of uncertainty. You give your heart and soul to a beautiful child, and yet you have this primal fear that sits in your gut, that one day the parent will come and take them back. Cerys was a shadow over my happiness in the early days of adoption, and now, years later she'd tried her best to wheedle her way into our lives. But it seemed she just enjoyed the mind games, she didn't want her child, and had already given up on Sofia.

The next morning, as she ate her toast and I put milk on my cereal, Sofia said; 'I'm staying late at school tonight.'

'Oh, okay. I'll be finished by 6 p.m., I could come and meet you?'

'Nah, I'm good thanks, not sure what time I'll be finished.'

'What is it you're doing?'

'An English revision session.'

'With Mr Roberts?'

'Yeah.'

'Just a few days before you break up for Christmas?' I asked, trying not to sound like I was questioning this. I was.

'The mocks are due in the new year, so he wants to do a final push — that's what he said: "A final push!"' she said this in Mr Roberts' Scottish accent, and made me laugh.

I had to learn to trust Sofia again. If I didn't, how could I expect her to trust me?

At the shop, I tried not to think too much about her staying late, and when she texted me at lunchtime with a funny cat meme and a complaint about Ruby's 'attitude', I knew we were back on track.

I sent her a text back: 'Hey, I thought we could go to Exeter on Christmas Eve and do some last-minute Christmas shopping? We can buy those shoes you want?'

They were expensive, but Mr Woods had given me a generous cheque to buy something from him for Sofia. 'She's had a tough few months,' he'd said, 'and so have you.'

'Yay' was her response, so I sent her a smiley face and got on with the job of Christmas perfume selling.

At 5.45 p.m., Mr Woods and I were just about to close the shop, when Ruby and Archie called in to buy some perfume for Ruby's grandma. They were giggling and touching each other and I felt for Sofia if she had to put up with this at school.

'Oh, have you just finished English?' I asked.

'No?' Ruby looked confused.

'I... Oh. I thought you had an English session with Mr Roberts after school,' I said, dread coming down like a big, grey blanket.

'No, there's no after-school stuff this week because it's end of term and the Christmas play's on,' Ruby replied, then squirted Archie with some Love at Midnight.

The minute they left, I called Sofia. She didn't answer. I wasn't sure what to think – then I remembered her sadness at

Cerys leaving to go home to Manchester. Had Sofia gone to say goodbye?

After saying goodbye to Mr Woods, I walked briskly through the dark streets, holding on to the hope that I'd get home and find Sofia in her room, headphones on, having not heard her phone. But as soon as I opened the door, I could see the flat was dark. I called her, but there was no answer. I phoned her again, no answer. Then I called the school, and asked if she was there, and if there'd been any revision sessions that evening. I received the same reply that I had from Ruby: 'The Christmas play's on all week, so there are no extra sessions.'

There was only one place she could be. My car still wouldn't start so I'd have to go on foot. But first I ran into the kitchen, picked up a kitchen knife off the block and, sliding it into my roomy handbag, I began marching to the respectable, tree-lined, Acorn Road.

When I arrived, I stood across the road where I'd stood before, watching. The lights were blazing, so someone was home, but I had no intention of going up to that door and knocking on it until I *knew* Sofia was there. If she *was* there and had simply gone to say goodbye to Cerys, then I would understand that this was the closure she needed, and I could live with that.

'Hello! Is that you out there?' a voice was calling behind me.

I turned to see the overfriendly old lady who'd talked at me the last time I'd stood there.

'It is you. Have you come to meet your daughter again?' She was shouting too loudly, and I was worried if anyone came out of the house, they'd hear her and my cover would be blown.

'I thought you said you had the wrong street last time, that your daughter was somewhere else?' she was smiling broadly and looking right into my face.

'I was... confused, it's the house I thought it was,' I said absently.

'So she's here, on Acorn Road, at the Richardsons' old house?'

'Yes,' I said this quietly and smiled like it was all quite normal for a mother to loiter behind a tree a few hundred yards away from the house her daughter was visiting.

'Why don't you come in for a cup of tea?' she asked.

'No thank you, I'm fine,' I said.

'I told you last time, you can't stand out here in the freezing cold, you'll catch your death. You can watch for your daughter through the front window.'

I thought about this for a moment. If I went inside and sat looking out I could see directly into Cerys's house.

'Thank you that would be lovely,' I said, linking my arm through hers so she'd move faster and we could get inside without being seen.

'I'm Margaret by the way, who are you?' she asked, slowing down to wait for my answer.

'I'm Julie,' I lied, and gently pulled her forward so we could get inside her house quickly.

Once inside, she chattered on as I went into the front room and sat in the darkness watching across the road. She was shouting to me from the kitchen, 'You make yourself at home, I'll soon have the kettle on.'

'Lovely!' I called back from my seat. The view was perfect, I was looking directly into the front room of Cerys's house, and they'd thoughtfully put a big light on so I could see everything. The first thing that struck me was, despite most of the houses on the road having Christmas trees and fairy lights in their windows, there was nothing to suggest Christmas at her house.

Cerys was wandering around the room chatting, with a vape in her hand, and I could see Jody, then I saw Sofia, and my heart jumped. My daughter was sitting on the sofa, laughing and drinking something that might have been alcoholic from a glass. I had to steady myself, how like Cerys to give a young teen alcohol, exactly what I'd expect from someone like her. She was as irresponsible and stupid as I remembered. I moved closer to the window, and as I did, a car pulled up outside. The driver's door opened, and someone climbed out, someone I recognised. *Oliver* was in the street outside.

At first, my mind couldn't merge the two elements, Cerys and Oliver. I wondered if his sister lived on this road too and what a coincidence that would be. But it was so much more than a coincidence. My mouth went dry as I watched him walk to the front door, and open it with his *own* keys. I saw him then appear in the living room, where Cerys, Jody and Sofia, all got up and hugged him, one by one.

THIRTY-ONE

'Oh there you are.' Margaret trundled in with a tray of tea. 'What are you doing sitting in the dark?' she asked, putting the tray down, turning on the light and basically illuminating the whole room with me sitting right in the window where I could be seen by anyone across the road who happened to glance over.

'Turn the light off,' I shouted, jumping down behind the windowsill before any of them saw me.

She jumped and immediately did as I said, and I felt bad about shouting at an old lady.

'I'm sorry,' I said. 'I didn't explain; it's my eyes, they can't take light,' I added, nonsensically.

'Oh dear, can I put a lamp on because I can't see where I'm putting the tray?'

I leaped up, my eyes now used to the darkness. 'Let me take that for you,' I said. Throughout this exchange, all I could think was, why? What in God's name was Oliver doing in Cerys's house? I was desperately trying to come up with an innocent explanation while trying to remember just how much I'd told him. Did *he* know I was connected to Cerys? Of course he did,

I'd mentioned her name enough times, I'd told him the whole story.

I put down the tray while Margaret continued to talk. I barely spoke, and gulped down my tea as I looked back out of the window and watched the four of them talking. But then I became aware that Sofia wasn't joining in, and as I moved even closer to the window, it looked like she'd fallen asleep on Jody's shoulder. I couldn't get my breath. Had they given Sofia something to put her to sleep? Surely not!

Then, all of a sudden, all the lights went out in Cerys's house. I wasn't going to sit here while they had my daughter in the dark. God only knew what they were going to do. So I made my excuses and ran. So much was going through my mind as I dashed down the hallway, desperate to go right over there and bash down their door. I grabbed the door handle and pulled, 'MARGARET!' I screamed. 'The door's stuck.'

'No it's not, dear, I always lock it when I come home, you never know. In fact, my neighbour Mrs Peabody—'

'OPEN THE DOOR!' I yelled, almost in her face.

'Oh goodness, you are in a hurry, aren't you?' she muttered as I danced on the spot with fear and frustration. 'Now where did I put my keys?' she was saying to herself as she waddled slowly back down the hall.

'Hurry up, I think my daughter's in *danger*!' I yelled.

Eventually, she announced that she'd found them and was about to explain to me exactly where they were as opposed to where she *thought* they were, when I just snatched them from her hand. I twisted and turned and shook that door, until it opened, while she gave instructions from behind. Then I threw the keys back down the hall, and ran out into the road, to see Cerys and Jody putting bags and cases into the back of Oliver's car.

What the hell? I hid behind Margaret's garden wall, and

while watching them, I called the police. And after five long minutes of me trying to explain the situation in a loud whisper, the person on the other end said, 'Can I check your address again please?'

'Acorn Road,' I said as loudly as I could without being heard by Cerys and Jody, who'd now been joined by Oliver who was putting a box in the boot. My concern was that as I'd reported Sofia missing before and she had turned up, they might not take this seriously and assume I was just an overanxious mother. 'My daughter is in danger, I think they've drugged her!' I hissed down the phone, probably making it worse as I now sounded hysterical.

'We'll send someone over as soon as we can,' was the response and I put down the phone, now in tears, not knowing what to do.

Cerys was teetering on little heels with carrier bags and Jody carried a small TV. They passed each other, one going into the house, the other coming out, and they giggled, and all I could think was where is my daughter? This was a full-on operation, and more and more stuff was being put into the car; it was clear they were going somewhere. They were leaving the rented house and doing a moonlight, but what were they going to do about Sofia? She was, presumably, still inside the house but hadn't come to the window and wasn't helping them pack up. Cerys was going to take her, she was going to do to me what I'd done to her all those years ago – she was going to steal my child. If the police didn't arrive soon, my daughter was going to be the next thing they carried out and packed in the back of the car. I couldn't breathe, I was desperate, so I called the police again, only to be greeted by an automated voice telling me to wait and someone would respond, but I *couldn't* wait! If they took Sofia, God knows what would happen to her. There was still no sign of the police, I was totally alone, I had no way of stopping them. So I called the only friend I had in the world.

'Nancy, you know that guy you sleep with sometimes who's in the Navy? Big guy, intimidating, lives in town, drives a fast car.'

'Oh that's Nathan. Yeah?'

'I'm on Acorn Road, I think he only lives around the corner?'

'I... Why are you telling me this?'

'Do you think you can get him to come here now? I really need help. Cerys has taken Sofia, I think they've given her something to knock her out.'

'Shit, is Sofia okay?'

'I don't know, and... I called the police, but they haven't come. Nancy, I don't know what to *do*,' I said, trying to swallow my sobs.

'Acorn Road? Put the phone down, I'll call Nathan.'

Within a couple of minutes, I could see in the distance, a figure running down Acorn Road. But my heart sank, had Nancy just come alone without Nathan? We couldn't stop them on our own, and now Nancy was heading this way. I just hoped she didn't draw attention to herself – or me. But as I watched her running towards me, I saw her veer off to the other side of the road, where Oliver was now loading more stuff into the car. Within seconds, she was stood by his side, and from my close proximity, I could see they were having a conversation. I almost collapsed, why was Nancy talking to Oliver? She was standing with her hands on her hips, and he was leaning on the car, his head down. My head couldn't untangle or decipher what was going on. If Nancy was in on this, then I was lost. I could scream and make as much noise as possible until a neighbour phoned the police, but that was all I had. In my head was still a small sparkle of hope that the police would arrive, but that hope was fading, and the longer Nancy was talking to Oliver, the more I felt that calling her was probably the worst thing I could have done. They were talking in hushed voices, and I couldn't hear what they were saying. Then out of nowhere, Nancy suddenly whacked Oliver across the face! She moved back, like a panther who'd just struck her prey, and she ran away. Oliver held his face, his head bowed. My finger ends tingled with shock, what the hell was going on?

THIRTY-TWO

Suddenly, bright lights lit up this weird tableau, and I had to shield my eyes. At first, I thought the police had arrived, but as the lights came closer, it looked like a big American truck, and its huge headlights were flooding the street with light.

As the truck pulled up, Nancy jumped out and walked towards me, and I stepped out into the brightness. Just then, Cerys and Jody appeared in the doorway and brought Sofia down the path, they were holding her up either side, she could barely stand. As soon as I saw her, I ran into the road, calling her name, vaguely aware of Oliver running in front of me, blocking me from her. But no one was keeping me from my child, and I leaped at him, desperately trying to push him out of the way.

'Nathan!' I heard Nancy yell.

He was here, it was Nathan in the truck, and somewhere inside, twisted around the fear and the anger and the mess, was a little flake of hope. Within seconds, Oliver was in a headlock, and being held down by Nathan, who pulled him aside so I could get to Sofia.

'What the *hell* are you doing?' I spat in Cerys's face.

Shocked at the sight of me, she pulled harshly at Sofia's arm. 'You're *hurting* her!' I screamed.

'Piss off, she's my kid, I'll do what I like!' She turned on me, her eyes narrow, her lips tight and mean. 'Now you know how it feels. I'm taking her back to Manchester where she belongs!' She was heading to Oliver's car, but as he was pushed up against it, his arms twisted behind his back, and the weight of Nathan bearing down on him, she turned back. 'Come on, Jody, move! We'll get her back in the house,' she said, but Jody was clearly upset and Cerys took over and started to drag Sofia roughly back up towards the front door by her arm.

That did it, no one hurt my daughter, so I jumped on her back, while she tried to spit and claw at me. Her desire to hurt me was so much stronger than her need to protect her daughter that she spun round, letting go of Sofia. But I instinctively caught her in my arms just before she landed head first on the concrete path.

Suddenly, Nancy appeared behind Cerys and wrapped her arm around her throat.

'Jody, you *idiot*, help me.' Cerys was screaming obscenities at her daughter.

Jody was sobbing, and shouting, 'Mum, stop, stop,' as Cerys tried to bite Nancy's arm, but Nancy wasn't letting go. The more she bit, the tighter her hold on her.

'Come on, darling,' I was saying to Sofia, holding her, guiding her away from this horror.

'Mum,' she said slowly. She was leaning on me, trying to stay upright and beginning to come round.

'You bitch! You thieving bitch!' Cerys hissed at me, her arms flailing, grabbing at me as Nancy yanked her back, and I held on to Sofia. We started walking backwards down the path to the gate, as Cerys yelled obscenities at me, and Nancy yelled them at her. Poor Jody had now run back into the house in tears.

'How could you?' I said. 'You knew we were happy, you

knew Sofia was cared for, she's living a good life, a better life than you could have given her. You hate me so much you want to ruin your own daughter's life, and you got *him* to help you by spying on me, faking a friendship...' I gesticulated with my head at Oliver, I couldn't bring myself to say his name.

Nancy had taken her arm away, and Cerys was now standing in the path, staring at me, a smirk on her face.

'Him?' She gestured to Oliver. 'It was *him* who got me to do this,' she snapped.

'Stop trying to pass the buck, Cerys, you never take responsibility for your own actions, do you?'

'I'm not passing any buck. He hates you more than I do... if that's possible.'

'Oliver doesn't hate me, he doesn't even know me, but presumably you've laid your poison there so he thinks he does.'

'You killed his son,' Cerys spat.

'I don't even *know* his son, Oliver's son killed himself.'

'He was Sofia's father, he was going to come back for us, his parents made him go away to university, said I was bad for him. Then you took Sofia, and he had nothing to come back for,' she spat.

It was beginning to make some weird, twisted sense, but I couldn't quite work it out.

'Oliver's Sofia's granddad, his son was Sofia's dad,' she said, her voice icy.

I was aware of Nancy groaning at this, but when I opened my mouth, I couldn't speak. I just looked at Oliver, who couldn't meet my eyes. *Now* it made sense.

I eventually was able to put a few words together, but I had so many questions, what I actually said was almost irrelevant to the bigger picture.

'So *you* planned all this, moved everyone to Sidmouth?' I asked, stunned, trying to process this.

'Yep, he paid for it all too.' Cerys smirked, she was leaning on the garden wall, arms folded, pleased with herself.

'So you came along for the free holiday?'

Cerys stepped forward. 'Yeah, I did. I came here for a holiday and so I could find you, you bitch! You... are a *liar*! You *stole* my kid.' It felt so rehearsed, but as she waved her arms and spat her words in short, sharp stabs, each one was a fresh wound.

'But you couldn't look after her,' I protested, trying desperately to simplify this, to bring it back to what it was, a child who needed love and care.

'You set me up,' she snarled. 'You lied to my social workers, you even lied to the newspaper about finding her, she wasn't in the street, she was in the nursery. Liar, liar, LIAR!' she screeched.

'Stop! Stop it, she's not.' Sofia still sounded groggy but was clearly upset about what Cerys was saying. 'Mum isn't a liar, she's been good to me, she's looked after me. She did find me on the street, didn't you, Mum?' She was looking at me, beseeching me to say yes.

I nodded.

'I could have been picked up by *anyone!*' She looked back at Cerys, close to tears. 'Where were *you*? You didn't care, but Mum did, and she's always been there for me.'

'I'm your *real* mother, she stole you, can't you see she's a liar, she made it all up.'

'NO! She didn't.'

'All these years you've left us alone, you never came to find Sofia, so why now?' I joined in.

'Because I wanted my granddaughter back.' Oliver was suddenly standing behind me. I spun round, unsure of what he might do, this man wasn't who I'd believed him to be. He walked through the gate, onto the path outside the house where we all stood.

'Don't you fucking dare touch her!' Nancy yelled at him.

'I'm not going to do anything,' Oliver said to her, his hands up in surrender.

'It's fine, he wouldn't dare,' I reassured Nancy.

'Where are the police, I thought you called them?' she asked me.

'Yeah, yeah I did,' I murmured, still in shock.

'Well I'm going to call them again.' She walked off, phone in her hand, with Nathan close by her like a guard dog.

My arm was now protectively around Sofia. If Oliver was here to take my daughter, I was ready for him, and had backup. Nancy was now just a few hundred yards away calling the police with her muscle-bound Navy man.

'This has all gone too far,' Oliver spoke calmly, looking from me to Cerys. 'I didn't want anyone to get hurt, but I admit, I went along with this madness.'

'It was your *idea*!' Cerys snapped at him. '"We'll get my granddaughter back, and we can all live together in my big house," that's what you said.'

'I know, I know,' he murmured, defeated, 'but you told me she'd been stolen, that you were destitute, I believed you.'

'She *was* stolen!' Her voice was permanently on high volume, she'd probably had to fight all her life to be heard, but Oliver was unable to match her energy – or her hate.

'I wanted to rescue you, give you a better life...' He looked at Sofia.

'I don't *need* rescuing,' she mumbled, unwilling to look at him.

'I know that *now*, I can see that your mother cares about you.' He looked at Cerys, 'She doesn't mistreat her, she doesn't lie, she didn't "frame" you to the social workers. I believed you, Cerys, I believed that Sofia was in danger, and when you called me asking for my help, I admit I fell for it.'

'Your granddaughter had been stolen, I'd been suffering all

these years since she'd gone, and in my grief I hadn't been able to work. Me and Jody were destitute, about to be thrown out of our flat because of *you!*' She spat, pointing at me.

'Ah, it's beginning to make sense now,' I said. 'You needed money, so you thought you'd scam your ex-boyfriend's dad!'

'It wasn't like that. I just told him the truth, that you scammed ME!'

I shook my head, I was trembling with cold and anger, the night was brittle, the air frosty, and I wanted to just walk home to our warm little flat. I was tired of defending myself, exhausted from the fear of what she might do and say. And to learn now that Oliver was involved too, I couldn't believe it, I wasn't sure how much more I could take.

Sofia was now looking up at Oliver. 'But why did you go along with it, why did you make my mum think you were her boyfriend?'

He looked guilty, but at the same time I detected a sense of remorse, and regret. He gave a deep sigh and leaned on the gate post. 'I'm sorry I did that, but we thought that that was the only way to make sure it was Cerys's daughter. She wanted to go to the police, but we couldn't just accuse your mum of stealing you, so I was making a dossier to give to the police to prove it was you.'

'But I *adopted* Sofia, there was no theft, whatever Cerys told you.' I glanced over at her scowling face, she was now sitting on the front doorstep, her arms wrapped around herself protectively, she knew she was on a sticky wicket.

'Yeah.' Oliver pushed his foot into the frosty grass, flattening it, a nervous gesture, trying to get control of his feelings, I supposed. 'You told me you had all the adoption papers and that's when I started to wonder just who was telling the truth.'

Cerys muttered her objection from the doorstep, angrily.

'Until then you'd just believed everything she said and went along with it?' I asked.

He shrugged. 'Sofia's my only living relative now, she's all I have, I think I wanted to believe she needed me,' he shrugged.

'But you have a sister, a daughter... a granddaughter?'

'He has no one,' Cerys butted in. 'They were all made up, he told you that when he bought your overpriced perfume so he could get in with you and ask you out. That was *my* idea,' she said proudly. 'Not nice being lied to, is it, Emily?' She smirked.

Oliver didn't respond to her, nor did I. But he looked at me, and in the light from the porch lamp, I saw regret and hopelessness in his eyes. He'd been played, and he knew it. What Oliver wanted from this was his granddaughter, but what Cerys wanted was to come into my life and mess with me, play mind games and hurt me for the hurt she felt I'd caused her. She thrived on this kind of behaviour, it was oxygen to her, she'd lived a life of conflict and violence, and she knew nothing else.

I tried not to look at her smug face, the mean lips, the cold, hard eyes. She was a product of her horrible childhood with a woman clearly incapable of love when it came to her stepchild. Cerys had been treated so badly, I felt sorry for her, I could see the pain etched in her face, and in spite of everything, a part of me wanted to wrap her up in my arms and hug her until she thawed. The maternal side of me wanted to show her that she was loveable, that it was possible for others to love damaged people like her. But still, I could never allow Sofia to be in her care.

What a fool I'd been to think I could hide the truth, when Cerys was always waiting in the wings for her moment. I just had to hope that whatever else was revealed, it wouldn't break my daughter's trust in me. Cerys knew so much, and was eager to share. I held my breath, hoping against hope she wasn't going to tell, because if she did, I might lose Sofia after all.

THIRTY-THREE

Oliver stepped back from Cerys now she had temporarily calmed down, and he probably assumed he didn't feel the need to shield Sofia and I, that she wasn't going to scratch my eyes out. He obviously didn't know Cerys; she was as unpredictable as she was violent, and those two traits made quite a cocktail. Again, I reminded myself that being locked in what her step-mother referred to as 'the nursery,' for days on end had probably created a frustrated, angry and deeply hurt child who was still lashing out.

'So your son? What you told me, that was true?' I asked, turning to Oliver.

He nodded. 'Tommy was eighteen, he'd got in with a bad crowd and started taking drugs, we were out of our minds with worry. He was our only child, we'd invested so much in that kid, we loved him so much... you know?' He looked at me, and I nodded, yes I *knew*. I knew only too well how much you can love a child, and the lengths you'd go to just to keep them safe.

'Anyway,' he continued, 'when we found out he'd got some young girl pregnant, we were devastated. We knew he wasn't old enough or capable of looking after a partner and child, so I went to see her. She said she didn't want to keep the baby because she couldn't afford it, so I said we would give her some money, and she only had to call us if she needed more. Which she did,' he added, looking over at Cerys.

'I had our Jody by then, I needed the money for her,' she snapped.

Oliver took a long breath, he was so much calmer and less angry than Cerys and I, but the hurt he'd suffered was present in his voice. 'Anyway, my wife never wanted to meet our grand-daughter, she was a mess after our son died, and as I told you, she was never the same; she sat in a stupor for years, but after she died, I called Cerys, asking if I could see my granddaughter, who I was still supporting financially.'

'Yeah, they gave me money, but made him go away to university at the other end of the country. They made him promise to never get in touch with me again. They didn't want me to ruin his life. It was okay that he'd ruined mine,' she added, anger ribboning her words, 'so I took their payment to stay away.' She grumbled something derogatory about how little the cheque was. But no doubt it had gone on drugs and drink and anything else Cerys needed.

'So he paid you off, and you took it?' Sofia asked, incredulous.

'Oh don't be soft. I bet you've never had to worry where your next meal's coming from, or found yourself pregnant to some spoiled brat.'

'I'm not that stupid,' Sofia said dismissively.

Cerys stepped forward in Sofia's direction, and both Oliver and I immediately reacted. He put his hand out to Cerys, and keeping my arm around Sofia, I gently pulled her away.

'The truth is, Sofia, that the minute shit got real, *his* son ran to mummy and daddy who rescued him. No one's ever rescued me,' she said bitterly.

Oliver bowed his head, he looked wounded.

'It was wrong of us to interfere with his life, and I'll regret it to my dying day. I hoped that by seeing you, Sofia, I could somehow make it up to him, to you... you were all I had left of him. So a few months ago, I called Cerys and asked how you were. She said you'd been stolen years ago, and she'd been trying to get you back, but needed help. I thought it was fate... my wife had just died, and here was someone who was telling me my granddaughter had virtually been kidnapped and I had to do something.'

'Yeah, and so I looked online – and there you were, all over Facebook and Instagram,' Cerys added.

'So you hadn't looked for me before. It was only when Oliver called that you thought to search for me?' Sofia asked.

Cerys shifted uncomfortably. 'I *did* want to find you, but even if I had, I didn't have the money to go to wherever you were and get you. Oliver said we could take you back to Manchester, and if Emily objected we'd take her to court. He said if we got you back we could all live rent-free in one of the houses he owns. I guess that's ruined now. You always manage to mess things up for me don't you, Emily?'

She folded her arms, her face empty, save a veil of disappointment and an absence of hope. But something else was creeping into those black eyes, framed by shadows, as a defiant, almost challenging expression took over her face as she turned to Sofia.

'She stands there all holier than thou making out she saved you, but you didn't need saving. She crept into your nursery, and *stole* you.'

Cerys's words bit into my flesh, and held all the pain and resentment of the years between.

'That's not true, you're being so mean, Cerys. I thought you were funny and kind, but you're horrible.' Sofia's eyes filled with tears. 'You're the liar!'

Cerys smirked. 'Am I... ask her, go on. Ask her what *really* happened.'

I still had my arm around Sofia, she was shivering in the cold. 'I'm taking her home,' I said. 'It's cold and I'm not standing here arguing with you.'

Oliver stepped forward. 'Please, Emily, please don't take her just yet, I want to talk.'

'Oh really? Like you've been talking to me these past few weeks, telling me lies just to get dirt on me so you can steal my daughter?'

'Steal *your* daughter?' Cerys walked towards me, her finger pointing at me, stabbing the air.

Sensing her aggression, Oliver moved between us, but she leaned to one side so she could make eye contact while yelling at me.

'*You're* the thief, not me! Sweet little Emily – the friendly nurse who'd been so kind in the hospital. You turned up at my door all simpering and sweet. "I've come for a visit to see how *baby* is doing," she'd said. So, of course I let you in.' She paused, glaring in my direction, waiting for me to respond.

I couldn't. The words had been held in so long, I couldn't let them go.

'She always turned up in uniform, didn't you, Emily?' Cerys was laughing at me, goading me as Oliver held her back. The loudness of her voice had attracted some onlookers, and I was aware of curtains twitching in other homes on the road. 'Always smiling, always cooing over you,' she addressed Sofia now, who glared at her from under her eyebrows. 'Oh yeah, she was always offering to look after "baby Sofia", as she called you. And I'll admit, I was happy to let her, it gave me the chance to go out with my friends, have a few drinks. I'd come back blind drunk and she'd put me to bed. It felt to me like she was the mother I'd never had, weren't you, *nurse* Emily?'

Cerys waited, her look was pure hatred and defiance, she

was daring me to respond, and waiting for my comeback. Sofia had also turned to look at me, as did Oliver, even Jody, who emerged from the house and stood by Cerys – they were all waiting for my response, my denial. And the longer she waited, the more Sofia's expression changed, from disbelief to concern. How I longed for Cerys's words to be gobbled up by the thick, heavy silence.

'I was your nurse, I took care of you and your baby,' I said calmly.

'We didn't need *you*. We didn't need some twisted cow who was checking my every move to try to get my kid off me. You had a dossier too just like Oliver, didn't you? You knew you could get her taken off me and have her yourself.'

'Don't be ridiculous,' I spat.

'I trusted her, why wouldn't I?' She continued to address Sofia, who was still and silent, just staring at her like she could *see* the words coming out of Cerys's mouth, each one a new story, a new horror to deal with. 'This woman had helped me breastfeed, showed me how to make you stop crying, how to put you safely in your cot in your nursery. She was always going on about being "safe", keeping baby "safe." But *she* wasn't safe, were you?' Cerys turned to me again.

I took a breath. 'She wasn't *safe* with *you*, Cerys, you *neglected* her.'

'I was seventeen, you stupid cow! I wasn't ready to be a mum, I still had my life to live. I thought you understood when I told you I couldn't cope, and that sometimes the baby cried so hard I wanted to shake her.' She paused. 'And yes, I locked her in the nursery the same way I'd been locked in, and I told you I was worried I might be repeating the same pattern. But instead of helping me, you wrote it all down and told my social worker.'

'You scared me, I knew she was in danger, and on top of all that, you were a drug addict.'

Her eyes were now filling with tears, her voice faltering.

'And some nights you'd stay with me and talk to me while I tried to go cold turkey.'

'And after I left, your first call was to your dealer,' I spat.

'But I *tried*.' She stopped again, and looked straight at me. 'I liked you, Emily...' She started to laugh, then she turned to Sofia. 'I fucking *liked* her, I thought she was my friend. But all the time she was in my house, pretending she was helping me to be a better mother, she was plotting to steal you from me.'

'Mum?' Sofia's voice cut through; she was asking me if this was true. I saw the pain and confusion, her face a conflict of love and mistrust.

I put my hand on Sofia's shoulder. 'I didn't *plan* it, darling. I can see why Cerys might think that,' I said, trying to be reasonable. 'At first I visited to keep an eye on you.'

'I needed my mum,' Cerys was saying now through tears. 'But she'd died when I was little, I never knew her.' She looked straight at me. I could see she was about to shoot some poisoned dart, and I flinched. 'But, of course, I don't need to tell you, Emily – *you* know all about my family history, don't you?'

Silence. Total silence as I took in her last sentence. *She knew.*

THIRTY-FOUR

The others were looking at me expectantly, waiting for me to respond to what Cerys had said about me knowing her family history. *She knew.* I took a breath, I'd lived a lie all these years, and like cancer, the lies had multiplied, one leading to another and spreading, until my whole life was consumed by lies. From what she said, and the way she said it, it was clear that Cerys knew the truth, and it was now time for me to dilute those lies with some truth. I had to explain, which meant giving Sofia the palatable version of how I came to be her mother.

'Cerys came into the A & E department of the hospital I was working at,' I said, addressing Sofia primarily, but also addressing Oliver and Cerys. 'She was just another pregnant teenager, she was scared and alone and said she didn't want her baby. She was also pretty abrasive and not easy to like.' I gave an apologetic shrug to Cerys.

'You tell it like it is,' she murmured, unsmiling.

'She told me her boyfriend was an addict and she also struggled with addiction. I was horrified that into this a baby was about to be born, so I helped her with applications for housing, went with her to the council and we secured a nice little house with a garden.'

'The area was rough as hell,' Cerys muttered ungratefully.

'Better than the streets,' I bit back.

'You were like a bloody stalker, you never left my side, you were always there, and by the time she was born, I couldn't do anything for myself.'

'That's not my fault.'

'Yes it was, you took over, from the minute you saw my bulging belly, you decided it was going to be yours!'

'It wasn't like that.' I turned to Sofia; she nodded uncertainly. 'I visited Cerys on and off in my professional capacity for the first two years of your life,' I continued.

'But then you stole her!'

She was shaking her head.

'I was a *nurse*, and I knew how a baby should be treated. The place was filthy, you weren't alert to danger, and the day I saw that so-called "nursery" with the damp, peeling walls—'

'She had toys and stuff...' she cut in.

'There was a dangerous mobile dangling over the baby's head. You told me you were scared of what you might do when she cried so much you couldn't take it. It was that, along with the bedbugs, that made me concerned about her. I knew you were too young, too out of it – I had to do something, I had to get her away.'

'From her own *mum*? Who tucked her in one night, and then woke the next day to find her cot empty?'

'It wasn't like that, you abandoned her, you never tucked her in, you put her in a cot and imprisoned her in a nursery so you could get on with your life. I saved her.'

She was furious at this, her face was mean and tight and angry as she spat words at me. 'You took her, she was mine and you took her, she was my baby, you ruined my life! Who do you think you are, Mother Teresa?'

'She may have been yours, but you didn't care for her. In all the time I was there in your home, observing, I never saw signs of a warm, nurturing love from you. And then there were the friends who seemed to hang around, smoking and drinking and having a good time while your baby was left alone. It seemed to me that your baby was an inconvenience.'

'She wasn't. I was young, I wanted to have a good time,' she argued.

'And I don't blame you for that, I understood, you were young, you'd been in care—'

'I was sent to my dad after Mum died,' she explained to Sofia, 'but my stepmum didn't want a cuckoo in the nest, and I hated her guts. She used to lock me in the attic, she called it the nursery, but it was more like a prison; horrible dark place. I'd sometimes be locked in there for days. She'd give me some bread and water, and yell at me through the door. If I ever cried or made a noise, she'd come upstairs and thump me for disturbing her. By the time I was seven, I was in a kids' home, not many laughs in there.' She rolled her eyes.

We all stood in silence. Cerys had suffered a horrible childhood, and she wore it almost proudly. Like a tattoo on her forearm, she showed it to everyone, begging for their attention, their sympathy, their love. She could never be a good mother, because she was still a little girl herself, vying for the adults' attention, and when neither myself nor Oliver responded, she pursued a different tack, to get my attention.

'You never told anyone at the hospital you'd been visiting me,' she started, then turned to Sofia, still trying to prove to her that she was with the wrong mother. 'She pretended she'd never seen you before the day she "found" you, and it didn't matter what I said, no one believed me. It sounded mad when I said a nurse who'd been with me when I gave birth had stolen my baby. My social worker thought I'd totally lost it. The psychiatrist said I had problems accepting responsibility, what the actu-al...' She was becoming angry just talking about it. 'Your husband knew. He came to see me, said he'd support me if I wanted to take you to court, that's why you left and came here, isn't it? You've got a lot to answer for, Emily. I'll never forgive you, my own sister...'

Sofia gasped. 'What?' She was staring from me to Cerys and back again, stunned.

'You two are sisters?' Oliver asked, confused, bordering on angry.

I took a breath. 'Cerys and I are half-sisters,' I said. 'We were split up when we were very young, when our mum died. I was twelve, she was just two, which is why she didn't recognise me as the nurse who looked after her.'

'I did my own digging once I realised what you were, I just had to google "psycho nurse", and there you were,' she laughed at this. Loudly. 'I had no idea, didn't even know I had a half-sister, but a distant cousin of my dad's told me that my mum had three kids, and I was the youngest.'

Sofia was shocked of course. 'That explains why we've all got red hair,' she said, which seemed like a strange thing to say, but she was clinging to what she knew. My daughter was flailing around and I couldn't help her; I just kept my arm tightly around her shoulder.

'So when you were protecting Sofia as a baby, you were protecting your niece,' Oliver said.

'Yes, I was, and my little sister – that was my plan. I did lie to Cerys, I told her I was the midwife visitor appointed from the hospital, which was only half-true. By then I *was* a midwife, but I wasn't visiting Cerys in any official capacity, in fact the hospital had no records and no knowledge of my visits. This was my own personal after care plan, because after I'd met her in the hospital, I realised quite quickly who she was, and decided I would help her. But I knew early on that she had issues, and realised that I could only do so much, and at some point I might have to step in. If she knew we were sisters it would change the dynamic, and she'd simply use me as a babysitter. I was married, trying for children of my own, I didn't want to be tied to someone like Cerys, who despite being family, was like a stranger to me.' None of this was a lie, but deep down, I also knew there might come a time when I might need to rescue Sofia, my niece from this life. It would have been harder for me, as a sister, to take Sofia from her mother. I had to appear detached, professional – 'the visiting midwife' – so Cerys would trust me, tell me things, be honest about the situation.

'Yeah, and if anyone found out we were sisters, it would be harder to pretend you found me, that you hadn't planned to take her,' Cerys sniped from the side, echoing my thoughts.

'You can see why I had to keep everything at arm's-length, Cerys always has her own agenda,' I murmured to Oliver, who raised his eyebrows.

'You can stop whispering sweet nothings to him,' she hissed, 'he's not interested in you. He was sleeping with that drunk mate of yours,' she added with a smug smile.

'Who, Nancy?' I asked, shocked at this, instinctively looking at her, standing with Nathan waiting for the police. She was too far away to hear the conversation. I felt sick, who the hell was this man I'd believed to be kind and gentle, and still too mired in grief for his lost wife to be intimate with *anyone*.

I looked at Oliver, who was staring at Cerys, his jaw twitching, clearly annoyed at her revelation, which suggested it was true.

'You and... *Nancy*?' was all I could utter.

'I... I had a few evenings out with Nancy,' he stuttered, clearly finding it hard to get the words out.

'Before me?'

He nodded.

'He wasn't interested in *either* of you,' Cerys started. 'He was trying to find Sofia, so he needed to find you. He went out every night trawling the pubs, and eventually he got talking to her, slept with her a few times and found out from her all he needed to know to track you down. That's when he prowled around the perfume shop where you worked.'

'I'm ashamed,' he said, 'it's all true, but you have to understand, I never meant to hurt anyone. It felt like a game, and the more involved I became, the more risks I was willing to take.'

'He's bloody mad, aren't you, Oliver? I think it's the grief,' Cerys said in an aside to me. 'He never got over Tommy dying. You blamed yourself,' she addressed him. 'Tommy was going to leave uni and come back to me, we were going to get married, but when Sofia had been taken off me, he gave up.'

I think we all took some responsibility for Tommy's death, from the drug dealers who pushed, to his parents who pushed, to Cerys who pushed. As for me, Cerys was probably right, I took the one thing in his life that meant something to both of them. Would Cerys have rallied round, might she have become the mother Sofia needed? We'll never know, but I just wasn't prepared to risk it.

Before we could talk any more, two police cars screeched to a halt outside the house, and out climbed several officers, who marched towards us, quickly followed by Nancy and Nathan.

'These are the two that were going to kidnap the girl,' Nancy was yelling, and after a short discussion, Oliver was being manhandled down the path, onto the road and bundled into a police car.

'I don't believe this,' Cerys hissed at me on the doorstep, as the police walked towards her. 'You kept me talking here just to give the police time to get here and arrest me.'

And still maintaining her innocence, and blaming me for her bad luck, Cerys was also manhandled into the back of a police car. She was yelling and kicking, and I remembered a little two-year-old doing exactly the same as she was manhandled into her father's car. I was twelve, and I stood on the pavement, tears streaming down my face, as I watched my little sister in the back seat of a car, crying at me through the back window.

THIRTY-FIVE

I remember the moment Cerys came into the A & E Department of the hospital where I was working that night. There was something familiar about this pregnant teenager with hair like mine. And when I took her name and date of birth, it was obvious this was no coincidence – this was my lost little sister. I told the truth when I said I didn't want to tell her because I didn't want to get close, and I might find it harder to report on my sister for neglecting her child. But the unwashed hair, the dishevelled appearance, the smell of weed and alcohol on her breath worried me. I knew even then that if, against the odds, this baby was born, she would be in trouble, and the only way she'd be out of trouble would be if she wasn't with Cerys. So, in truth, I decided I was going to be Sofia's mum before she was even born and I put my plan into action straight away.

The day after she'd been seen in A & E, I put in for a transfer to midwifery, where I soon became a trainee midwife. So I was ready and waiting the day Cerys came in to give birth, and it all went smoothly, and I held Sofia in my arms within minutes of her being born.

Once Cerys left the hospital with her newborn, I stuck like

glue. My sister was right, I was like 'a bloody stalker' and turned up at least twice a week, in uniform, with my notepad. In my defence, I didn't set out to 'steal' Sofia as such, I told myself that if the first few months went well, I would perhaps leave Sofia with Cerys. I'd then turn up to visit, and act all surprised and announce the 'shocking' news that we were sisters. I'd go on to be Sofia's auntie, support my sister and we'd all live happily ever after – but life isn't like that. In the first few days I knew this wasn't going to happen, because Cerys was off her face on drugs a lot of the time. I tried to help her come off them on several occasions. 'Do it for Sofia,' I'd urge as her teeth chattered, and her body screamed out for opiates, but the demons always won.

I stayed with her for two years, and if she'd got clean, if she'd shown any kind of care for the child, I wouldn't have taken Sofia. But she was getting worse, and as the baby became mobile, she was in even more danger, both inside and outside of the house. Cerys's friends were always around, they were loud, they all smoked weed or drank, they were young and stupid and didn't know what they were doing. I couldn't sleep at night for worrying about what might happen to this vulnerable baby girl in that house of horrors.

So one day, when I knew the situation was becoming dangerous, I went round to the house. Cerys was in the kitchen, smoking weed, and not really with it. I asked where Sofia was, and she said, 'In the nursery.' My blood turned to ice, and I took the stairs up to the room two at a time. When I tried to open the door, my worst fears were confirmed. The door was locked, and with my heart in my mouth, I called Cerys, but I was greeted with only a heavy silence. I twisted the handle and banged on the door to try to open it, but nothing would budge it, so finding strength I never knew I had, I lunged at the door, and after a few attempts, managed to break the lock.

As I opened the door onto the filthy room, I was greeted with the dank, musty smell of neglect, and the sound of whimpering coming from the corner. Trembling, I moved across the room, and there on the floor, hiding behind a battered old teddy bear was Sofia, her face was wet with old and new tears. She was clutching the teddy, and pushing herself against the wall, clearly scared that I was going to hurt her. It was then I knew the time had come, and very early the following morning, I returned. I knocked on the door, and when Cerys didn't appear, I went round to the back door, which was always open. Cerys was sitting in the same chair in the kitchen she had been the previous evening, I wasn't convinced she'd moved. Her head lay in her arms, and when I lifted her hair to see her face, it was clear, she was out of it, completely gone. So I went straight upstairs to the so-called nursery, where, thanks to my lock break the previous day, I was able to gain access immediately. Sofia lay fully clothed and asleep in the cot she was now far too big for. Her mother had obviously plonked her in there the night before so she couldn't climb out and get in the way of her partying. I had no doubts as I gathered her up in my arms and carried her downstairs to where her mother was sleeping off whatever she'd imbibed the night before.

I quietly carried the little one out of the house, and placed her gently in the back of my car. I then opened my boot, and took out the hypodermics and pills I'd brought from the hospital and left them on the kitchen counter. I had to make sure this wasn't misconstrued by social workers, and I didn't want Cerys denying anything, it had to be watertight.

I then left the house, and drove Sofia to the local library, where I told the librarian that I'd found her on the street. The local papers covered it, and the story got bigger and bigger. I couldn't go back on it after that. I'd naively hoped I'd be able to take Sofia home with me that day, and the social worker would be grateful. But, of course, there was a lot of red tape to get through first, and Sofia had to be placed in approved foster care for the time being. I was so upset – what if the foster parents were worse than Cerys? What if Chris and I weren't accepted as adoptive parents, and someone else adopted her? I'd have done all that for nothing, but I talked to the social worker, made her my friend, and after a tense few months, Sofia was put up for adoption, and she helped me to begin adoption proceedings. I wanted children, I always had, but Chris wasn't so keen; we were in our late twenties, and he still had ambitions for us to take off and travel the world. I didn't share those ambitions, but I knew when he met little Sofia, with her mop of red hair, he would be smitten, and he was. Chris was a teacher, I was a nurse, and we were both clean as a whistle, so after a lot of meetings, observations and red tape, we were approved, and less than a year later, we officially adopted Sofia.

And for the first few months we were blissfully happy, just the three of us. Chris was beginning to settle to the idea of being parents and his plans to travel were put on a back-burner. But soon after Sofia became ours, I received the first death threat from Cerys claiming I'd framed her and stolen her child. I knew there was no proof, I'd made sure of that, but I was scared, so I registered the note with the police and the social worker. Then, more notes were pushed through the door at all times of the day and night, and when Chris opened one, I knew it was time to tell him the truth.

So one evening, after I'd bathed Sofia and put her to bed, I sat him down, and told him Cerys was my sister, how she'd come to the hospital pregnant and, from that moment, I'd vowed to make sure this baby survived. I explained how I'd visited, babysat and told him about 'the nursery' – both Cerys's childhood horror, and how she used it as a punishment for Sofia. I also told him how I'd planted the drug paraphernalia in her kitchen, and lied about finding Sofia in the street, when really I took her from the locked nursery.

I'll never forget his face, he was horrified, said what I'd done was immoral, and this wasn't an adoption, it was child theft. But he hadn't seen the nursery, he hadn't seen the way Cerys lived, and how Sofia would be in permanent danger if she stayed there. To my horror, he threatened to go to the police and report what had happened because I'd committed a crime. He said he couldn't be part of this and didn't want anything to do with me or Sofia; he said he couldn't live with himself knowing what I'd done. The way he looked at me made me realise it was over for the two of us, and if he went to the police I'd lose Sofia too, and that wasn't going to happen. So that night, I walked out and left him and Manchester for good.

I'd lived in fear of Chris finding me, and turning up in Sidmouth with the police, that's why I'd thought it was him behind the break-in, and the person spying on us. But after the showdown with Cerys and Oliver, I googled Chris's name and found a photo of him in an Australian newspaper. He was teaching at a school there, his class had won a prize and he was stood there tanned and smiling with the kids. He obviously decided, like me, it was easier to run away than to face what I'd done.

THIRTY-SIX

THREE MONTHS LATER – EARLY SPRING

I'd like to say Sofia and I arrived home from Acorn Road that night and lived happily ever after. But you can't erase the past and what happened between us all will echo through the years in the same way that what I did echoed through the years. I still lived with the guilt and wondered if one day someone might just believe Cerys, question who the nurse was who visited her and her baby, and ask why that woman was the one to find her baby and adopt her.

One day I would tell Sofia the truth but felt she had to be a mother herself to understand why I did what I did. She needed to feel what it means to be a mother, and how you would sell your soul to the devil to keep the child you love safe from harm. I held on to the belief that I did the right thing all those years ago, even though I still hid behind lies.

I was scorched with guilt at how Sofia had to cope with the revelations about herself, her past, and her family. It would take a long time, and a lot of care for her to heal, and for our relationship to get back on track. She had to learn to trust me again, and I knew that wouldn't be easy.

As for Cerys, she managed to slip away from responsibility

as she always had. After being arrested that night, she was taken to the police station and told the police that Oliver had *forced* her to go along with his plan to abduct Sofia. She said he threatened to hurt her and Jody if they didn't do everything he said, and she was given a suspended sentence. I was shocked at how she'd apparently convinced everyone that she was the innocent party, but then I remembered her stepmother, the way she beat her and locked her in the nursery. It was amazing that she'd even survived that, but that was the key – Cerys had learned how to survive and swerve, and could pretty much withstand, or escape from, anything.

My biggest fear was that she might come after us again because after the court case she started posting some pretty vicious posts on her Facebook account. Most of these posts centred on what seemed to be an increasing obsession with revenge, and justice, which I know were aimed at me. She clearly believed I set her up again, and kept her outside the house talking that night while Nancy called the police. It seemed her inability to take responsibility for her predicament was part of a paranoia she suffered: she was always the victim, it was always someone else's fault – and she was dead set on meting out her own punishment, which was chilling.

I never really knew my little sister until I met her in the hospital at sixteen years old, and though she had no idea I was her sister, I sometimes wondered if I was the only person who'd shown her anything like parental love? It made me sad to think she felt so betrayed by me, and I didn't blame her for not trusting me after what I did. We were both young and impulsive. The only way I could live with myself was to say it all worked out in the end. But still, I was terrified of opening the front door and being faced with a hissing, clawing Cerys hellbent on revenge for what she perceived to be a set-up and my second betrayal.

Discovering that she was the one who burgled our home

and had left the first missing piece of the mobile with the note was chilling. It indicated just how far she'd go, not for her child – but for revenge. But what I didn't tell anyone, was that I had taken the mobile from the nursery the day I took Sofia, and for years it had been hidden in drawers under my bed. I don't know why I took it, my mind was fizzing that day when I found Sofia whimpering in the corner, but I felt it might be something familiar for her, something from her birth mother when I eventually told her she was adopted. So when I was concerned that Sofia was being brainwashed by Cerys, it was me who sent the plastic cow to our address in the post and added the nursery rhyme. When Sofia discovered the photo of the mobile, it reminded me that I still had it somewhere, and the cow seemed significant to her. I hated myself but I had to do it to make her realise how dangerous Cerys was. Just as the social workers had needed signposts to point out that Cerys was using while responsible for a toddler. It also scared Nancy, and in the end, I reckon the thought of Sofia's 'crazed' mother turning up at the door focused her mind, and she finally went home.

So while Cerys went on to live her life, Oliver, meanwhile, was sentenced to two years behind bars after pleading guilty to attempting to kidnap a child. I felt no satisfaction, no sense of justice being achieved. In fact, I'd hoped after the court case, he'd be free. He'd been through enough, and was still crazy with grief for his beloved wife and son. I realise now that like me he was also just a parent trying to find his child. He believed that by taking Sofia back, he could somehow conjure his son, and Cerys had given him plenty of justification for doing that by telling him I had stolen Sofia. And like me, he was simply trying to make a wrong right, but in doing so, caused more damage. We were more alike than I'd realised, and because of that I felt disappointed by Oliver, and a little hurt. He'd strung me along simply so he'd have evidence against me for the police after he'd kidnapped my daughter. Fortunately, he found nothing to suggest that I was a bad mother, and I never revealed anything to him about what I'd done. However, had we developed a proper relationship, who knew what I might have shared with him? So in the end it worked out for the best.

After learning of his relationship with Nancy, we talked about what had happened in the aftermath.

'I feel bad because I basically told him where you lived, where you worked, all about you,' she said. 'So, unwittingly, I helped make it happen.'

I told her we were all being manipulated, on the surface by Oliver, but he was a lamb to the slaughter, being encouraged and egged on by Cerys. I also realised that her attitude towards me during those difficult weeks of her recuperation was all about him, and I asked her if she still felt angry towards me.

'No, of course not, but I hated you back then,' she confessed. 'I'd really fallen for Oliver, but he kept saying I couldn't tell anyone about our relationship, he wasn't ready to go public. I thought he might be married.'

'Me too,' I agreed.

'But when he dumped me, I was so devastated – that's when I took the overdose. So to then see you and him together was the worst, I was so hurt, I thought he'd chosen you over me.'

'I had no idea. I wish you'd told me.'

'I know, but I didn't want to be Debbie Downer and ruin things for you, it's not like you get much man action and I didn't want to ruin it,' she joked. 'Besides, when you called me that night from Acorn Road asking for help, I realised I'm all you've got, same as when I called you after he dumped me and I tried to kill myself. We were the first one the other called – we need each other.'

She was right. She was annoying, and sometimes selfish, and always loud, and yet she made me laugh, and yes, we needed each other. This whole episode had brought Nancy and I so much closer, and after what happened I never took my friends for granted, because whatever happens, they will always be there for you.

Mr Woods was another person who was there for me, and after that awful night at Acorn Road, the first thing he did was to give me a week off. 'You need to be home for Sofia,' he'd said. 'You two now need to heal.' Once back at work, he'd listened when I had shared my concerns about Cerys's threatening messages, and her current state of mind. 'We'll never be free of her,' I'd said. 'Now she's found us, Cerys will always be a shadow in our lives. She'll want Sofia's attention when she's bored and demand to be at her graduation, her wedding, her first child. It will all be tainted for me. I'm being mean and self-ish, but I can't help how I feel, and I know that will probably give her the most pleasure – ruining things for me.'

'Those feelings are perfectly understandable,' he'd said. 'She's your daughter, why would you want to share those special times with a stranger? That's what she is in essence.'

'But Cerys is her birth mother, and it might be difficult to refuse because I think Sofia may want her around,' I'd mused.

'She may be her biological mother, but from what you tell me, she's a disaster,' he'd said. 'Sofia has you, and the years you've been there for her, you're her real mother in every sense.'

I found this comforting, and he was right, no one could take away our past, me and Sofia, and our shared history, shared humour, even our shared genes.

So as we started to try to move forward, the story of Cerys and Oliver's planned kidnapping was slowly emerging. We heard snippets of information from the police, and Sofia was in touch with Jody – they are sisters after all. It all added up now, Cerys fed Jody (Pink Girl) all the information about me seeing Oliver and this was used to make it seem as if I was letting Sofia down. It was no coincidence that Oliver wanted to meet the day after I'd told Sofia she was adopted. In her distress, Sofia had messaged

Jody as the only friend she felt she could trust, and that's when Oliver's plan started to move. He took me out of town for coffee and sandwiches, while Cerys did something to my car so it wouldn't start. Oliver knew I drove an old Fiat – because I'd told him, therefore she had no trouble finding it parked near our flat. This gave Jody the opportunity to meet Sofia outside school and point out how her mother didn't care, because she was with a man. And things had escalated from there.

I thought as we'd entered the new year, that we had begun to put it all behind us. However, one evening as we ate dinner, I felt the familiar icy stab in my chest when Sofia asked if she could go to Manchester.

'Oliver's asked me to visit him in prison,' she'd said. 'He's my granddad and—'

'And he's in prison for attempting to kidnap you,' I reminded her.

'He's not a bad person, Mum, he lost his son, then his wife. I'm the only blood he has left – I'm his granddaughter.'

'But you're only sixteen, I think you'd need to be accompanied by an adult anyway,' I said, and offered to go with her. But to my surprise, and fear, she'd already contacted Cerys to ask if she would accompany her.

I expressed concerns for her safety, but tried to be reasonable, despite feeling very hurt. I offered to take the day off and go with her on the train to Manchester and wait outside the prison, but Sofia was adamant she would go alone.

'Mum, I need to do this.'

So, the following week, she had set off with her backpack, and I'd tried to accept that this was her life and her wishes and at sixteen she was old enough to do these things by herself. But still I worried. I'd spent the day working, to take my mind off her being in Manchester in a prison and with Cerys – it was hard to know what was more scary. I couldn't rest and constantly checked my phone to see where she was, just hoping against hope she'd be okay.

'She's a sensible girl, she'll be fine,' Mr Woods said when he called me from Exeter to check on the shop. Even though he'd had to go for a meeting, he was aware of what was happening with me, and how anxious I was.

'Thanks, but it's Cerys I'm worried about,' I said, biting my nails.

And when Sofia had texted me on her way home from Manchester later that day, I'd wept with relief. I ran to meet her at the station, and she'd told me that Oliver, who she'd only met on the night of the kidnapping, was sad.

'He looks very old, Mum. He said he was worried that he'd be beaten up, but he's helping some of the inmates with their appeals, so he's staying safe. I like him.'

'I liked him too,' I'd agreed, even though it sounded like a strange thing to say.

'And how was Cerys?' I was scared even to ask.

'She's a bit of a mess. Jody's gone to live with her boyfriend's family, she's only fifteen and Cerys is trying to get her back, she says they've stolen her.' She rolled her eyes at this. 'Cerys seemed so unhappy. God, Mum, you should see her flat, it's disgusting.'

My stomach dipped. Presumably Cerys had invited Sofia back there, and I was glad I hadn't known this at the time, I'd have been out of my mind with worry. But over the next few weeks the fact that Sofia had been to Cerys's flat the day she visited Manchester became significant, and even more worrying, but not in the way I'd expected.

THIRTY-SEVEN

Yesterday morning, I'd turned on the radio, and the first news story had turned my blood cold. A body had been found on the tenth floor of a block of flats. In Manchester. I'd listened as the reporter explained, 'The body appears to have been there for several days, neighbours only realised when a strange smell began to emerge in upper floors.' Just hearing this made me nervous and jittery, even though the name of the deceased wasn't released. I couldn't put my finger on why, but it felt weird, and in the afternoon, while I was at work, I had found myself checking my phone every few minutes for news updates. Then at 2 p.m., I had checked again, I was standing by the counter in the shop and grabbed onto it, my head was reeling. The dead woman was 'thirty-three-year-old mother of one, Cerys Morton'. My sister. My nemesis. My daughter's mother.

At first, I'd assumed she'd taken her own life – but the report had said the police were treating it as a murder investigation. Then when I got home from work, Sofia and I had been scared by a loud thumping on the front door at about 7 p.m. After everything, we were still jumpy, and I made her stay in the kitchen while I answered it. When I opened the door, two police officers from Manchester were on the doorstep.

'We'd like to ask your daughter some questions about her visit with Cerys Morton in Manchester last week,' one of them said.

A creeping chill began to envelop me. 'Does she need a solicitor?' I'd asked, too quickly.

'Not unless you want her to,' the taller of them had replied. So I let them in, and asked if I could be with her while they asked their questions. Sofia was sitting at the kitchen table, the blood had drained from her face. 'Of course you can stay with her,' the taller officer had said to me, as he sat down and reached for his notebook. 'We just want to ask a few questions, nothing too hard,' he joked, looking at Sofia, who stared back, horrified at the intrusion.

'Now, Sofia, can you give us the exact time you visited Cerys Morton last week, talk us through what happened.'

Sofia told them, and repeated what she'd told me about Cerys being unhappy.

'Can I ask, what is your relationship with the deceased?' the other one asked.

I waited for Sofia to answer, and for a moment she seemed to hesitate.

'She's the woman who gave birth to me,' she said.

'So she's your mother?' he replied.

'No, this is my mum.' She gestured towards me, and I saw Cerys's defiance in the arch of her brow.

'Did you have a parental relationship with the deceased?'

'No, not really, she turned up a little while ago and tried to kidnap me, so I went to see her to say goodbye.'

'Goodbye? Why was that?'

Sofia hesitated. 'I just... knew I wanted to end it. I knew that she would always be... a problem...' She put her head down.

I almost died at this. Sofia was putting herself in the frame here, and if I tried to advise her not to, it would look like I thought she was guilty.

'Why did you think she'd be a problem?' the officer asked.

'Because she was a mess, her flat was a mess, her life was shit and I just didn't feel I could cope. Her other daughter had moved out, and she was asking me to go and live with her, but I said no.' Sofia glanced quickly at me, then back at the officer. She hadn't told me this, and I wondered if perhaps Sofia's refusal had caused Cerys to become angry? Had there been some conflict between them? I wondered again if I should have insisted on a solicitor, but it was too late now.

'And what was her reaction, when you said no?' he asked.

Sofia shrugged. 'Pissed off, sulky.'

He took a breath and looked through his notes while the other officer took over.

'According to forensics, Cerys Morton died just a few hours after you left. We can't pin it down exactly, but that's why you're a vital witness.'

I was shocked, I assumed she'd died a day or so after Sofia had left. Was this a coincidence that Sofia had been there the day she died, or had she killed herself because Sofia had rejected her?

'When you left that day, can you remember how she seemed, her state of mind... were you aware of any phone calls or texts she may have received?'

Sofia shook her head, but didn't say anything, which I worried could be perceived as slightly uncooperative.

'It seems that you were the last person to see Cerys Morton alive,' he continued, 'so anything you can remember, however insignificant it may seem, could be vital to the case.'

'But I thought Cerys killed herself, so surely it's not a *case*, is it?' I asked.

'At the moment, we don't have much to go on, but the

victim ingested poison. Whether that poison was given to her or self-administered is what we're trying to work out.'

Sofia and I were both quite shaken when they'd left, this was a horrible thing to happen, and I was worried about how this would affect Sofia. She seemed edgy.

'You okay?' I asked.

'Yeah, I just feel like my emotions can't catch up with what's happening. I find out I'm adopted, then I meet my birth mother, now she's dead.'

'Yes it's been a tough few months for you, love,' I agreed, hugging her. 'And it must be even harder knowing you were the last person to see her,' I remarked, wondering if she'd pick up on that. But she didn't.

So the next morning, I decided to have a proper talk with her.

'I want you to be really, really honest with me, even if you're scared,' I started, as we sat together on the seafront drinking coffee from paper cups.

Sofia turned away from the sea to look at me, her expression was one of confusion. 'Talk to you about what?' she asked.

'Cerys, Oliver, everything that happened. Her death – does it make you sad?'

'Yeah, of course, but I'm glad I got to say goodbye.'

'Why do you feel bad about it?'

'To be honest, I try not to think about it – no point in going over and over stuff.'

There was sunshine, a spring breeze and a wonderful calmness in the air as the sea gently lapped over the stony beach. But I felt no joy, Sofia seemed cut off, unable to articulate her thoughts like she always had, and I wondered if that was just as a result of the recent revelations. Or was it something else?

'It's just that I was thinking the other day, it was good that you said goodbye to her.'

She nodded. 'Yeah, she wasn't a terrible person. But she would have been a terrible mother.'

As much as I didn't want to hear my daughter had done something horrible, I needed to know so I could protect her. 'What made you suddenly want to go and see her?' I asked outright.

She put her head to one side, considering this. 'No reason, really. Mr Woods made me think about it. I wanted to say goodbye to Cerys because I knew I'd never see her again and he said I shouldn't ever let people go without saying goodbye. He said he still missed his wife, but was glad he'd had chance to say what he wanted to, so I thought I should talk to Cerys, and I told her that you were my mum, nothing could change that.'

'Did she accept this?' I asked, doubtfully.

'No, of course not – that's when she said I should move in with her.' She rolled her eyes at this. 'But now she's dead, I'm glad I took his advice, I feel like I got closure, though Mr Woods didn't use that word as such.'

I chuckled. 'No, that's not a word Mr Woods would use. I'm glad you saw Cerys though... given what happened.'

She nodded. 'Yeah, I feel like things are coming together. I spoke to Ruby yesterday too.'

'Oh, good, I hope you two can be friends again. Just because she's going out with Archie, it doesn't mean you can't be friends. I know you liked him, but there'll be plenty more fish in the sea,' I said.

'I didn't like Archie in that way, Mum, it was Ruby I liked,' she said quietly.

I continued to stare out at the sea, the sky was still blue, the clouds were still hanging in there, and I was still anchored here on Earth, but its axis had just moved slightly. 'You mean—?'

'I'm gay, Mum.'

'Oh... okay.' I needed time to process this, not because I had any problem with my daughter being gay, I just couldn't believe I hadn't realised.

'I was with Ruby. Archie and I were mates and she decided she was straight because she found the alternative too difficult.'

This was a huge revelation and made me realise that however close we are to our kids, however well we think we know them – we don't. Sometimes they are like strangers and we have to get to know them all over again.

I continued to stare out at the ocean. 'Good for you for standing by who you are,' I heard myself say.

'Thanks, Mum.'

I put my arm around her. 'I reckon she's punching,' I said. 'You can do better than Ruby.'

I saw the familiar eye-roll, and turned back to watch the waves, marvelling at the unexpected joys of being a mum. The things children say, the wild ideas, the love, the wonderful, sometimes scary surprises they just throw at you like little hand grenades. As we sat together staring out at the great big sky, I felt like we'd been through hell, and come out the other side. Perhaps we might just have a chance at happiness now. But little did I know what was just around the corner.

THIRTY-EIGHT

Satisfied there were no suspicious circumstances surrounding Cerys's death, the police closed the investigation and her body was released. In many ways, I was relieved that Cerys had taken her own life and ashamed of myself for even entertaining the idea that my daughter had anything to do with it.

Cerys's funeral was held in her hometown of Manchester, and both Sofia and I wanted to pay our respects – after all, she was family, to both of us. As my car was still out of action, Mr Woods had kindly driven us to Manchester, an eight-hour round trip, for which I was very grateful.

The service was a sad affair, with just a handful of people. We were the only ones who sent flowers, and no one cried. I talked to a couple of Cerys's so-called friends, but they didn't shed much light on who she was or why she took her life – in fact, they were adamant she hadn't. But Cerys didn't let people get close, and they didn't know her, neither did I, and I was her sister.

As we drove home from the funeral, Mr Woods stopped to get some petrol, and Sofia went to the bathroom at the service station. I was now briefly alone in the car, and finally able to shed a tear for my sister, who'd lived such a lonely, sad life. I took some responsibility for her anger and hurt, but in taking Sofia that day, I believed I'd saved her.

In need of a tissue to wipe my eyes, I opened the glove compartment in front of me. Inside, was a little plastic bag containing petals, one of the essentials of Mr Woods' work as a perfumier. But something struck me about the packaging, it wasn't from our usual supplier in Exeter, the address on the package was Manchester, and on the pack there was a warning. *DEADLY: Ingesting a single leaf can kill an adult.*

I gasped, feeling my heart thumping in my throat.

'We'll never be free of her,' I'd told him. *'Cerys will always be a shadow in our lives. Sofia's graduation, her wedding, her first child. It will all be tainted for me.'*

I looked up to see Mr Woods approaching the car and quickly pushed the package back into the glove compartment, but in my rush, some of the dried petals escaped.

'I thought you girls would like a drink and something sweet for the journey home?' he was saying, as he climbed back into the car.

'Thank you,' I murmured, unable to focus, trying to detangle the mess in my head.

He opened the carrier bag and took out his own drink before handing the bag to me.

'I thought Sofia might like mint chocolate. I was thinking, imagine a perfume made from chocolate and mint?'

'Mmm, lovely,' I replied, absently taking the bag from him, and turning to see him taking a swig from his bottle. *Strawberry-flavoured milk.*

'I smell apricots?' he said, wiping his mouth with the back of his hand. He was smiling, and looking around as Sofia got back into the car.

'Apricots?' I repeated, trying not to flush.

He twisted the top back on his drink and stuffed it into his door pocket, before starting the car. 'Yes, it's oleander, white oleander,' he said, sniffing the air. 'I'd know that lingering sweet scent anywhere.'

'I opened the glove compartment, something fell out,' I said. 'That might be what you can smell?'

'Ah yes.' He pulled out onto the road, and drove for a few minutes.

I didn't know what to think. Was I being crazy, had the past few months made me paranoid? Mr Woods was my boss, my landlord, just a kind old man – wasn't he?

I glanced behind. Sofia had her headphones on, her eyes closed, tapping her feet, blissfully unaware of anything.

'Did you find what you were looking for, Emily?' he suddenly said.

'I'm... I don't know. I was looking for a tissue... I'm not sure what I found.' I turned to look at him. 'I think it might be poisonous.'

'Only if ingested,' he said, without taking his eyes off the road. 'Hard to imagine, isn't it? Those innocent pink and white petals betray deadly toxins racing throughout every single part of the flower.'

'So it could *kill* someone?'

'Ground up into a powder and sprinkled into vodka it could?' He said this almost boastfully, as he turned the wheel extravagantly.

I considered this for a while as we drove along.

'Cerys?' I croaked.

He didn't answer me straight away. I had the feeling he wanted to savour the moment, the way he savoured French perfume.

'I had to do *something*, you told me she was a shadow in your life—'

'I didn't ask you to do *anything*!' I cried.

'You were dreading your own daughter's wedding, Emily,

and everything else that should be bring joy to a parent. I wasn't having that, and neither would you. No one wants shadows tainting the good times – do they?' A smile played on his whiskery lips.

'But you didn't... you *couldn't*?'

'It was my promise to Dorothy, that I'd look after you both, and I always keep a promise.'

'But... how did you... when?'

'I let Sofia see her first, I felt it would be good for our girl, give her the chance to say goodbye. I didn't want her to live with guilt, it's not good for a person. So when she went to Manchester, I followed her, as I have often followed one or the other of you.' He smiled to himself. 'You two keep me very busy with your social lives and your friends.'

I was looking at him in horror, and he half turned to me; he seemed surprised at my reaction.

'I don't follow you *all* the time, but sometimes I like to check on you both. I wander past the flat at night. Sometimes I've stood in your garden to make sure no one's breaking in, Dorothy tells me to.'

'She doesn't... she doesn't...' I groaned.

'And I sometimes stay all night in the back garden, just to make sure no one bothers you, that you're safe.' He smiled to himself. Then he glanced over at me. 'I even stand on the seafront, under a street lamp watching the house some nights. I keep you safe, just as I promised her,' he continued, like I wasn't even there. 'In Manchester I followed Cerys and Sofia back to her horrible little flat. And after they'd said their goodbyes, I paid her a visit.'

I was numb with shock, and as the grey landscape passed me by, I tried to process what he'd just told me.

I slowly turned to look at him. 'You mean, you... you *killed* Cerys?' I heard myself croak.

He nodded at this like he'd simply swatted an irritating fly. 'I did, I took away that awful shadow hanging over your life.'

I was now terrified for Sofia and I, locked in the car with him. With Mr Woods. A murderer. I stayed silent, the blood rushing through my head, as Mr Woods carried on talking.

'If you ask me, it all started last summer when Sofia started hanging around in the park again. Even when I was young, that was where the troublemakers went, but back then it wasn't drugs – it was cigarettes and loose young women. That Zoe was loose, you know. I was as worried as you about Sofia being friends with her. I remember you saying she was a bad influence.'

Zoe?

'She died in Scotland, a drugs overdose...' I murmured.

'Scotland wasn't far enough,' he replied. 'I was worried she might come back, but we couldn't have that, could we?'

I was going to be sick.

'Eat your chocolate bar, Emily, that's your favourite one, isn't it, with the nuts in?'

I nodded, slowly, unable to speak.

'You see, I even know your favourite chocolate. Dorothy always said, "You're the father she never had," and you've told me that yourself often enough.' He turned to me and smiled.

'Mr Woods—' I started to protest.

'We're family, Emily. I always wanted a daughter just like you did. And you didn't give birth to Sofia, but you're the best mother she could have – so let me be the best father?'

I just needed to stay calm, not let Mr Woods realise how horrified and scared I was. I had to get Sofia and I home, bolt the doors, and call the police. The landscape sped by, other cars passed us on the road, life continued as other people went about their business. The car was locked, and we had a long journey ahead, so I clenched my knuckles, and tried to breathe, while screaming inside.

It had always been my dearest wish for my unknown father to come into my life. As a child, I would wish every night before I went to sleep that he would turn up the next day to protect me, make me safe, and scare the bogeyman away. And here he was now, a man who loved me like a daughter, and Sofia like a granddaughter, he'd protected us, made us safe, and scared the bogeyman away. He'd also *killed* for us. Twice.

Be careful what you wish for...

A LETTER FROM SUE

Thank you so much for choosing to read *The Nursery*. If you enjoyed it and want to keep up to date with all my latest releases, just sign up at the following link. Your email address will never be shared and you can unsubscribe at any time.

www.bookouture.com/sue-watson

This book was inspired by the idea of being an adopted child. My father was adopted and luckily was very happy with his adopted family. He never knew who his birth family was, and chose not to look for them, and as a family, we respected his decision. But, as his daughter, I have always wondered about that half of me.

So when I recently read about a woman who was desperate because her adopted children had been approached by their biological mother, I was fascinated. Before the internet and social media, a meeting between adopted children and their birth mothers was managed very carefully, with the feelings of all parties considered, and not before the child was eighteen. Now, however, birth parents might find out who and where their child is on platforms like Facebook, and who could blame them for reaching out?

On the other side of this is the adoptive parent, who, emotions aside, has a responsibility to make sure their child is safe. Given that sometimes children are adopted because their safety is at risk with their birth family, the adoptive parent may, understandably, be very scared at this sudden relationship forming online without their consent or supervision. The very thought of this both scared me and pulled at my emotions, and I just knew I had to write *The Nursery*.

I hope you enjoyed *The Nursery* and if you did, I would be so grateful if you could write a review. It doesn't have to be as long as a sentence – every word counts and is very much appreciated. I love to hear what you think, and it makes such a difference helping new readers to discover one of my books for the first time.

I love hearing from my readers – so please get in touch, you can find me on my Facebook page, Instagram, Twitter, Goodreads or my website.

Thanks so much for reading,

Sue

www.suewatsonbooks.com

 facebook.com/suewatsonbooks

twitter.com/suewatsonwriter

ACKNOWLEDGEMENTS

As always, my huge thanks to the wonderful team at Bookouture who are amazing.

I'm so grateful to my fantastic editor, Helen Jenner, who was with me every step of the way, inspiring me with her ideas and knocking the book into the best shape. Thanks also to Jade Craddock, my long-time copy-editor, who helps provide the final polish and ties up all those loose ends so neatly.

Big thanks to Ann Bresnan, my American friend and reader who always finds the things I miss, and spots what might get lost in translation. Thanks to her, my US readers aren't confused by my British turn of phrase. Likewise, big thanks to Harolyn Grant, my girl in Canada, who casts her eye on the details and lets me know what is and isn't working. Both these ladies are a wonderful safety net, and I'm indebted to them!

As always, a huge thank you to my long-suffering husband, Nick, my amazing daughter, Eve, my lovely mum, the rest of my family, and all my wonderful friends. I don't know what I'd do without them.